The Critic

By Dyanne Davis

Other Titles By Dyanne Davis

The Color of Trouble
The Wedding Gown
Misty Blue
Let's Get It On
Forever And A Day
Two Sides To Every Story
In The Beginning (As F.D. Davis)
Many Shades of Gray
Another Man's Baby

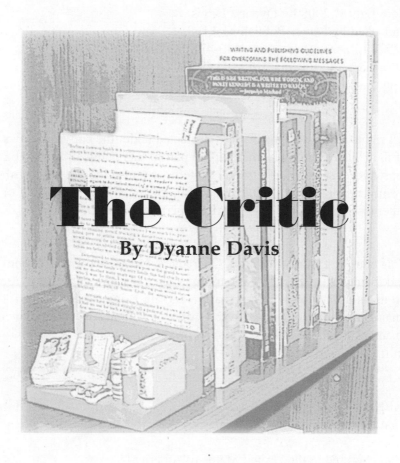

The Critic

By Dyanne Davis

Parker Publishing LLC

Zora is an imprint of Parker Publishing LLC.

Copyright © 2008 by Dyanne Davis
Published by Parker Publishing LLC
12523 Limonite Ave., Ste. #440-438
Mira Loma, California 91752
www.parker-publishing.com

This book is a work of fiction. Characters, names, locations, events and incidents (in either a contemporary and/or historical setting) are products of the author's imagination and are being used in an imaginative manner as part of this work of fiction. Any resemblance to actual events, locations, settings, or persons, living or dead, is entirely coincidental.

ISBN: 978-1-60043-032-9
First Edition

Manufactured in the United States of America

Cover Design by Jaxadora Design

Acknowledgements

As always all praise honor and glory goes to God. It is with profound appreciation that I acknowledge your having allowed me to be able to hear the voices and tell the stories of some who may not have been told had I not listened.

To my sister, Jackqueline Toreas Jackson. I'll give a plug here for one of your favorite writers, E Lynn Harris. Why not? Since every time you come to one of my signings you're looking for one of his books. (LOL)

To the yahoo ladies, of the Dyannedavisfans. You ladies are the greatest each and every one of you. You're all extremely important to me whether you're a lurker or an active participant. To the active participants, Viola, Brenda,Patsy, Lynda, Kim, Debby, Tracy, Alvena, Nikki, Lisa, Brenda, Mona, Patricia, Linda, Haronica, Joy, Anne Marie, Stephanie, Thelma, Stephanie, Desta, Irene, Tarra, Rita, Seta and Abigail. To Brenda Willis, thank you for making my site a professional one that I can still enjoy.

And as always to my editor, Sidney Rickman. You have helped to make this insane process fun. We make a truly wonderful team. I have been truly blessed to have you with me as we try one thing then another, from romance to vampire, women's fiction and now a try at humor.

It is with deep pride that I once again thank Windy City RWA for allowing me to volunteer and serve as president for two terms. By the time this book is on the shelves my term as president will be over but not my reign. Melody Thomas, friend and past president dubbed me Queen Dy and I'm keeping the title. I love it. I wish the incoming board much success and to the rest of my current board, I offer my sincere thanks for a job well done. I count it a privilege to have served with you. We've left our posts with more members, a healthy bank account, and a feeling of camaraderie. WE DONE GOOD! LOL. Jackie Wallis vice-president, Adrienne Maynard-Treasurer, Theresa Stevens, Secretary.

Barbara Harrison, Chris Foutris, Frederricka Meiners, Kelle Z. Riley, Deb Pfeiffer, Terri Stone, Susan Gibberman, Lauren Ford, Luisa Buehler. Deb Larson, Mary Frances Madonia, Sharon Nelson, Todd Stone,Tracey Lynn Smith, Janice Morretti, Jean Newlin, Sherry Weddle, Jacalyn Schuuer, Cathie Linz., Jimmie Morel, and last but not least, Haley Hughes who was my very first Myspace friend and is also my first face book friend. Thank you Haley. To all of you Thank you for volunteering in one way or another during my time as president. It was much needed and appreciated.

Kathy Sullivan, Kathy Thigpen, Vercyna Smith, Renita Williams, Rebecca J, Kwaben, Valeney Liontonia and Norin Leahy, you ladies all make me laugh and give me so much joy.

And bringing up the rear, the most important two people in my world. Bill, my love, my hero, my romance story come to life, you are loved by me and you have my heart. But you always knew that, didn't you? To our son Bill Jr. You continue to make me proud.

Dear Readers,

I want to take a moment to tell you a little about the reason I wrote this particular book. I belong to Romance Writers of America along with 9,500 other writers. By the time, The Critic comes out next year, I will no longer be able to say this so I will get as much mileage from it as I can now: I am proudly serving as president of Windy City RWA, my local chapter. This is my second term and we do have term limits. A good thing.

Anyway, back to the reason I wrote this book. It began as a joke merely for the members of my chapter and was intended to be a short story. But as with most things, it took on a life of its own. Although it was meant originally as a book for romance writers, I'm hoping romance readers will enjoy it as well.

I had a lot of fun writing this book. It's not angst filled and wasn't meant to be. It's meant to be fun, perhaps a bit of a whimsical look into the life of romance writers. I hope you enjoy the book as much as I enjoyed bringing it to you. I hope it makes you laugh because that is my intention.

My local writers chapter is fictional (sort of), and I want to assure you that no romance writers or romance critics were harmed in the telling of this story.

The American Romance Writers organization of my novel is a product of my imagination. To all aspiring romance writers out there: I strongly encourage you to join the real romance writers' organizations, Romance Writers of America. There are 144 chapters and special interest chapters as well. To write you must be informed. To be informed you must know where to look. Look no farther than Romance Writers of America. This is the best advice I can give you.

www.rwanational.org

Sincerely,

Dyanne Davis

Dedication

This book is dedicated with light, love and laughter to each and every member of Windy City RWA, past, present and future. It was with your love, encouragement, teaching and sharing that my dreams became a reality. It is my fervent prayer that all of Windy City members' dreams come to fruition. You ladies and now Todd were the source of inspiration for this book. Thank you. And since this is the last time I can say this, thank you for making me your president for two terms. You're the best group of writers that RWA has to offer.

1

His eyes called to her and she was drawn by the dangerous whiskey color that looked gold when the camera came in for a close up. His mouth was full and sexy, and the thought of being kissed by those lips... Mercy. Her eyes dropped lower, caressing the contours of his body. A small sigh escaped her as her eyes lingered on his massive chest. The thought of laying her head on that chest caused an internal tremble.

She took a swallow of the cold lemonade in her hand, then swiped at the beads of condensation on the glass and rubbed the moisture across her forehead in hopes of quenching the fire.

Toreas Rose wanted badly to be able to reach out a hand and touch Jared Stone. Mentally shaking herself, she looked even lower, sighing again at the sight of legs that appeared powerful and oh so masterful within the dark mustard colored trousers which were a perfect match for his bronze skin. Jared was one truly gorgeous Black man.

Toreas watched spellbound as Jared's tongue slid out of his mouth to anchor his top lip, then lave his entire mouth. God, how she wanted to suckle that tongue, to have it inside her mouth, to have it...

She didn't know how it had happened, but Jared Stone had crawled inside her brain and hooked her. To her, he was the epitome of a hero come to life. Toreas hated admitting it, but she was falling for the man on the screen, a man she knew she'd never meet in real life. But she could dream, couldn't she? For months she'd watched him and indulged in her secret crush. In her safe home he existed just for her. It would be better to never meet a man like that.

She hadn't heard the sound of his voice in weeks. She'd kept her television muted, just to enjoy the yummy sight of him. Listening would have been distracting. Now that he'd swiped his lips with his tongue, though, Toreas needed to hear his voice and restored the sound to the program.

"Romance writers are a bunch of empty headed, bored women, and the women that read that trash are even worse."

Toreas started. She couldn't believe the words that had come out of her lover's mouth. Well, the lover in her mind.

The sound of glass shattering on the ceramic tile caused Toreas to look down in surprise. Lemonade was spreading across the floor. While her attention was concentrated on Jared Stone, the glass had slipped from her hand.

"Romance writers, please," Jared sneered. *"What good do they do besides further feed the fantasies that addle-brained women already have. It's all nonsense. Black women should not be buying into that crap. There is no such thing as true love, or love at first sight, or happy endings. If you ask me, romance writers are doing a disservice to the public by deluding women, regardless of race."*

She couldn't believe it. Toreas was riveted to the screen, unable to move, certainly not to clean up the floor. She stared at the man who for the past several months she'd been thinking of as the role model for the hero in her mind. She'd thought his looks perfect: golden brown skin; beautiful light brown eyes with flecks of gold that she could see even on her television screen when the set lights hit him just right; full mouth that seemed just made for kissing; hair always neatly done in a half dread, half braided look. Toreas didn't know what it was called but on Jared it looked good.

She studied the tight fitting body shirt he wore. It was obvious the man was proud of his body as he never bothered to cover it with a suit coat. He was tall and well muscled, but not too, with lean hips that flared into seemingly well toned legs.

His voice and his walk had totally captivated Toreas the first time she'd seen him. Now the words being spoken in that same voice had her wanting to turn off the set. She couldn't believe he was tearing down everything that she wanted in her life. In essence, Jared Stone was destroying her dream before she had a chance to accomplish it.

She was a romance writer.

Well, she wanted to be a romance writer, but so far she'd met with nothing but rejection. It was becoming increasingly depressing to continue. Jared Stone mouthing off didn't help the situation.

"The whole lot of them are stupid, the women who write that thrash and the ones who read it. They're just plain stupid. They should all get a life."

Toreas groaned inwardly. How had she ever fallen for such an arrogant man? His words were a real turn off. Well, enough fantasizing. With a flick of her wrist, she turned off the television, mourning the loss of something that never was.

✍

"Drivel, that's what I said and I'm standing by it." Jared slammed the second book that he'd picked up onto the table and glared at the women around him. "Well?"

Somehow Toreas found herself again watching Jared's talk show, and again he was attacking romance writers. This time several writers had attempted to change his opinion, but he was having none of it. He was brutal. Toreas winced. How had she ever been attracted to the man? She wanted badly to hear him say something that would make him redeemable but there was nothing. Sadly, she clicked off the set again.

But habit forced her to tune in again the next day and the next. It appeared he was dedicating a segment of each show to bash romance writers. Maybe if she gave him some time he'd stop. She waited a week. This time was the worst. This time he'd managed to get romance readers to come on the show. He was treating them worse than he'd treated the writers on his previous show.

"What is it you like about that drivel?" Jared was asking.

"It gives us hope," the woman answered.

"Hogwash. Hope for what? Do you think your husband is suddenly going to go and put out a fire for you or rescue a kitten from a tree? Think again. If you don't love the man as he is, then let him go so he can find a woman who's not out to change him, one who's not judging him on things from some writer's imagination."

Toreas waited while Jared tried to alter the women's opinions. When that didn't work, he attempted to charm them, then preach to them. Toreas couldn't help watching. Who the heck did the man think he was?

"Look, ladies, all the money you spend on buying these books you could spend on making your home a more comfortable place."

"But the books are a means of entertainment. They don't cost that much. Women work hard in the home and outside the home, and they should spend their money any way they choose. The fact that you're able to be on the airwaves, albeit on a local show, calling women who write romances and women who read them stupid is offensive. You have no right to try and tell women what they should read or how to spend their money."

Jared responded in a fake voice that dripped of rationality. "Think about it: the money could be spent instead on a good meal, a school book for a kid, an educational toy, whatever. You'll have to admit I'm making more sense than you ladies."

Stunned, Toreas shook her head at the television and at Jared Stone. Before the women could respond Jared was saying goodbye and asking people to tune in the next week.

That was it, the last straw. Toreas was done with fantasizing about Jared Stone. As he'd said, it was stupid. Besides, she now saw him for what he was: a know-nothing romance-critic. Too bad she'd ever turned up the volume. She could have remained happily unaware of that nonsense he was spouting as though it were gospel. She dialed information, determined to call the television station and ask for an apology.

Had she not been a fledgling romance writer maybe she could have forgiven Jared. Maybe. But his assault on romance readers, that she couldn't forgive.

Toreas was one of those readers. She'd loved stories of romance since she could remember. Her most vivid memories from her formative years were of reading stories of love, passion and lust. She'd loved the short stories in *True Confessions and Bronze Thrills*. She had become familiar with writers such as Donna Hill and Francis Ray who wrote stories for the magazines and followed them when they moved into full length novels. She remembered how eagerly she'd purchased her copy of *Entwined Destinies* by Rosalind Wells, believed to be the very first romance by an African American author featuring African American characters. If nothing else, Toreas Rose was indeed a fan of romance. Were she not, she could relegate her crush on Jared to the back of her mind where it belonged.

Toreas sat frozen in a panic on the makeshift stage. She was supposed to be defending the romance genre with the assistance of several members of her local writing chapter.

For weeks, her blood had been boiling over Jared Stone's consistently rude comments. But here she sat, mute. Her calls, letters, and emails had seemingly been ignored, but one day out of the blue she'd received a call from someone named Derrick, who'd informed her that he was the station manager and owner.

She had been invited to come on the show to defend romance novels. All Toreas had wanted was for Jared to stop trashing the world of romance. She'd never expected to meet him face to face, to have to…

She had been in a state of panic until she'd gone to her writers' meeting. After she relayed the station's invitation, several of the writers offered to join her. Whether it was for the exposure they would receive or truly to assist her she didn't know and didn't care. She only knew that she wanted someone sitting beside her when she met Jared Stone.

Now she was here. Now she had her chance to finally tell the man to back off, that romance was a two billion dollar a year business. But what had she done so far? Nothing, not a darn thing but yank on her skirt and watch the others battle Jared. And they were losing. She glanced quickly at her watch, praying this slaughter would soon be over. Five minutes to go. Thank God.

Suddenly electrical impulses flooded her body, seemingly jumpstarting her brain in the process. She shouldn't and couldn't let the opportunity for rebuttal pass. She had to speak up, force her tongue away from the roof of her mouth. She had to stop thinking how much better Jared looked in person than he did on her television screen.

When she looked up, her eyes connected with Jared's. He had a look on his face that said she was dead meat. That fact alone should have stopped her from drooling, but it didn't. She watched as he gave a sardonic grin in the direction of the camera, then turned back toward her. He stood, his eyes pinning her in place. On Jared sardonic was sexy.

"Tell me, exactly what does ARW, stand for?"

This was a question she could answer. She knew the proper response, only the words refused to come out.

"American Romance Writers."

Toreas glanced in the direction of her friends, not sure which one had answered the question but relieved that she had. She looked away, hoping to avoid Jared's attention.

It didn't work. He was coming closer to her, asking her another question. Heat was flooding her body as the blood drained from her brain, leaving her speechless.

"So, ARW is a union?"

Here was another one Toreas knew the answer to. She was working her tongue, trying her best to loosen it. Her jaws were moving and her head was twitching.

She could only imagine the image she was projecting. Her breath was coming in short gulps as she watched Jared approaching. His eyes… If only they weren't so darn beautiful, so…

"ARW is not a union, rather a professional organization for romance writers, numbering almost 29,000 members."

Toreas and Jared turned at the same instant to look at the speaker. Toreas's look was one of gratitude, Jared's of annoyance. It was Toreas he wanted on the hot seat, not Elysa.

"Thank you but—" Jared attempted to interrupt Elysa.

Toreas smiled slightly to herself. Now he would be the one cut into little pieces. Elysa knew her statistics.

"You want the complete answer, don't you, Mr. Stone?"

Toreas watched as her friend continued with facts Jared didn't want to hear.

"We have a monthly magazine dealing with things writers want and need to know. There are attorneys who write articles advising us on contracts and other professional issues."

Well done, Elysa. As the thought flitted thorough her head, Toreas glanced down once again at her watch. This was the longest five minutes she'd ever lived through. Worse yet, Jared didn't appear the least interested in Elysa's answer. He was staring at her.

"You've been very quiet, Ms. Rose. I understand you're the one who called, objecting to my calling the trash you produce 'bodice rippers.'"

Her friends were looking at her, trying their best to give her support. Toreas heard Liz attempt to speak only to be silenced by Jared.

"I'm talking to Ms. Rose, the lady who wanted my bosses to muzzle me. I want her to answer this one."

Now he stood directly in front of her. "You're what, 5'1", 5'2?" He tilted his head to the side to study her. "A hundred pounds? Do you consider yourself a heroine, Ms. Rose?"

Toreas was aware that Jared was laughing at her without making a sound. Her cheeks were warming from the nearness of the man as well as her seeming inability to talk. She could only blink, wishing him away, It wasn't working.

"What would you do if a big bad villain invaded your space, Ms. Rose?" He turned to leer at the camera. "You wouldn't mind demonstrating now, would you?"

Toreas saw Jared's challenging leer and that was the catalyst that enabled her to come out of her moronic trance. In one fluid motion she stood and pushed her chair away from her with the tip of her foot.

"Thanks for asking, Mr. Stone. I don't mind showing the women in your audience how to defend themselves. I do, however, need your permission in case you get hurt." Toreas smiled as sweetly as she knew how and repeated, "Just in case."

"I don't think there's any danger of me getting hurt, Ms. Rose."

"Then I have your permission?"

"Of course, do what you need to do."

Before she could reason herself out of her ill-timed action, Toreas's hand closed into a fist and shot out in Jared's direction, landing a solid-fisted punch in his stomach.

As the man doubled over, she heard him groan and she couldn't resist grinning before saying, "That's what I do to villains, Mr. Stone."

Her wrist had wrenched sideways against his hard abdomen and now a searing hot pain shot up from the tips of her fingers all the way to her shoulder and made a home at the base of her neck.

That punch had hurt her more than Jared Stone, of that Toreas was sure. Darn Kelle anyway for teaching them self-defense. The punch was part of last night's lesson.

For several moments everyone seemed frozen as Jared glared at her. Her friends were looking at her with wonder. Wondering if she'd lost her mind, that is.

Toreas looked up into the red eye of the camera and her mouth dropped open. How could she have forgotten she was on television, if only locally. She shouldn't have lost her temper like that.

She looked back at Jared who'd at least stopped glaring at her. His dark eyes were now golden brown and were registering surprise.

He was watching her as if she were some new species he'd never seen before. Good manners dictated that Toreas should at least apologize but she couldn't.

In that instant Jared pounced on her, capturing her head in his hands and kissing her soundly on the lips. He then moved away from her.

"So what am I now, the villain or the hero?"

Uncaring now of either the camera or her friends, Toreas aimed a kick at Jared's shin. But he was out of range and was grinning wickedly at her. Then she felt soft but strong hands pushing on her shoulders. She looked up into the eyes of both Elysa and Liz a moment before landing in her chair.

Toreas could feel the heat invade her entire face and then go into the very roots of her short curly afro. She was glad she'd not apologized to the man. And she was glad that the natural red tones of her brown skin hid most of her embarrassment, at least from the camera. In person, now that was a different thing.

Her hand gripped the chair. She knew she was scowling at Jared. She had to. His kiss, though unexpected, had stirred longings within her, but surely not for him. Mercifully the show ended and she was able to leave.

Feeling the vibrations in the air behind her, Toreas knew without a doubt that Jared Stone was near her.

"I want you on another show." His voice was gruff and he stopped just as Toreas turned toward him. "You embarrassed me in front of my audience and they loved it. You're a hit."

Toreas eyed the man talking to her from a safe distance. He evidently considered her dangerous or crazy. She didn't know which. Kelle would be happy to know he considered her dangerous, but disappointed that Toreas had suffered more pain from the punch than Jared.

The hot blazing pain she was still feeling told her she'd not delivered the punch as instructed. She'd be sure to ask Kelle to show her again.

"Ms. Rose, are you listening to me?"

Toreas brought her eyes up slowly to face the man she'd attacked. *Crazy*, that's what he had to be. Did he really think she'd agree to come to another taping and have him annihilate her?

"No, thank you, Mr. Stone. Your hospitality for one evening has been more than enough." She smiled sweetly. "But if I ever want to visit hell again, I'll call you."

Was that a twitch at the corner of his mouth? She glared at Jared, taking in his thick black hair and golden brown skin. *And was that a dimple peeking out from his left cheek*? She couldn't be sure. The man had not actually smiled.

"Ms. Rose, if you come back, I promise I'll be on my best behavior. You can even punch me again. The audience went crazy when you hit me."

"No," Toreas answered. "I don't want to be anywhere near you." This time she meant it. The man was making her forget the reasons she had appeared on his show in the first place. He was the enemy. He hated her, hated her entire genre. She had to remind herself of that little fact as she felt her body swaying in his general direction. She couldn't keep her mind off his kiss and wanted another.

"If you don't come back I'll sue you for assault."

"And I'll sue you for sexual harassment," Toreas retorted. "You did kiss me without my permission."

"Then give me your permission for the next kiss, only give it to me on the next show."

Jared was grinning at her as if thinking she kissed strange men every day of her life. He was crazier than she was.

"You're nuts," she answered.

Toreas glanced over at Liz who was still staring at her as if she'd lost the last few marbles she possessed. She glanced toward Elysa, Barb and Wendy. Yep, they were all eyeing her with a strange look on their faces. She could tell her friends were wishing they were anywhere but with her at the moment. Instead of helping their cause she'd single handedly lit a keg of dynamite with one well aimed but badly delivered punch.

Toreas walked out the heavy green doors, praying her friends would follow and that she would not be arrested before she could leave the building.

She stood next to Elysa's van, wishing she had come alone. But she hadn't. Elysa was the driver for the group. Toreas had no choice but to wait. So she waited for them to come out, wondering why it was taking so long.

The heavy metal doors finally opened and Toreas breathed a sigh of relief. At least now she could get in the van and start to forget this horrible day.

Darn! Her mouth dropped open in astonishment and she rushed to close it. Her friends were not alone. Jared Stone was tagging along, standing strategically behind Liz as though he didn't trust himself to be too near Toreas.

"Ms. Rose, won't you please reconsider? I think you owe me that much." Jared grinned. "That punch hurt."

"Why would you want me back on the show? You didn't want to hear anything I had to say."

"You didn't say anything."

"You didn't give me a chance."

"You had sixty minutes. It was up to you to use them wisely."

Toreas could only stare at the man, the sight of him making her weak in the knees. Her former crush was battling with her new dislike. Was it any wonder she was a bundle of nerves, of contradictions? Jared Stone was making her crazy.

"Will you do it?" Jared asked again.

"For ratings?"

"Of course," he answered, then frowned. What was wrong with the woman? She was in the business, she had to understand how things worked.

"You want me to come back on your show and be humiliated again so the ratings on your show will go up?"

"Yes. Besides, I was the one humiliated. The audience loved you."

"I will not come back on your show and punch you again."

"Then come back and apologize."

Toreas's head tilted just a wee bit and she knew once again she was going to act without thinking of the consequences. "One should only apologize if one is sorry."

"And you're not sorry?"

"Are you sorry for the way you treated us on your show?"

Jared moved a bit closer to the woman, hoping his towering height would at least intimidate her. It didn't. He saw the sparks flying from her eyes straight at him. At first he thought it was a trick of the sun, then looked again and blinked. Toreas Rose had beautiful eyes. Jared blinked as he looked into her eyes, eyes that flamed when she was angry.

He felt a lump appear in his throat and a throb begin in his groin. He couldn't want this little bitty woman; it must be the punch. Maybe she'd somehow damaged his mind as well as his pride.

Jared wanted more contact with the woman, another chance to prove to himself that romance writers were evil, that this little woman standing in front of him held no interest for him, that he wasn't getting a hard-on as he stared at her. He shook his head as if trying to shake away the lie.

"Ms. Rose, please come back on the show. You would really be doing me a favor and you would help your group as well."

"Are you crazy? What just took place in there didn't help my group. It made us look stupid, as though the things you'd said were true."

"But there is always interest in controversy. What just happened today between the two of us will be great for both of our careers. Think about it. This thing can really get big if we work it right.

"I have no plans to work it right," Toreas said indignantly. "I don't want to do you any favors. I don't like you."

"I don't like you either. That's what would make it so great. Every week you could come on, hit me, flip me, kick me, I don't care, and every week I'll grab you and kiss you." He smiled. "Think about it, the sizzle."

"Let me get this straight. You want to trash us on television every week and you now want me to be a part of this ridiculous plan."

"Yes."

"You're on every weekday. Why don' you want me on every day?"

"Overkill. Why do you think I only talk about romance writers for a small segment of the show sometimes not at all? Too much and the viewer would become bored. If you came on the show once a week they would be excited. This could get really big."

"You are crazy, aren't you?"

"If you don't come back I can guarantee you that things will get worse."

"I don't care."

"You're lying. You care or you never would have called the station to complain." This time there was a definite pulling in his groin and Jared couldn't deny that it was in direct response to the fire coming from Toreas's eyes. He groaned inwardly with the realization. And with that realization he knew he'd do anything to see her again, to dispel his body of the notion that it was attracted to this itty bitty romance writer. *Yuck, perish the thought.* Jared took a step back, grounding himself in the reasons for his feud in the first place. He hated romance writers. He sent a message to his libido. *Snap out of it. We have work to do.*

"Ms. Rose, if you don't reappear, I'll...I'll..."

"You'll what, Mr. Stone?"

"Until this job I worked in advertising, then public relations."

"What's that supposed to mean to me?"

"I was very good at my job." He narrowed his gaze. "I have never failed to get extensive press. Generally it was for a client but in this case I'll be my own client. I made big bucks putting the spin I wanted on things. Your coming back on the show would work for both of us and for your entire organization. Not to accept my offer is selfish. You can't put your dislike of me before what could be good for your friends." He smiled. "Now will you come and help me milk this feud?"

"No."

Jared stared at her for a moment, not believing she'd really said no again. He'd given her plenty of legitimate reasons why she should come. He rubbed his chin, thinking of a new tactic. "I'll sue your chapter."

It was a bluff. It had to be but the panic on Liz and Elysa's faces told Toreas they didn't think so.

"I'll tell you what, Mr. Stone, the three viewers who were probably watching you, if they complain, send me their addresses and I'll apologize to them. As for the people in your audience, I don't think anyone would waste their time coming to watch your show live, so they're probably plants. If not, tell them to write me and I'll apologize to them as well.

Now she'd done it. She'd gone and insulted the man. Toreas's head was beginning to pound. She'd been too nervous to eat breakfast and the need for some protein was evident.

That had to be it, or maybe she simply had low blood sugar. Sure, that would explain it. She didn't normally go around punching people or being nasty.

Jared was staring at her. She had the feeling he was undressing her and she resisted the urge to cover her body with her hand. He was probably deliberately trying to unnerve her. If that was his game, it was working.

Toreas wanted to beg Elysa to unlock the van. From the look in his eyes, she had the distinct impression that Jared Stone was preparing to kiss her again and she couldn't believe it. Yet part of her was wishing he would. She needed to get away from him, from those beautiful brown eyes. He was the enemy.

Toreas walked to the opposite side of the van, away from the man and the scorching looks he was sending her way. She couldn't understand why her friends were still talking to him, trying to pacify him.

She was wishing they would all start pummeling him with the

books they'd brought, the same books he'd sneered at and refused to read. He'd treated them the same as he had the last groups of writers who'd braved his vindictive remarks.

At long last Elysa opened the door and Toreas scampered inside, making sure to keep her head turned away from the building and away from Jared who stood outside watching them drive away.

Liz peered at her from the front. Toreas was crouched down, almost into the cushions.

"What was that all about? Why did you hit him?"

"I don't know. When he got in my face, I thought about what Kelle taught us last night and I just reacted."

"Did Kelle tell you to hit the host of a TV show that we're trying to turn around?"

"But we weren't turning him around, he was being nasty."

"Then why didn't you speak up? You're the one who started it, remember? We only came to back you up. Then you sat there frozen, that is, until you decided to play Bruce Lee. You should have ignored him."

Liz was right and Toreas knew it, but darn, they were her friends. Shouldn't they be on her side? "Look, it's just a local show. There's a good chance no one we know is ever going to hear about this. Besides, I asked for his permission before I hit him. Didn't you hear me?"

"Oh, we heard you alright, but judging from the look on your face, you would have hit him with or without his permission."

Toreas did her best to keep the smirk from her face. Of course she would have hit him. She'd wanted to, if for no other reason than the fact that he'd ruined her fantasy. Of course there was the more realistic issue of his treatment of them as a whole. Toreas found herself grinning as she looked to the front of the van toward her friends. Sure, she'd wanted to hit him because of the readers. Yeah, right. "I am sorry I hit the guy so hard."

"Then why can't you go back on the air and apologize to him? It would be easy to just pretend that the two of you staged it. Jared told us his plan. We all think it will work for all of us. I don't understand why you won't do it."

"Would you go along with his plan?" Toreas couldn't believe what she was hearing. And these were her friends.

"I wouldn't have hit him," Liz said with a smug look on her face.

"You know," Elysa chimed in, "you had better be glad that this is real life and not some story in a book."

Toreas turned her attention from Liz to Elysa. They were both giving her a headache. She was wishing now she had ridden in the car with Barb and Wendy.

"Why should I be happy that this horrible day is my life?"

Elysa smiled before answering. "If this were a book, the readers would not accept the heroine losing her temper and slugging someone on television. The least they'd want to know is what motivated her to do it. She's supposed to be an adult and have control of her temper."

"You're right." Toreas glanced out of the window. "What happens in real life would never be accepted by either an editor or a reader, but, then again, I'm not a heroine. I don't always have a reason for what I do."

She sighed heavily, deciding to give it one more try. "Why are you putting all the blame on me? Kelle's responsible also. I didn't even want to learn karate."

She was pouting like a child but she couldn't seem to stop herself. "What about Jared kissing me? I should have slugged him again." She wasn't going to mention the attempted kick.

Toreas could feel her face getting hot and knew without a doubt she was blushing and turned her head toward the window.

Still, she saw the looks that passed between Elysa and Liz, could even hear the gears grinding in their little writer heads. "Romance writer falls in love with romance critic." Never in a million years. But she could bet they were both writing their first drafts in their heads.

"Listen, whatever the two of you are thinking, forget it." She laughed. "I'm a writer too, remember. I can see where you're headed."

This time her friends joined her in laughing, their anger at her for possibly damaging their careers forgotten.

"Well, it was an interesting day. We have to say that much. It's a lucky thing only a few of us came with you."

"But the entire group knew we were coming. I told them," Toreas said looking at Liz and knowing she was trying to figure out a way to help her.

"You know how everyone is. They're not going to even remember what you or anyone told them if they're not reminded a thousand times. I asked Jared when the show would air and he said there would be a week delay. Maybe we shouldn't mention the air date to the rest of the group."

Good old Liz. Toreas knew she would come through in a pinch. She was her angel, her confidante, her friend. She couldn't blame her for being angry over a chance to have their genre featured in a good light. Now Toreas was angry with herself for screwing up the chance to educate the public on the hard work that was involved in writing romances. Now she could only console herself with the fact that she hadn't punched out a supporter. That would have been worse.

"What about Barb and Wendy? What if they tell someone what

happened today or tell them when the show will air. How are we going to keep them from reminding the group that we came on Jared's show today." Toreas was smiling, knowing the answer to her question, just wanting Liz to say it.

"I'll call them. You knew that, didn't you?"

"Yes." Toreas answered, then closed her eyes and leaned back to begin forgetting.

2

Toreas popped in her microwave TV dinner for one, poured herself a glass of seltzer water and sat down to watch the evening news. A picture of a man with his arm in a sling came up on the screen. It was Jared Stone.

"Toreas Rose, a member of American Romance Writers, has been accused of attacking Jared Stone the popular host of *Straight Up, No Chaser*. The show is the flagship of the independently owned Chicagoland television station KGB. The station reported that while he was hosting his regular show, Toreas Rose, a romance writer, had attacked him for no apparent reason. Jared Stone has vowed that this incident will not stop him from expressing his honest opinions on the show."

Toreas listened to the announcer in disbelief, her glass slipping from her hand and landing near her feet. Thank God it was only seltzer. She stared at the cracked glass and frowned. If she didn't do something about Jared Stone she'd soon have to switch to plastic.

Without bothering to do more than throw down a towel, Toreas turned her attention back to the TV. She almost laughed at the pitiful look on Jared's face as he smiled wanly for the camera. He attempted to move his arm, which was in the sling, then grimaced and allowed a look of pain to cross his handsome face.

That fake, she thought. *I didn't punch him in the arm, it was his stomach*. But she began to feel alarm as he mentioned not only the name of her local chapter but Liz, Elysa, Barb and Wendy as well. *Only three days*, she thought. *How did Jared manage to get so much coverage in such a short span of time?* She groaned as she remembered his threat. Dang, he must have been really good at his public relations job.

She turned to another channel to see if anybody else was carrying the ridiculous story. Apparently they were. This time she listened closely as she heard the announcer asking, "Do you plan to sue Ms.

Rose, Mr. Stone?"

Toreas glared at her screen as Jared turned toward the camera and smiled. "I never wanted this to happen." He glanced at his arm. "I won't sue. Not if she's willing to come back on my show and say she's sorry. After all, I thought romance writers wrote about love, not violence."

The nerve of him. She'd rather die first. Was that a dimple she saw? Actually it was two dimples, one on each cheek

Toreas shook her head. What was she thinking of? She didn't care about Jared Stone's dimples.

She closed her eyes against the flecks of gold dancing in his brown eyes. Somehow she knew this act was for her. He was grinning at her from her television, making it personal. Toreas inadvertently rubbed her finger along her lips, remembering his kiss.

No, no, no. She couldn't possibly want him to kiss her again. It had been way too long since she'd had a man in her life. This was too unbelievable, something she wouldn't even write. She hated sappy, predictable romance stories and sure as heck wasn't going to allow her real life to become one. She would avoid the man like the plague.

Go back on his show? No sir, no way. If she did, this time she might carry a gun and she might use it. Nope, give it another week and this story would die down.

Toreas thought about an Ex-President. Hardly anyone even mentioned him using the White House for his little tryst anymore. Heck, she was a long way from being famous.

A week at most, then it should have run its course.

The phone rang and without even checking her caller ID she knew it would be Liz. Still, from force of habit she looked and groaned.

"Did you see him on the news?"

Toreas could feel herself beginning to squirm. "Well, we can still be thankful that it's not national."

"Are you crazy? Not only did they mention our names but they mentioned our group and ARW by name. This thing is not going to go away."

"Come on, Liz." Toreas stopped. She had to try and convince herself as well as her friend.

"Listen, he's on independent television, he's not much more than just a small time cable guy trying to get some free publicity for the station. If I ignore him, eventually he'll go away."

"Maybe, but you know we can't keep this contained locally any longer. *KGB* may be independent and it might not be anywhere near as large as *WGN*, but it is a lot bigger than just a local cable show. Everyone's going to find out."

Toreas sighed and glanced at her dinner, no longer hungry. "Yeah, I'm dreading the next meeting. I'm sorry I hit the guy and that I got the rest of you involved in my mess."

"You're sorry?"

"Of course I am. I don't know what came over me. I just hit him without thinking."

"Then tell him that," Liz snapped. "You can end this thing before it goes any farther."

Her support base was slipping. If Liz wanted her to tell the guy she was sorry, what would the rest of the group think? What would Kelle think about her blaming her self-defense class for her own boorish behavior?

"Liz, that's my other line. I have to go now."

"I didn't hear anything."

"Well, I did. I'll talk to you later."

There was not another call waiting but Toreas wasn't in the mood to be scolded. She wished she had never contacted the station, had never gotten angry at the way Jared was portraying romance writers and readers.

Now she'd made the whole thing worse. To top it off, Liz had not mentioned once that Jared was faking and she had been there. Liz knew the guy wasn't seriously injured and definitely not his arm.

Why wasn't anyone sticking up for her? *Probably because you're wrong.* The thought popped into her head from out of nowhere. It didn't matter. She still wasn't going to go back on that darn show, not ever.

No sooner had the thought formed in her mind than the inevitable began. Her phone rang. One after the other, the members of her group called or emailed and asked her what she had done to Jared Stone.

It no longer worked to blame Kelle, so Toreas attempted to minimize what had happened by saying Jared had kissed her and she hit him.

Technically what she said was true. She just had the order of the events wrong. She found she got more sympathy from her polished version, though. She'd thought it would make her feel better. She had wanted sympathy. Now she had it, but it was all a big fat lie. Besides, there was a good chance they would see what happened when the tape was shown.

Toreas sighed and shook her head, wishing again as she had in the past weeks that she'd never turned the sound up. If only she'd kept it muted she would have never heard the mean things Jared Stone was saying. He would still be her hero. She could feel herself glaring and had to wonder if the real reason she was so angry with Jared was that he'd shown her hero to have feet of clay.

Moaning in despair, Toreas took her phone off the hook, no longer wanting to talk to anyone. Her stomach was all tied in knots from worrying if Jared would really sue her. Heck, she didn't have any money. She'd never even sold a book. How would she pay him?

✍

She dreamt that night of brown eyes with flecks of gold and dimpled cheeks, of soft sensuous lips kissing her until she was dizzy.

Toreas awoke with a start, realizing she had been dreaming of Jared Stone, her worst nightmare.

For the next several days she busied herself on her computer and fielded the calls, refusing to do any more explaining. She had already sent word over the loop that she had lost her temper and punched the man. She didn't know what the group really thought; she had been too afraid to open her emails.

God. And they'd wanted a chance to appear on *Oprah*. Toreas shuddered to think what would have happened to her if she had done to the queen of talk shows what she had done to Jared.

Well, that's different, she told herself. *The queen doesn't care much for us, but at least she doesn't go around trashing us either.*

She had to wonder what Jared's agenda was. Didn't he have anything else to talk about? Why his sudden interest and increasingly vicious attacks on a group of writers who had done nothing to him?

Apparently the station had given him her number because Jared was calling her repeatedly. The man was tenacious, she had to give him that. He alternated between threatening her and trying to charm her. When that failed, he'd tried to reason with her, convince her it would be good for her. No way would Toreas's being around Jared be good for her. Her emotions where he was concerned were too conflicted.

Even now with everything that was happening she couldn't stop herself from turning the television channel to Jared's show. For a few moments she watched him with the sound muted and then she closed her eyes and turned up the volume.

Is there such a thing as love at first sight? This reporter recently attempted to ask romance writer Toreas Rose. Her answer was, "No comment." That sounds like a big fat no to me. The writer knows how to throw a punch but does she know the first thing about love? For that matter, it appears Ms. Rose doesn't even know how to apologize when she's done something wrong. Believe me, I've held out the olive branch to her. I would think that as a romance writer she would want to come on the show and see what would happen. Maybe we could have real chemistry if she'd only give it a chance. Wouldn't a true romantic

*wonder? Maybe coming on my show would give her new material for a
book. How does she know what could happen if she doesn't give it a
chance? Maybe I could be the man of her dreams. But will she give either
of us a chance to find out? The answer to that, dear viewer, is a no. Stay
tuned and I'll bring you more tomorrow on the world of romance and
Toreas Rose.*

Toreas was furious. Jared Stone couldn't just use her name like that.
And what he said, surely it had to be considered slander. She frowned,
trying to remember. No, he had not lied, but still he'd insinuated
things. She reached for the phone and immediately put it back down.
That was how their war had gotten started in the first place.

Yet the next week Toreas found herself once again turning the
channel to *Straight up-No chaser*. Surely by now he was talking about
something else. Jared stared into the red light of the camera as if he'd
been waiting for her. It was funny, the way he smiled as though he
knew she was watching. What was wrong with that man?

"Toreas Rose, are you out there watching? I know you are," Jared
purred. "Today we're going to talk about, you guessed it, romance
writers. Toreas, just this past month alone I've counted thirty-seven
stories of the amnesiac bride. Do you really think that many women
are walking around marrying guys when they've lost their memory?"
Jared snickered. "Maybe that's the reason women write romances and
other women read them. Maybe you've all lost your memories. Toreas,
I'm extending an open invitation to you to come on my show and tell
my viewers your side of the romance story."

Toreas didn't know what else Jared said because she turned off the
set. The man was infuriating. He was definitely better at looking
pretty than keeping his mouth shut.

This was the last straw for her. Someone had to do something. If, as
he claimed, he never read the stuff, why was he defaming it? And why
did he have so many accurate statistics?

It was all a mystery, one she didn't care to solve. Jared Stone could
rot in hell as far as she was concerned.

☙

Toreas walked into her bi-monthly writers meeting with
trepidation. Not only hadn't that stupid incident with Jared blown
over, it had gotten worse.

The late night talk shows had picked up on it and Jared was all over
the place looking pitiful, pretending that he was injured.

On *Letterman*, he'd even produced a document that he claimed was
from his doctor. She knew it had to be forged. There was nothing
wrong with the man. She was the one who'd used Ben-Gay for a week
and slept with a heating pad.

Her entire family was up in arms over this nonsense. Her brothers, Michael and Billy, were ready to move to Chicago to protect her.

When her father phoned her from Georgia, that was the topper. He was ready to fly to Chicago on a moment's notice and kick Jared's butt properly. It had taken some doing to reassure him that the newspaper articles and news stories were exaggerated and were only the very clever work of a crafty publicity hound.

"Listen," he'd told her. "I don't like what the man has accused you of. I know you were raised better than to attack someone and especially not in public—not on television—unless the man molested you. Did he?"

Toreas could hear her father's voice raised in anger. Molested no, kissed yes. But she knew better than to even joke about that. Her father was serious.

"Tesa, did that man molest you?"

"No, Daddy, it's just his way of thinking he's clever. He's going for ratings. I had no idea an independent station could garner such attention. I guess I forgot about satellite TV. You don't have to worry about me. This will die down if I refuse to respond."

"It hasn't so far," her father growled. "I can make it stop tomorrow."

"Daddy, it's my problem. I'll deal with it. Don't worry."

"I knew something like this would happen. I should have never allowed your mother to influence my decision to allow you to move to Chicago. Your wanting to write was one thing. I never thought your leaving home was a smart idea. One thing I haven't changed my mind about is your new friends. I don't want you hanging around with those women in that writers' group. They're putting bad ideas into your head, making you write trash. We raised you as a Christian and what you want to write has nothing to do with Christianity."

"I know, Dad. If it's not edifying the kingdom, it's of no value." She said what he wanted to hear. What good would it do to tell him that her group had not influenced her? That she'd smuggled romance novels to Sunday school tucked between her bible and her lessons. Talking disappointed—He'd be even more disappointed if he knew she had a massager, and not for back rubs.

"Don't forget our agreement," her father continued. "It'll soon be two years. I expect you to honor your word. I want you to come home where I can keep an eye on you."

"Daddy, I'm a grown woman."

"That doesn't matter. You're always going to be my baby."

Toreas remembered the agreement well. She'd known when he proposed the deal that it could be the same for her as making a deal with the devil. When her father had challenged her to quit her job and take two years to concentrate on her writing, to become a professional in that time or stop, she'd known the risk she was taking. She knew he was aware of how many people failed after a decade of trying. Still, the offer was the best one she'd had, so she'd accepted. His monthly checks had supplemented her savings, allowing her to live in Chicago and write full time. Living in Chicago hadn't been part of her plan but she'd thought it best to see something more of the world than Georgia. Her mother had agreed.

A shiver trailed over her spine, bringing Toreas back to her meeting. She glanced at Becca's scowling face and at her fiery red hair. Hair that was so red that she could have been gifted with it only from the devil himself. That color couldn't be found in a bottle. It was all her own and now it appeared to be ready to burst into flames as Becca fixed her with a glare that would have melted a glacier. If only Toreas hadn't been thinking of her father and the deal she'd made with him, those thoughts of Becca would have never popped into her head.

"I hear you've been very busy making things hard for all of us. It would have been nice if you had bothered to answer any of my calls or the dozen emails I sent you."

And it would be nice if we were having this conversation in private, Toreas thought. But then again, what she had done had affected the entire group, hadn't it?

"Listen, Becca, I'm sorry and I want to apologize to the group for any embarrassment I may have inadvertently caused."

She looked around the room, gauging the temperature, wondering if everyone was freezing her out. Some of the faces were trying hard not to smile and they almost succeeded, that is, until Kelle spoke.

"I understand you hurt yourself more than you did Jared," Kelle said.

Toreas was pretty sure that was a smirk she saw on Kelle's face. "Yeah, I think I might have delivered the punch wrong." She was still standing as though waiting for permission to sit.

"I guess you'll pay more attention next time. If you hit a guy right he shouldn't have the strength to get back up and kiss you, nor should he want to."

Kelle's gaze darted around the room. Toreas noted her usually calm veneer was now agitated. She took teaching women self-defense seriously.

The fact that the failure of one of her pupils to carry out her instructions to the letter had caused injury to the student and not the perpetrator angered her. The entire chapter knew Kelle's stance on this issue.

Her look was so fierce that Toreas started laughing. She knew she shouldn't, but she couldn't help herself, not even after Becca started ringing her bell for attention. She couldn't stop.

Her laugh was infectious. One after the other, the women started laughing, that is, all but Becca. With her red hair, a pitchfork would have been all that she needed to complete the look she was giving them. Yep, her look was telling them all to go straight to hell.

The woman was in league with the dark angel, the big kahuna himself, the old red one. Satan.

Toreas sank back into a chair, staring at Becca with tears of amusement running down her face, smearing mascara in uneven tracks. She did her best to pull herself together.

"I really am sorry." She bit her upper lip, needing to feel grounded, needing to stop the now almost hysterical laughter she was feeling. Becca was glaring at her and all the women who continued to laugh.

"This isn't funny," she began. "This affects all of our careers. Think about that, ladies, while you're laughing, smiling, or smirking."

Becca had raised her voice but it wasn't the tone that stopped the laughter. It was her words.

"Toreas, you started this by going on that show. Correction, by calling them. We never gave a darn about the man. Most of us had never heard of him. Now the whole world knows who he is and we're all just one big joke."

Toreas squirmed in her seat as Becca's look pinned her.

"Those readers you wanted to defend, do you think you've helped them? I'll tell you the answer. No. Now they'll have to go back to hiding romance books in brown paper bags."

Brown paper bags? Where does Becca get this stuff? No one uses paper bags anymore, they use plastic. The image of a group of romance readers hiding their books was hysterical. It was only with strong-willed determination that Toreas didn't start laughing again.

She had hoped that Becca was done. No such luck. It seemed she had only paused long enough to allow what she was saying to sink in.

"Toreas, you're an adult, not a three-year-old. You should know how to control your temper."

"I thought it was only in fiction that people can be perfectly controlled," Toreas answered. "I thought a real person is allowed to be imperfect."

"What are you talking about?"

Toreas watched as one by one Becca froze them all with a glare, and then sat back in her seat. Okay, she had to stop being childish. It wasn't fair to try and blame her friends for not supporting her when what'd she'd done was affecting all of them. They were a great bunch of women and she was lucky to have them as part of her support system.

Only right now she could feel her support giving way as though it had been built on sand, and she didn't like the feeling.

She was aware of what they all wanted her to do. It seemed a simple enough thing, to go back on the show and tell Jared Stone she was wrong. If it would end there, maybe, just maybe, she would consider it. But she doubted that had ever been Jared's intention and now that he'd gotten national attention, there was no way he was going to let her off with a simple apology.

Toreas licked her lips, eyeing the huge bottle of water that Lauren brought with her to each meeting and wishing she could have a drop. There wasn't even any spit in her mouth. How the heck could she go back on television when she couldn't even talk to her group?

She cleared her throat several times and sighed loudly. "I can't go back, he would crucify me. I couldn't even talk when I was there."

Liz glanced over at her. "She's right, Becca. When you see the tape you'll see she sat glued to her seat, scared to death."

"Yeah, she couldn't even name our group or tell him what it stands for. The most basic things she couldn't even answer. It was pretty disgusting."

Thanks a lot, Wendy. Was that supposed to be support? Toreas wanted more than anything to glare at Wendy, but for now she decided to let it go.

Now not only was her tongue glued to the roof of her mouth but it seemed her butt was glued to the chair. She wiggled trying to get comfortable, wanting something to drink. She eyed Lauren's water again. She didn't feel her legs would carry her to the fountain in the hall. God, what she wouldn't give for a drink right now.

"Can't you just write him a note?"

Elysa was staring at her with something akin to contempt. Toreas stared back. "I supposed I could. What would I say?"

"You're a writer, use your imagination."

Becca turned in her direction. "It's agreed then. You'll write the man a note and get him off our backs."

"I'll write the note, but remember, he was on our backs before any of this happened."

One after the other she could feel rather than see the women looking at her, thinking that if she just wrote the note the problem would go away. *Fine*, she thought. I'll write the darn note. *Then they'll see it won't matter.* They were still looking at her. She kept forgetting people couldn't read her mind. "Okay, I'll write the note."

"Now that that's settled we'll move along with the business portion of our meeting." Becca appeared pacified for the moment and was now smiling her usual cheery smile. Toreas had no idea what the meeting was about. She only knew she felt backed into a corner. Her only support had come from her friend calling her a coward. At least it was better than Wendy practically calling her stupid and Toreas was still smarting over that comment. When the rustle of bodies and chairs being shoved back caught her attention, she knew the meeting was over.

"So are you coming with us to the restaurant?"

It was Lauren. Toreas looked at her and at the partially empty bottle of water that was now nestled in Lauren's arm. For some strange reason she wanted to rip the bottle away and pour the remainder of the contents on the woman's head.

She didn't know why, just that she wanted to do it. Instead she smiled. "No, not tonight, I'm going to go home and write that note." *And try and figure out where this sudden violent streak is coming from,* she thought. *Lust for Jared Stone.* The words slammed into her mind and she groaned, praying that wasn't the reason for her odd behavior.

True to her word, the moment Toreas was home she did as she'd promised. She wrote Jared a note. She chose plain white stationary, the cheap kind she had stopped using eons ago. The ends were yellowed with age but she didn't care. That was all Jared Stone deserved.

> *Mr. Stone,*
> *I'm sorry that you're the rudest*
> *person I've ever met, and that I allowed you to*
> *antagonize me to the point of violence. I'm also*
> *sorry that you appear to have nothing better to*
> *do with your time than to harass romance writers*
> *and readers. Perhaps you do this because*
> *you've never been loved. Could that be the*
> *reason, Mr. Stone? Did some woman find your*
> *disagreeable behavior a real turn off? Are you*
> *more the villain than the hero? Think about it.*
> *As for our little mishap, I've assigned to myself ten*
> *percent blame as one of the responsible parties*
> *involved in your unfortunate incident. The other*
> *ninety goes to you.*
> *Sincerely,*
> *Toreas Rose*

Toreas reread her note and laughed, knowing there was no way she could possibly send it. She pulled out another sheet of paper and wrote a real note of apology. It was short, quick and to the point. *"I'm sorry for my bad behavior."* She shook her head and left the note on the table. She'd take the final step and put it in the envelope later. Right before she went to bed she could put it off no longer. She hastily grabbed what she'd written and without bothering to check, crammed it in the even more yellowed envelope and licked it shut, making a face from the awful taste of the glue. "That's as much of an apology as you're going to get, Mr. Stone," she muttered out loud.

To her surprise she found herself caressing his name on the front of the envelope. She suddenly felt hot and found it hard to swallow. She pushed the envelope away from her. *Whatever you want, Jared Stone, you're not going to get it.*

3

Jared Stone sat in his office reading his sudden influx of fan mail. He would have to thank that Ms. Priss, Toreas Rose. Prior to that, his fledgling career at a two bit independent station had been about to come to an end. Derrick wasn't making enough money to keep paying him what he was getting. Now there was new blood and renewed interest. And with that interest new sponsors had picked up *Straight Up—No Chaser*.

Heck, he'd only taken the job to get him out of Los Angeles. What he knew about hosting a talk show was about as much as that Rose woman knew about romance.

She had been nothing like he expected. He had watched her from the moment she came on the stage. From the fury of her calls he had expected some Amazon to come storming out. Instead, what he saw was a timid, mousy little woman who sat with her feet tucked under her and looked scared to death, as if she thought the camera was aimed under her skirt. True, he could tell that with major overhaul the woman would be a knockout. But he wasn't looking for a knockout, he was looking to obliterate the romance writer.

Still, her golden bronze skin was the stuff millions of women spent tons of money and hours in the sun to acquire. Hers was natural, as was her hair that she was wearing in a throwback to the sixties. On her the curly afro looked wonderful and she had to know that. So he wondered at the contradictions in the woman. He'd looked at the way she tugged on her overly long skirt while glaring at the camera. He'd frowned at the hideous oversized sweater the woman had worn. The other women had reeked of femininity, but not Toreas Rose. She reeked of vagabond, waif, homeless, and he'd be damn if he hadn't found her intriguing, especially her fascination with the camera.

She'd treated the thing as if it were the enemy out to steal her virginity. She kept glaring at it as though she thought someone was trying to get a shot underneath that skirt she kept tugging at. Even if it had been aimed in that direction, the cameraman would have had to do some fancy footwork to get a shot beneath all that billowing material. The darn skirt was so long it nearly dragged the floor, even when she was standing.

Jared tapped his finger on the desk, remembering when he'd first locked gazes with Toreas. The woman had stopped her fussing and stared straight ahead at him, their eyes locking for a moment, long enough for Jared to think to himself, *Wow, I had it wrong, she isn't mousy at all*.

But the moment had passed as the intensity of the woman's stare burned straight through him. Her glare was personal and he wondered why.

True, he had been taking potshots at romance writers and readers for months, but his reasons were his own. He had never planned to turn it into a full scale war. He was only venting until he got over...

No, he wouldn't think about that. He would only think about how much fun he was having tormenting the hapless woman. The woman intrigued him and it had nothing to do with her looks. First, she'd called and demanded that he be stopped. Then when she was given an opportunity to talk, she froze.

Without warning she'd punched him. He'd seen that she was every bit as surprised as he was. But for some reason the woman refused to apologize. There was more to her than met the eye. He didn't think she was as helpless as she appeared at first glance.

Jared looked down at the latest letter he had received from yet another romance writer. They were coming out of the woodwork.

If he had known there were so many of them maybe he would have had a better battle plan before he began his attack. Maybe he would have included a way to surrender without losing. Part of him felt sorry for the women and Toreas Rose in particular. But ratings were ratings. And he did owe Derrick a favor. Not only that, he really wanted his friend to make a go of his station.

Jared exhaled noisily, running the scenario over and over in his mind. Maybe he should leave the romance writers alone. But then again, they were indirectly responsible for ruining his life. He deserved a little harmless revenge.

The women were definitely keeping him amused. To date he had received over a hundred letters from women all over the country. At least a dozen of them came from the same chapter, the one Toreas Rose was a member of. They were all apologizing for her behavior, calling it unforgivable. He couldn't help noticing that not one of the women mentioned his behavior, how badly he had treated the women, or the hostility he'd created when he stepped in front of Toreas Rose. And no, not even his boss had admonished him for kissing her.

Jared had expected another punch, had even been prepared for it but it never came. For a brief second she'd merely looked at him. Then her eyes went cold and he released her.

He was beginning to feel a familiar warmth creeping up on him but he refused to allow it free rein. Yet he could not keep his tongue from coming out of his mouth and slowly traversing the length of his lips as though searching for the taste of her.

The kiss had been brief but memorable. The woman had soft full lips. He smiled. They were also sweet, reminding him of fresh washed strawberries.

Okay, that's far enough. He stood and paced around the room, needing to release the sudden restriction in his throat and elsewhere. He didn't want this woman. Only a darn fool would even have the thoughts he was having, but heaven help him, he was having them.

A romance writer? No way, no way. Not after what they'd done to him. In taking Gina from him they'd taken away his opportunity to fulfill his promise to his mother. She'd never asked for much from him, just for him to get married and give her grandchildren before she died.

He'd known it was motherly manipulation, but still, he'd given her the promise. Why not? His mother was as healthy as a horse. It had only been when she'd turned up the guilt that he'd convinced himself that he cared enough for Gina to marry her and give his mother grandchildren.

Two weeks after Gina's betrayal his mother had been killed in a car accident, leaving Jared feeling guilty for having never fulfilled his promise. Of course common sense told him his mother's death was a tragic accident and that even if he'd married Gina there would not have been time to give his mother the grandchildren she'd wanted. Still, unbearable grief over losing her had made him focus on his promise to her. He'd been close to both parents, and after his father died suddenly of a massive heart attack, Jared had grown even closer to his mother. After the accident he'd needed someone to blame for his failure to keep his promise, whether they deserved it or not, he'd blamed romance writers for taking Gina from him, thus robbing him of the chance to produce the grandchildren his mother had wanted.

Sure, the past weeks had been a lot of fun and he'd called in a lot of favors to go national, but now it was getting dangerous. He was beginning to feel again. It was time to stop the game. Jared turned as his office door opened and Derrick rushed in, his face red with excitement, a bag clutched in his arms.

"Jared, you won't believe it. Another bag of mail just came for you.

Man, you've gotten more mail in the past two weeks than this entire station has received in two years. You're a hit."

Jared peered at Derrick. "Don't you know how to knock?" He wasn't really annoyed at the intrusion but at himself for what he'd been thinking. He watched as his boss, the owner of the station, looked down toward the floor as though he were a little kid being scolded. He'd forgotten how sensitive Derrick was in certain areas.

"Sorry about that, man. I just got excited," Derrick apologized.

"We've gotten all the mileage we're going to get out of this." Jared paused, knowing how his next words would be received. "I'm thinking of backing off, leaving the women alone."

"But you can't. I've taken out a full page ad in both the *Chicago Tribune* and the *Sun Times*, an opinion poll asking people to vote if they think she should come back on the show."

"There's no way she's going to do that." Jared ignored the hitch in his throat.

"It doesn't matter; the whole thing will give us more publicity. Advertisers are even calling, wanting time on your show. Man, this feud is turning into a real cash cow."

Jared gazed at his friend. He had been the one to rescue him from the hell his life had become in Los Angeles. He'd visited when he realized what a deep depression Jared had sunk into after his mother's death. He'd begged Jared to help him out with his struggling independent television station by coming back to Chicago and hosting a show. They'd both known what Derrick was doing. He'd made up a job for Jared to get him out of L. A., to help him come out of his depression. He looked at the pleasure beaming from the man's ruddy cheeks. How could he deny him a chance to make a go of his dreams? The feud with the writers was bringing money to the station.

A tiny ping of conscience nagged at him. He was positive Toreas Rose was receiving some flack from this. He could tell from the comments in the letters. He would feel like a real heel if he didn't try once again to dissuade Derrick.

"Listen, what if what we're doing actually ends up hurting the woman? I never intended it to go this far. I only wanted to push the romance writers a little, you know, make them squirm."

Even as he said it he knew that wasn't what he'd been after. He'd wanted the women to admit that sometimes the stories they wrote broke up relationships, that after reading romance some women might become bored with reality and want something new and different, maybe even a man who looked like a cover model.

It wasn't far-fetched. That's what had happened with Gina. In the beginning Jared hadn't known about her addiction. He'd found out

Gina was a voracious romance reader when out of the blue the writers held a conference in Los Angeles and had a contest to choose a hunky male for one of those bodice ripper novels.

The writers had used good promo. Jared had to admit to that. They'd even hired the firm he worked for to get the guys in town interested in coming out and posing. Jared hadn't been able to believe at first how many men wanted to be featured on those covers.

Anyway, the writers had secured a suite at the Bali, one of the most prestigious hotels in town and had charged the women who attended fifty bucks a pop, serving them only champagne punch and cheese and crackers, but offering them the opportunity to see the beefcake parade and vote for their choice of best male hunk out of a field of 200 male models or model wannabees.

Gina had wasted no time in buying a ticket for the event. After seeing the buffed guys strutting their stuff, she'd fallen in love with one of the male models.

So yes, Jared had good reason to hate the writers. He'd been on the verge of telling Gina that he wanted to make their relationship exclusive, that he thought he might be on the verge of falling in love with her. That is, he was thinking he might be, but he never got the chance to find out. Gina was suddenly gone from his life, just like that.

Her departure sent his confidence into the toilet. But it was his mother's death two weeks later that sent him into a deep depression. His unfulfilled promise to her weighed heavily on his heart. Derrick's visit had been nothing less than a godsend. The last thing he'd wanted to do was remain in a town with Gina, the woman, who could have been the one to help him keep his promise and the man with the toothpaste ad grin.

To add to the irony, because of his involvement with the event, Jared might have been the one who sent the guy over to the writers' convention in the first place. He hadn't bothered to find out. It would have been too much like pouring salt into an open wound.

"Are you listening to me, Jared?"

Jared closed his eyes and shook his head gently to dislodge the memories. He owed Derrick. "Yeah, I'm listening."

"Well, listen to this. So what if the women's feelings get a little bent out of shape? In the long run this will help their careers. They'll probably all sell tons of books."

Jared attempted to smile. "You're probably right, but I was just thinking of something that woman Liz said. She said they worked hard to make people understand what they do, that they're not just a bunch of bored, air-head housewives."

"Who cares? Our ratings are hitting the roof."

Jared speared his friend with a look and tried again to back off. "Shouldn't we care? This doesn't feel like fun anymore."

Derrick was glaring at him, wringing his hands. Jared watched as the veins began to pop out on his neck.

"You owe me, man."

Jared walked toward him. "Don't pull that on me."

Jared stopped when he saw the fear enter Derrick's eyes. Oh yes, this had all gone much too far. He smiled weakly at him, and then smoothed his hand down the side of his slacks trying to push away the thought of what he knew he was about to do. "You're right, I do owe you."

"I shouldn't have used that on you. I'm sorry about that. But I thought you wanted to get back at Gina. I'm the one helping you with your little vendetta."

Derrick was fast talking him. Jared knew that, but it was working. It was making him forget the honey brown woman with the short afro and the strawberry-flavored lips and remember instead the conniving blonde bombshell who'd left him cold. Maybe Derrick was right, maybe a few more weeks of this wouldn't hurt anyone.

Then his hand hit on the discolored envelope and he knew what was in it. He opened it up and took out a sheet of paper surprised to see that Toreas Rose had apologized. Then he realized a second sheet was stuck to it. He read the second sheet and laughed out loud. *This was what Toreas Rose thought was an apology?* He looked again at the first apology, knowing she'd written it after she'd written what she'd really wanted to say. He wondered what would happen when she realized she'd mailed it with the one she'd obviously intended to send.

Jared knew it, had known it all along. The woman had guts. He didn't know what had happened to her when she was on the show, but she was anything but the wimp he had first pegged her for.

He looked at the note and laughed again. The paper looked as if it had probably belonged to her grandmother. It was that yellow with age, nothing like the flowery stationary the other writers had sent. There was no personal header, nothing. He much preferred the note he knew he wasn't supposed to see versus the note that read, *"I'm sorry for my bad behavior."*

He read her words on the second sheet of paper carefully. She was actually telling him the whole thing was his fault, something none of the others had had the guts to do. He happened to look up and noticed that Derrick was eyeing him with a question in his eyes.

"Don't worry." Jared laughed again. "I think this might continue to be fun. Listen, do you have that letter from Becca Kamp, the chapter president?"

"Yeah, do you want it?"

"Turnabout's fair play. Toreas Rose spoke to my boss, now I think I'll speak to hers."

As Derrick went off in search of the letter, Jared's mind strayed once again to the soft, full, luscious lips that tasted like strawberries.

✍

It was two days before Toreas realized her mistake. She was dumping her waste basket when she realized she didn't see any yellowed note paper. She dumped the contents of the can on the floor and searched the trash frantically. *Oh no*, she thought. *Please, God, don't let Jared read that note.*

Toreas rubbed her hand across her head that was now hurting. There was no way Jared Stone had not read the note. She wondered why he hadn't called her. She thought to call him and explain the note she'd not intended to send. Then she dismissed the thought. She didn't want to talk to Jared; he would only ask her to come back on the show. To ask him not to show the note would mean she'd owe him a favor. She didn't think it safe to be in Jared's debt. She'd just have to wait for the shoe to drop, to see what he planned to do with the note.

4

There was excitement in the air. Becca was ringing the bell for all she was worth and there was a secret smile on her face. *Oh, oh*, Toreas thought. The hairs on the back of her neck prickled. Something about this meeting wasn't right.

Becca had been bugging her for over a week, wanting to know if she'd received any response from her note of apology to Jared. Then suddenly without warning she'd dropped her attack.

"Ladies, take your seat."

Becca was preening, tamping her hair down with the palm of her hand. *That's not like her*, Torcas thought. Usually Becca contained her fiery hair with fancy barrettes.

No, there was something wrong. Toreas sat back in her chair to wait for the bomb, the knots in her stomach her surefire signal that something was amiss, something big and coming soon.

"Ladies, we have a special guest tonight."

Toreas watched as Becca paused for effect. The knots were pulling tighter and when she looked down at her arm, the hairs were standing on end.

"I know this was not on our calendar but I'm sure this speaker will be able to help some of you with ideas you might be working on."

Becca smiled then. "He's very anxious to talk to our group and perhaps he can give us the male perspective on romance. Also, as an added treat, he's in television and has agreed to allow us to pick his brain. He also worked for several years in advertising and public relations. Please, let's welcome…"

Toreas stared at Becca with horror. Then she turned quickly toward Liz, wondering if she knew. She didn't need to hear his name. She knew who it was. Jared Stone. Oh God, no. Not here. This was supposed to be her safe place.

"Now let's welcome Jared Stone."

When Becca started applauding, the door opened. Obviously the two of them had worked out that little signal beforehand.

Toreas attempted to clap. It was the only polite thing to do, but she couldn't. How could Becca do such a thing to her? Hadn't she seen the polls in the papers? The man had gotten the entire state involved in their feud; now he had been invited into her home, so to speak.

Toreas could hear the gasps of surprise, the quick intakes of breath. Even she had to admit the man was handsome, but so what?

They were behaving as though they had never seen a handsome man. My God, they frequently had various cover models come to their meetings, so there was nothing special about Jared Stone. And if she didn't look at him she could keep telling herself that.

Jared stood in the middle of the room smiling at the women, caressing each one in turn with his eyes, making each feel that he was there for her alone.

Toreas was doing her best to keep her eyes down on her open notepad. She had to find something else to look at.

Jared's voice was smooth and rough at the same time. Toreas curled her toes inside her shoes and gripped her pen for all she was worth. She didn't want to look at him.

She heard him talking, laughing easily, and answering the women's questions. All the time she felt the heat rising in her face, reaching out toward him. She wanted to keep her head down but it was as though an invisible string was forcing her to look up into his eyes.

He was looking at her, and he was laughing at her. Though he was answering the women's questions, it didn't matter. She could tell he was laughing at her.

"Mr. Stone, could you tell us why you hate romance books so much if you haven't read them?"

"Because they're nonsense. There is hate at first sight, not love." He smiled in Toreas's direction. "I think if you kissed a woman the moment you met her, sparks would fly and she'd slug you. What do you think, Ms. Rose? Would you hit me if I kissed you?"

"Not if you had permission," Toreas answered, feeling her skin warm with embarrassment. *Oh lord*, she thought, *what in the world has gotten into me?* She chewed on her lip, knowing how Jared would take that.

"If I asked you for permission would you give it to me?"

"No," Toreas said under her breath and began scribbling notes on her paper, wishing Jared would go away.

"Why not, Toreas? Isn't this the stuff romance is made of? Isn't this the stuff you write about?" He came and stood directly in front of her and grinned. "Shouldn't you be writing this down?" He glanced at the paper in front of her. "Are you?"

Toreas covered her paper with her hand and glared at Jared.

"Mr. Stone, you haven't answered the question. How do you know so much about romance if you don't read it?"

Good. It was Liz. Now the whole group would be able to rip him to shreds, something they had failed to accomplish on the show. Toreas settled into her seat and sat back to watch Jared squirm out of this one.

"Well," he smiled a lazy smile then directed his gaze toward Toreas. "Let me ask a question. Ms. Rose, how do you conduct your research?"

It was an innocent enough question. Heck, they'd had many sessions on just how to answer that very question but with the eyes of the entire group on her and Jared's tawny gaze doing things to her that she shouldn't even be thinking, she couldn't answer. She gripped her pen harder. Why was he intent on staying on her?

She refused to allow the silence to overtake her again. She pried her lips apart with her tongue.

"The stories are fiction, Mr. Stone. You figure it out."

Kelle and Lauren glanced at her and she glanced back at them, knowing what they were thinking: *There she goes being nasty again.* The carefree mood Jared had managed to bring into the room was seeping away and it was all her fault.

"Exactly my point, Ms. Rose. You can't write about love and passion if you've never experienced it. You can't write about characters falling in love at first glance unless it's happened to you."

"How do you know it hasn't," Toreas asked.

"Has it?" Jared smiled while Toreas squirmed. "I'm only trying to help you with your stories." He laughed out loud when Toreas glared at him and rolled her eyes.

"Ms. Rose, I've read enough romance novels to know that when a strange man kisses a woman she generally kisses him back." He tilted his head, enjoying the blush that stole over her skin. Damn. This was even more intriguing; a black woman blushing. He decided to press his advantage.

He stared into her eyes, holding her gaze, watching as she swallowed. He was making her nervous. He smiled gently when he saw her biting her lips, wishing his own lips were there to cushion the sharp edges of her teeth. He found he had to swallow himself before he could continue. "Have you ever imagined yourself as a heroine in a romance novel, Ms. Rose?"

"Why would I imagine something like that?"

"If you could imagine it then maybe when a strange man kisses you, well, I'd say you'd know what to do. And hitting him wouldn't be your first response. Participation in the kiss would be."

It was time to wrap up his questioning of Toreas. Her eyes were as large as...Well, Jared had no comparisons. He'd never seen a woman open her eyes so wide. But she was looking as if she wanted to bolt. "I'm sorry for having kissed you without your permission, Ms. Rose. But I had really thought that writers experienced things they wrote about. I never meant to offend you." He smiled. "I would be willing to kiss you again if you want. That is, if you want to use more than your imagination. If you want your stories to be believable, I have a suggestion. Maybe some field training would work wonders." He then had the nerve to turn to Liz and smile.

"Perhaps you're right. Maybe I have been rather harsh on you ladies. I've only skimmed a few hundred romance books and they all seemed pretty alike to me. Maybe yours are different, I don't know. I guess it's my fault for not taking you ladies up on your offer to read some of your work. If you will forgive my oversight and my behavior, we can remedy that situation. Reading some of your work could help my perspective."

The shuffle of bags being opened was almost deafening. With his sexy smile and dimpled cheeks, he had managed to charm the women into forgetting that he was dissecting them a little at a time every day.

The women pooled their collection in the middle of the table. Becca leaned toward Jared, actually wetting her lips with her tongue. Toreas couldn't believe it. What was wrong with her friends? Had they taken leave of their senses?

"Mr. Stone."

Toreas listened as Becca practically purred.

"We have an assortment here. You can take them all or pick out a few."

He straightened then. He had been leaning against one of the tables, half sitting, half standing, but when he stood erect and turned toward Becca, Toreas couldn't take her eyes off the man's lanky body. God, he was tall.

"You ladies have all been so wonderful to me," he turned and smiled at Toreas, "especially since we've been having this little disagreement."

Please God, no, just do this one little thing for me and I promise I'll try and behave.

With a sinking feeling Toreas knew God wasn't listening, because it was obvious to the entire room that the man was looking in her direction. She closed her eyes and wished for a hole to open up and swallow her. Jared laughed and the sound washed over her, forcing her to open her eyes and look at him.

"I'm as ready to put an end to this as you ladies are. Anytime Ms. Rose wants to come back on the show, she and all of you have an open invitation. I promise, I'll be on my best behavior. Now let me take at look at your books. I think it's time I really read a romance."

He began shuffling through the pile. "I want to read Ms. Rose's book. Where is it?"

"I don't have one there. I'm still working on it." Toreas felt her entire body blush. She was embarrassed to admit to Jared that she was unpublished.

It was worse than saying she was sorry. She felt naked and so very ashamed. She looked at the pile of books to avoid seeing him laughing at her. She would have to hit him, and this time she would do it right.

"Then I would like to read what you're working on. Maybe I could be of some help."

He was standing in front of her again but luckily there was a six-foot table between them.

"No."

"No?" Jared repeated. "Why not? Just show me a few pages, something to give me an idea of where you're coming from."

He sat one hip on the table in front of her and stared. She could feel her heart doing a double dance tap. She wanted nothing more than to shove him off the table.

Maybe she did want something else. Maybe she wanted him to grab her and kiss her again in that caveman fashion, the way he had done almost a month before.

But women didn't want that anymore. They didn't want to be dominated by a male. Neither did she. Definitely not by this male. Yet here she was having a hard time breathing. The hairs on her arms were tickling her and her senses were on full alert.

Toreas pushed her chair back, away from the table. She couldn't continue to sit that close to him with his tight butt right there in front of her, begging to be touched.

"I don't want you to read my work. It's that simple."

"You're not still mad at me, are you?" He looked around the room. "Ladies, I'm sorry if there are any hard feelings, but you have to understand I have a job to bring in viewers any way I can."

His voice was soft, beguiling, and Toreas herself was tempted to believe him as she listened to him.

"You're in the same line of work," Jared continued. "We're all trying hard to make a living. If the public is on your side you're hot."

Toreas eyed her friends. They were lapping up every word. Who wouldn't? She felt her reserve starting to melt just a bit and realized she was no different from the others. She wanted to believe Jared

Stone was not a monster, just a working stiff like them.

"Ms. Rose, if you'd come back on the show it would more than likely help your group. You don't even have to apologize." He smiled at her.

Toreas felt all eyes turn on her. She refused to blush again. "I've already said I'm sorry."

"Oh that, I have it right here." He held her yellowed envelope in his hand. "It's…hmmm…interesting. Both sheets." He smiled at her then. "Would you like me to read one to the ladies?"

Heat flooded her cheeks and she knew very well that she was blushing. She glared at Jared and the condemning note he held in his hand. So that was his game. He was threatening her and she was not going to take it. She should have known. Let him read the darn thing to the group. She'd never intended to send it anyway. She refused to allow him to blackmail her. She didn't care now what he did.

"I wrote it to you but if you want to share, be my guest." Toreas smiled at him. "Go ahead, Mr. Stone. Read my note."

Jared's head dipped and he speared her with a look that sent shivers through her entire body.

"No, as you said, this was written to me. The words that are in here will remain between the two of us, our little secret. I promise. How's that, Ms. Rose?"

Jared was beginning to enjoy this, maybe a little too much. He had openly challenged Toreas and she hadn't even flinched.

He looked at the woman, short in stature but mighty in spirit and a surge of desire filled him, something he had not felt in months. And for a romance writer of all people.

A loud commotion outside the door pulled Jared's eyes from Toreas Rose. He recognized the voices and a worry line pulled at his brow. Darn it. He was enjoying the women.

Without waiting for permission, Derrick burst through the door, followed by Josh, the cameraman, and Stella, the wannabe reporter.

Jared's eyes swung around the room. The women were eyeing him with suspicion. Becca was giving him a wounded look, relaying her feelings of betrayal. He had promised to give the group a fair shot. He was there as a guest speaker, not to ambush the women.

For a few seconds Jared stood helpless, not knowing what to do. He watched as though he were on the outside looking in as Stella's hawk-like gaze searched for and found Toreas.

Within seconds Stella had a microphone shoved in her face and was questioning her.

"Ms. Rose, do you really consider the note you sent to Mr. Stone to be appropriate after the violent, unprovoked assault on him?"

Jared could tell Stella was salivating with self- importance. She was behaving more like a lawyer than a reporter, firing question after question, not really waiting for an answer.

"Ms. Rose, you said the fault for your hitting Mr. Stone was his. Did you mean that?"

Toreas glared at the reporter then turned to Jared. She smiled slightly. "Is this what you meant by keeping this between us, Mr. Stone? Is that how you keep your promises?" She shook her head, allowing the disgust she felt at Jared to show on her face. Now it was time to handle the witch who was shoving the mike in her face.

"The note you're referring to was mailed by accident. I also included another or didn't Mr. Stone think to give that one to you? Now get that camera and your mike out of my face now, or I will…"

Jared was doing his best to relay to Toreas and the rest of the chapter that he'd had no part in the ambush but it was too late. He watched as Toreas shoved the mike and Stella away from her.

He wanted to warn her that she was giving them more ammunition but knew she wouldn't listen. If he wasn't the enemy before, he knew he darn well was now.

"Now that I think about it, I think the note you're referring to that I wrote to Mr. Stone was less than what he deserved." Toreas swiveled her body around to face him.

Her look caused him to cringe. He had sensed a change in her before. She had begun to thaw. Now he knew she wouldn't let her guard down again.

"Mr. Stone, I'm going to ask you and your crew to leave. This is not what we agreed to. When you asked to come, you said you only wanted to give us information we might be able to use. You've totally disrupted our meeting."

Both Toreas and Jared turned toward Becca. Stella was poking her camera in the faces of nearby women and asking questions. They all answered "no comment," looking stunned by what was happening.

"Ms. Kamp, I didn't know about this." Jared felt Toreas's eyes on him, freezing his blood in his veins. He was no longer welcome.

When he looked at Toreas, he had the strongest desire to touch her, to look into her brown eyes and have her believe him. Instead, he looked away from her as he hustled the crew out of the now too quiet room.

"Thanks a lot, Derrick. Why did you come here?" Jared growled once they were alone in the hall.

"It was too good an opportunity to let pass. We got some great stuff."

"What stuff? The women didn't answer you and Ms. Rose didn't back down."

"We didn't want her to. We want the feud to continue."

"This is slimy, you know that, man. I'm not in this anymore."

"We're not asking you to be. I'm doing all the work. We're getting great coverage from this. We're going to sell this tape to the networks. We're going to send a copy to the papers, along with Ms. Rose's note."

Jared stopped dead in his tracks. "I have her note."

"Yeah, but we made a copy."

Jared stared at Derrick. He was actually smiling at his ingenuity in stealing Toreas's note. Jared couldn't believe it. "Don't put her note in the papers. I promised her."

"Promised her what? You didn't know about this, right?"

Jared stared at Derrick. "I promised her the note would be between us."

"You work for me. The mail is mine."

"My name's on it."

"Then sue me. Look, Jared, you owe me. Remember?"

"I remember, but it's not a debt I plan on paying forever." He glared at his supposed friend, angrier than he'd ever been at Gina.

"Don't use that note. You can continue the war, just don't use the note, or I'm going to buy every paper that it's in and shove the article down your throat."

Jared stood his ground, watching as his boss swallowed several times before answering.

"Okay. You're getting soft, Jared. We won't use the note. I have a better angle. I'll use that shot of her shoving Stella. That'll work better anyway."

"Derrick, she had a right to shove that mike out of her face. Besides, she didn't really shove Stella. Stella was just sort of in the way." Jared laughed.

"Tell you what," Derrick grinned. "We'll air the tape and the people can decide."

Jared started toward Derrick, then noticed Josh fiddling with the camera and stopped. He shook his head and turned away. All of this had been started why? Because of Gina's leaving him. A woman he didn't even want anymore.

He was at a loss to explain why he didn't want her anymore, except to think somehow Toreas Rose's punch to the gut had knocked some sense into his brain.

In the past month Jared had derived more pleasure, perverse though it might be, from annoying Toreas Rose than he had the entire time he was dating Gina.

If he admitted the truth to himself, it was only after Gina left him cold that he thought he had been in love with her.

Now when Jared thought of Gina, which wasn't often, he realized she was the reason the phrase "high maintenance" had been invented.

✍

Toreas Rose sat back down and looked questioningly at Becca. "Why did you let him come?" she asked.

"Well, he said he wanted to put this whole thing behind us. I met with him and he convinced me it would be good for the group. He made some good suggestions."

Becca absentmindedly tucked a strand of her red hair behind her right ear. Toreas knew all too well what had happened to their president. The man had charmed her. Until the rest of his crew burst in, all the women had sat enthralled, giggling like a bunch of high schoolers.

Even Toreas had felt the magnetic pull of Jared's smile, of his eyes traveling over her body. She remembered his hands on her face, his lips on her own and she no longer blamed Becca.

How could women who were forever writing about finding "Mr. Right" be blamed for making this Herculean god into the perfect hero? He was. A perfect blend of good and evil. A smile that could melt a woman and send her screaming for that something she had tucked away in her underwear drawer if she didn't have a man in her life.

But this was real life, not fantasy. It wasn't a chapter in a book and Toreas had no idea how to handle it. It wasn't that she was a virgin. That would have been ridiculous. She was almost thirty.

It was just that the two men she'd had long term relationships with had been nothing to brag about. They had never made her eyes roll back in her head. They had never made her melt with their smiles.

So Jared had been correct when he insinuated she needed real life experience. She would never admit to anyone how uncomfortable writing love scenes made her.

It had taken her forever to get over letting a man touch her in her most private areas or how reluctantly she'd returned touches.

Yes, she'd admit it. She was a prude. The very idea of oral sex she found dirty and disgusting. The human mouth was not made for such things. Toreas shuddered when she thought of the other things she had either read or written. And no, she had never experienced any of it.

Maybe part of it could be blamed on the fact that she had been raised a strict southern Baptist and her father was a long time deacon of the church. Maybe the other part was her two brothers, Michael and Billy, who'd chased away every boy who'd even looked at her. It had taken Toreas's moving to another state to lose her virginity.

It didn't help that every time she made love she chastised herself in the middle of the act for fornicating. On more than one occasion she'd wondered if she was the reason sex was no big deal. She couldn't even use her massager without first turning out the lights. Even then, her fears that she was committing a sin didn't allow her to fully enjoy that small pleasure.

She'd tried countless times without success to put God out of her bed, but he refused to leave. She had almost married her last boyfriend, Fred, just to stop feeling guilty. They had made it as far as city hall. They had been standing in front of the judge when an overwhelming feeling came over her to run and she did. Her relationship with Fred had ended then and there.

Toreas clenched her teeth and sighed, bringing her focus back to the present. She looked around the room. The group was silent, waiting for someone to speak. She knew how they felt. When Jared left the room his energy had gone also and the room filled with over thirty women now seemed empty.

Stop this foolishness, she scolded herself. *What would a man like Jared Stone ever see in a plain 'rose' like me?* Toreas felt the blush coming. She didn't want Jared Stone. She hated the man. He was obnoxious, a liar. She could just imagine the number of prayers she would be sending up if she was involved with him.

Get hold of yourself, girl. Look what he did to you, to the group. He'd ambushed them. He'd invaded her private sanctuary. And he'd looked at her and she'd felt a thaw.

A wicked thought snuck across Toreas's mind and she smiled. *Jared Stone would definitely push God out of my bed.*

5

The morning papers blared the news. *"Romance Writer Toreas Rose at it again."* There was a picture of her shoving the wannabe reporter. Toreas groaned and headed for the kitchen to make herself a pot of coffee. She desperately needed the caffeine.

The previous evening had not been her fault. Still, the women had shifted the blame to her. Already she'd received several emails and calls asking what she had really written in that note.

She slapped her hand against her forehead and yelped with the force of the blow. She hadn't intended to hit herself so hard. Why didn't she do what she should have done in the first place?

If only she'd only kept her hands to herself. She was a proper Baptist girl who couldn't give herself permission to enjoy sex, something everyone said was a natural act, but she could punch a man and then not apologize.

She groaned again and this time not from the smack. Her grandmother, proper Southern woman that she'd been, would roll over in her grave at the actions of her wayward granddaughter.

The phone rang before she had finished pouring the cup of coffee. She glanced at the clock, then continued with putting cream and sugar in her cup.

She knew it was Liz. And she knew she would continue calling until she answered.

"Hi Liz." She answered the phone without even checking to see if the caller could be someone else.

"Okay, tell me what's going on?"

"What are you talking about?"

"You and Jared Stone. I mean, what's with the two of you? I saw the way he was looking at you last night and I saw you blushing. What is it? Do you have a thing for the man? Is that why you got us involved in this in the first place?"

"My God no. I hate the man." How in the world had Liz been able to tell that she was blushing? Was nothing sacred?

"So what that you hate him?" Liz continued. "That means nothing. I hated Mike when I first met him. It took me awhile to discover he's my soulmate."

"Forget it. Jared Stone is not my soulmate."

"How do you know if you don't give yourself a chance to find out?"

Toreas sighed and took a big gulp of her coffee. She could have this conversation only with Liz. Anyone else and she would have turned stone cold, refusing to answer. But Liz was different. For one thing, she would never let it go.

"Liz, listen to me. First, I'm not interested in the man. Second, if I were, he belittles what I do, what you do. Think about it. How could I ever want a relationship with him?"

Liz laughed. "Did you see his butt? And did you see…"

"Stop." Toreas refused to have this conversation. "I wasn't looking at his butt or any other part of his anatomy." She crossed her fingers for the lie she'd told.

She'd be darned if she'd admit to Liz that not only had she noticed Jared's butt but she'd wanted to reach out and grab it when he plopped it in front of her face.

"I don't believe you."

"I don't care," Toreas laughed. "That's my story and I'm sticking to it. Now can't we please talk about something else? We've talked about nothing but Jared Stone for over a month. I'm feeling so depressed I can't even write."

"Are you serious? I haven't been able to stop writing and neither has Elysa, Kelle or Lauren. Wendy called me to say she's finished a whole chapter already."

"So what are you guys doing? Finding a way to bring Jared and me together?" Toreas closed her eyes. Wouldn't it be something if her friends could write into existence all her dreams? She sighed again. Since when had Jared Stone become a part of her dreams?

"I don't know about the others," Liz laughed loudly this time, "but as for myself, honey, you are nowhere in my plans with Jared. He's my fantasy. If you want to be with him, I suggest you either write it or go for it."

"Go for what? Never mind. Liz, you're impossible." Toreas was blushing from her thoughts. "I think I need to stop talking to you and get some work done." With that said, she muttered goodbye.

Toreas poured her second cup of coffee. Liz had gotten too near the truth. Okay, the man was gorgeous. He had the most beautiful eyes and the softest lips and the gentlest hands. She stopped, catching her breath and fanning herself with hands that wanted to be doing something else. The very idea was dumb, about as dumb as a lot of the stories she herself had read. No wonder Jared was trashing them.

Oh my God, she thought with a start. *I want him and I want a bodice that he can rip off.*

✍️

Jared awoke with something he hadn't expected. He had dreamt of making love to a short golden brown woman with dark brown eyes that shot fire when she was angry. So what he had wasn't a total surprise. What he didn't expect was to be turned on so completely by the woman.

She wasn't his type at all. He liked his women tall to match his own stature. At 6'7" short women always appeared too delicate.

If he could find a woman six feet tall he was in heaven. And one that was mostly legs to wrap around him... Well now, he didn't have the words for that.

He looked down at his condition, remembering his dream. Toreas Rose's size had not mattered. But the memory of her angry eyes glaring at him the night before brought him back to reality. "Ahhh, Jared, get hold of yourself."

He heard the thump of the paper hitting his door and turned in that direction. *Why put off learning whatever Derrick had done?* He opened the door, expecting to turn at least to the middle of the paper for the story.

It was blaring out at him from the front page and he scanned it quickly. When he had begun trashing the writers, it was purely out of vengeance, vengeance that he had now worked out of his system. But the story had taken on a life of its own. Now it was all about ratings and profits. He felt like a traitor to the women.

Jared slammed his door, then kicked the plant stand and immediately swore, knowing there was not now the slightest possibility of making what he had dreamed a reality.

It was probably for the best. He needed to stick with what he knew. Him with a goody, goody two-shoes? Someone he'd undoubtedly have to train? No, that was not what he wanted. He wanted a woman who knew how to give pleasure as well as receive it.

He looked down again at her name emblazoned in the paper. Toreas Rose definitely wasn't the woman for him. He could tell in the easy way she blushed. That had been a real surprise.

He knew lots of African American women turned red in the face when they were angry but he couldn't remember seeing one of them blush. Then again, maybe he hadn't noticed because none of them had intrigued him the way that Toreas had.

He tried to remember the things he didn't like about the woman. Her loose fitting clothing was a sure sign that she was more than likely uptight. Reluctantly, he admitted to himself that intrigued him. He would love to be the one to teach her to open up. They were as different as night and day but for some strange reason he wanted the woman. Not forever. Just for a night. But all his well honed instincts told him she was not a one night stand. And he was not a man of commitment. Not anymore.

Maybe Derrick was right after all. Maybe he should just keep the war going and get all the mileage he could out of it and then return to California.

But for a moment last night Jared thought he had detected a hitch in her breath when he sat in front of her. She'd refused to meet his gaze, so he wasn't at all sure if she was reacting romantically to their close proximity or was just disgusted by him.

There was only one thing Jared was sure of and that was that he wanted to see her again. He didn't understand why it mattered so to him, but he wanted to change her opinion of him. He wanted her to believe that her name in the morning paper was not his idea.

He smiled. At least the paper had spelled her name correctly and usually for most people in the entertainment business, that was enough. But a private person wouldn't want to be in the paper. How did he know Toreas Rose was a private person?

He padded on bare feet to make coffee, his mind fixated on a tiny woman in loose fitting clothes. How did he presume to know this woman so well when he'd only seen her two times, not counting his dreams?

Would a private person write romance? Would a private person call the station to complain, and then accept the offer to come on television? Would a private person punch the host on his own show? Would a private person let the war go on so long without attempting to resolve it?

Would Toreas Rose, the woman with the dark brown eyes that smoldered with an inner fire do all of those things? Yes, but without a doubt he knew she was a private person. As he began to salivate thinking of her, his early morning surprise returned. He was hard as a rock.

✑

Toreas was trying her best to write but she kept thinking of Jared's bottom sitting in front of her face and she kept getting flushed.

The hero in her book was now flat by comparison. No matter how hard Toreas tried, she couldn't breathe life into him. Her words were stilted and dull. She knew this, so she paused in her writing.

What if I do a little research? She wondered if learning was a sin. Maybe she could call her father or the pastor and ask them if the pursuit of knowledge was a bad thing? But what would she answer when they asked about the nature of the knowledge? Maybe she should just put it out on the loop and go with the most favorable answers.

She suddenly needed a glass of water because she was wanting things she'd never wanted before, dirty things, and she couldn't get them out of her head.

Maybe she should just follow Liz's advice and pursue Jared. She didn't want him, she couldn't, not really, not for anything more than research.

She read back over the last pages she had written. Yes, she needed someone like Jared to make the hero in her book come alive. "Once. What would it hurt?"

She wouldn't go into anything with any expectations. She wouldn't fall in love with him or anything like that. That would be stupid.

But she could go to bed with him once, just once, for research. She thought of all the advice she'd been given. It all said to write about what you know and to do meticulous research.

Well, she was admitting it. She didn't know much. That's why her characters were boring, that's why she had yet to sell her first manuscript. She had to do this for the good of her career. She was going to make the first move toward Jared Stone.

She wouldn't fool herself about the type of man he was. She would remember all the times he'd humiliated writers and readers. That alone should be enough to protect her heart.

She wanted only one thing from Jared Stone. She wanted him to make her eyes roll back in her head, to make her feel that delicious shiver again and she wanted his touch all over her when he kissed her again.

That's three things, she thought and smiled. But all of that came with the main dish.

Toreas looked down at her baggy pants and oversized sweat shirt. First, she might have to do something to get the man to notice her. So far he'd only been pretending with those smoldering looks.

She'd never taken him seriously on any of it. How could she? Look at her. She needed a major overhaul if she intended to use him for research.

She felt several rapid heartbeats. Her hands were shaking and for a fleeting nanosecond she felt faint. What she was planning was ludicrous. She didn't know the first thing about seducing a man and certainly not a man like Jared.

Oh my God! If Daddy could hear my thoughts, he wouldn't be talking about kicking Jared's butt. He would be flying here to beat the living daylights out of me. And Granny…

Toreas was almost relieved that her beloved grandmother was no longer alive to witness the acts she was contemplating. She was afraid, but it felt good.

She felt alive, more alive than she could ever remember feeling. And if the deed was only a third as good as what she was imagining, she would be in heaven.

What if it was the same with Jared as it had been with her only two lovers? What would she do then? *That's easy*, she thought. *I'll write him as a terrible lover and I'll write my heroine as a wildcat. That's why it's called fiction.*

She worried for a moment about how easily she was willing to throw away her values. Was it really for research? "Yes," she answered herself, research and nothing more. "In fact, I think I'll make Jared the villain. And when my book is published I'll send him a copy with a note telling him he inspired it. He has too big an ego not to read it." She smiled. Now she could truly believe in her plan.

It would serve the man right to see himself in print in a bad light for a change. She latched onto the newspaper she had carelessly tossed away.

Jared deserved to be taught a lesson. She walked to the mirror and gave herself the once-over. Yeah, but did she have what it took to teach him that lesson? When it came down to it, would she even know what to do? She sure as heck didn't have any erotic tricks up her sleeve. Erotic was for other people, sexy people. She craved being the sexy erotic woman who would make Jared Stone swoon with real desire.

She felt the muscles in her stomach tightening. There was no one else around but she could still feel the blush covering her entire body. She wanted erotic. She wanted to believe there was a difference in that and porn. No, she *needed* to believe there was a difference in the two. She no longer wanted what she'd had in the past. She wanted the things she read about, had written about. At least she wanted some of them. So for that reason alone she had to believe there was a difference.

She knew for sure she wanted to feel shivers running through her body. And she definitely wanted to take her time kissing Jared, tasting him just to see what he tasted like.

Her previous boyfriends, while attractive, had been soft. They weren't the kind of men who produced shivers. In fact Fred's lips were mushy. Even his body was. She was sure he'd only had to shave once a week.

She thought of the slight stubble she'd noticed on Jared's face last night. He probably needed to shave twice a day. His face was hard, his body was hard, yet his lips were soft witout being mushy.

No wonder her hero lacked sensuality. She had only known soft men, so gentle in bed that she sometimes wondered if they'd even completed the act.

She had written entire scenes in her head during the act and was always surprised that they had finished without her even knowing they'd begun.

It was high time for the sake of research that her knowledge of men broadened. She needed a three dimensional man, not some cardboard character with no zip in the sex appeal department. Toreas needed Jared.

6

Toreas was practically giddy with excitement. She was about to embark on the biggest adventure in her entire life. She was going to shed her good girl image, once and only once, for research.

With trembling fingers she dialed the number to the television station before she could talk herself out of it.

"May I speak to Mr. Stone please?"

"He's not in. May I ask whose calling?"

Toreas recognized the voice of the owner of the station. She sighed loudly and stretched her fingers, trying to rid herself of the desire to employ a few more of Kelle's techniques.

Now she had two things on her list: seducing Jared Stone and becoming Kelle's number one pupil. *Here I go again drifting off into space*, she thought as she heard the gravely voice on the phone asking her once again who she was.

"This is Toreas Rose. Would you give Mr. Stone my new number and ask him to call please?" She heard a noise, then the sound of fumbling but no answer.

"Sure, Ms. Rose, I'll give him the message."

That was definitely a click she heard. *Oh God*, Toreas thought and slapped her hand against her forehead. He was taping her. She muttered a hurried goodbye and replaced the phone.

Yes, she was definitely going to learn the roundhouse kick, the reverse punch, the uppercut, and the snap kick. She would work with Kelle every available minute. She thought of her two older brothers who used to pick on her. She was going to learn to kick butt.

✑

"Jared." Derrick rushed at him. "You won't believe what happened, who called for you."

Jared stared at Derrick's face. He was happy. No, more than that, he was ecstatic. It probably had something to do with grabbing the front page this morning. Well, he'd let him have it. Hadn't he decided just an hour ago that nothing was going to happen with Toreas Rose? "Who called?"

"That Rose woman. She left her number and she wants you to call her back."

Jared stood in shock. "You mean she left her home number? But she went to all the trouble of having it changed."

"Yes," Derrick answered him, his mouth open in astonishment. "Why don't you use my phone here and call her back?"

Jared eyed Derrick with suspicion. "Just give me the number. I'll make the call from my own office."

As he took the slip of paper from his boss's outstretched hand, something about the whole episode seemed too easy. He glanced back over his shoulder and saw that he was being watched not only by Derrick but by Josh and Stella as well.

Something was up and he had a good idea what it was. Jared closed his office door and pulled his cellular phone from his pocket, checking at the same time for any suspicious devices attached to his office phone.

Toreas answered on the first ring, something he had not expected.

"Ms. Rose, this is Jared Stone. I understand you called."

"Yes. I saw the paper this morning. I think it's time we called a halt to this. Since the popular consensus is that I started this, then I suppose I should make the first move to end it."

She waited for Jared to answer her. She wished she could tell what he was thinking. "I'm sorry for my previous behavior on your show."

Again she paused and waited. Still nothing. "It shouldn't have mattered how much of a jerk you were being, or how uninformed, or how insensitive, or how rude—"

"Excuse me, but is this the apology?" Jared could feel his lips pulling into a smile as he wondered what the woman on the other end was doing.

Was she playing with her hair? Biting her nails? Or was she thinking about hitting him again?

"You're right." Toreas closed her eyes, determined to take the leap. "Maybe we should meet. Perhaps we could find a way to end this." There, she'd said it. The words were out.

He heard her but he didn't know if he believed it. "Are you saying that after last night and the paper this morning you're willing to meet with me? Ms. Rose, you wouldn't be planning on another attack would you?"

"Touché, Mr. Stone. Last night and the paper this morning are my reasons for calling you. I really wanted to apologize, something I should have done properly before. But you owe me one also, Mr. Stone."

"You mean for the kiss?" Jared asked. He was suspicious of Toreas's motive. She was too agreeable. He imagined she was blushing on the other end of the line. The woman got embarrassed on the phone talking about a kiss. What could he possibly want with her?

"Listen, Ms. Rose, tell me what kind of a punch that was you hit me with?"

"It's called a flat-fisted punch."

"Where did you learn it?"

"From Kelle."

Jared could feel her smiling and he rather liked the image. "Is Kelle also a writer?"

"She's so much more than that," Toreas bragged. She's a scientist and a 9th degree black belt. She's a karate master."

"A scientist who writes romance?" Jared was not being solicitous. He was truly under the impression that only bored housewives wrote those things and even more bored women read them. That's why he'd been so surprised to learn of Gina's passion for the books. How could she possible need to read about romance when he was providing her with all that she could handle?

He braced himself for the impact of pain to his chest. Jared waited, but the pain never came. Instead of the pain he felt himself smiling as he listened to Toreas explaining that in her group alone they had doctors, lawyers, teachers, librarians, computer programmers, artists, nurses and yes, mothers and wives.

She was going into a spiel about the number of romance readers and how they fell into the same occupational fields as the writers, when he interrupted her.

"Why didn't you speak up like that when you were on the show?"

"We were trying, you didn't give us a chance."

"I'm not talking about your friends Elysa or Liz or the others. I'm talking about you. You sat there the entire time and didn't say a word. Then you hit me."

His voice carried a note of surprise even now. "You have a bad temper, don't you?"

"No. And usually I'm adult enough to control my emotions. I'm not offering this as an excuse but I grew up with two older brothers and they would tease me unmercifully."

"Did you hit your brothers?"

"No, I never did."

"Then why me? Why start with me?" Jared knew he was making her uncomfortable but he wanted to keep talking to her, to hear that little catch in her voice, to imagine her blushing as she tried to answer him.

"I didn't choose to start with you. Like I said, it just happened. Kelle taught us that punch the night before."

Jared laughed then. "Was that your preparation for coming on the show? Most people just gather notes."

He imagined her licking her lips. He knew she was blushing. It carried through in her voice. He smiled to himself, thinking how easily they talked-that is, until a whirring sound in the background caught the attention of both of them and changed things.

"Mr. Stone, are you recording this conversation?"

"No. What would give you an idea like that?"

"Your show is after ratings and I, unfortunately, seem to have provided you with the perfect ratings booster."

Jared stopped smiling, not admitting that he'd had the thought earlier that Derrick and Josh were up to something. And he'd heard the sound also. Still, he didn't appreciate being accused of something so underhanded.

"Ms. Rose, I called you on my cell phone. Not that I ever had any intentions of recording you."

The entire mood had changed. He could sense it and he wanted to continue with the light-hearted banter, but it was too late.

"Where would you like to meet?" he asked instead. "You could come to the station. We could talk in my office."

"No, thank you."

Toreas could feel the words freezing in her throat. She was going to lose her opportunity. How was she ever going to get the chance to seduce Jared if she kept being nasty?

The more she thought of it, she didn't know if she would be able to go through with it. This simple conversation was beginning to make her feel as if she were being grilled.

Realizing that, she changed the tone and insulted him once more. This time unintentionally. But she'd remembered the earlier click from the station when she was positive she was being recorded and the hurtful words just tumbled out.

"Are you listening to me?"

Jared's voice jerked her back from her thoughts. She was trying to remember her plan. Her great seduction. Quick, what would a heroine say? Meet me at the bar?

"The pie place next door to your office would be better for me," Toreas said.

She wanted to die. Frumpy little writer in her frumpy little clothes suggesting meeting at a pie place. *Great mood for a seduction*, she thought in dismay. She heard Jared answering her, the playful tone gone from his voice.

"Good. Lets say 3 P.M., Ms Rose. I have appointments until then."

"That's fine…" She paused. "No cameras, Mr. Stone." She couldn't resist taking one last shot.

Toreas had barely hung up from talking to Jared when she began pushing buttons again. She had to call Liz. She was excited and she wanted to tell someone her plans.

"Liz, I'm going to do it."

"Well, hello to you too. Now what are you going to do?"

"I'm going to take your advice. I'm going after Jared Stone. Well, at least once. For research."

Toreas heard noise on the other end of the phone and called out to Liz. It sounded as though her friend might have fallen.

"Are you crazy?" Liz screamed. "That must be it. You've completely lost your mind. First, I was only kidding with you. And besides, you told me you hated the man."

"Like you said, my feelings have nothing to do with this. I do hate him. I just want to use him for research."

"What kind of research?"

"What kind do you think?"

"Oh my God. You can't be thinking of doing what I'm thinking. Tell me you're not that dumb."

"What are you talking about? This was your idea, remember?"

Toreas could tell Liz was becoming agitated but so was she. At last she'd decided to end this ridiculous feud but look at the thanks she was getting.

"I thought you would be happy that I'm getting him to stop attacking us."

"Don't you dare put this on me," Liz snapped. "If you go to bed with the man it'll be because you want to, not for the good of romance writers."

Toreas was hurt and a little ashamed that her good idea was being met with such harsh disapproval. She decided to try again.

"Liz, you said you guys are writing about Jared and you told me to go after him."

"What I told you was that you were not in my fantasy with Jared. I said either write about it or go after him if you had a thing for him. I did not tell you to use the man for research. Besides, why do you want to listen to me now? If I give you an honest critique on your writing you get all bent out of shape."

Toreas couldn't prevent the loud sigh from escaping. Okay, so this conversation was not going the way she'd imagined. She had thought more along the lines of Liz saying, "Go for it, girl," but she wasn't. What she was doing was scolding her and Toreas was puzzled.

Maybe Liz was worried about her. All right, she'd think of something to say to ease her mind.

"Liz, don't worry."

"Are you attracted to Jared?"

"No."

"Then don't go sleeping with the man for research. That's dumb."

"I'm only doing this to bring some pizzazz to my hero."

"What happens if you get pregnant? You'll blame it on me like you blamed hitting him on Kelle."

Toreas sat on her sofa stunned. She heard Liz laughing and wondered what part of the conversation she'd missed.

"I can just hear you now. 'Liz made me do it.' And then you'd probably want to sue me for child support."

Toreas waited for her friend to compose herself. "I need some help."

"With what?"

There was suspicion in Liz's voice. She couldn't blame her, not really. None of the things that had happened to her in the past weeks made one bit of sense.

Yeah, her life was beginning to feel like a romance novel, and a bad one at that. Who would believe that real life could be so strange?

If she wrote about the past weeks it would read like a—Oh my God, like a sappy romance. She wanted grit. Now here she was about to indulge in the wildest fantasy she could ever imagine, something that could only happen in real life. No self-respecting author would dare attempt to fool a reader into believing something so trite.

"Liz, tell me what to wear."

Toreas was hoping to pull Liz over to her side. She needed someone's help, anyone's help, in telling her how to go about seducing a man she professed to hate, but who intrigued her nonetheless.

"Wear anything, I don't know. I'm not getting involved in this. What are you going to do if he says no?"

It was Toreas's turn to laugh. "He's a man. What man do you know who is going to turn down free sex with no strings attached?"

"What are you going to say to him? I hope it's something better than that."

This entire conversation was growing wearisome. All Toreas had intended was to have her friend advise her if she should dye her hair or hot comb it, or maybe even perm it, or buy a short skirt or a new lipstick, not scold her about her plans. She was fully aware of what she was about to do and it didn't matter. She was determined. After all the abuse she'd suffered at his hands, Jared Stone owed her.

With or without Liz's help, she would find a way to entice the man. And she would be up front about it being strictly for professional reasons.

She thought of his lips on hers, his hands on her face. *This is all for my book, nothing more than that. He's not a potato chip. I can stop at just one.*

7

Toreas did her best to avoid looking in the mirror. Liz had been absolutely no help. She hadn't given her one word of advice to make this meeting with Jared easier. Liz didn't want her to go, that much was obvious.

Toreas wanted to arrive at the pie shop before Jared. If she was sitting there first, maybe the butterflies would go away. What did she mean, butterflies? It felt more like rocks lying in the pit of her gut making her nauseous.

That voice was bothering her again, pestering her, trying to remind her that she was a good Baptist girl. She was in enough trouble already with past deeds that hadn't been planned. Now here she was purposely planning to sin, and sin big time.

"All right already," she wanted to shout to the steady voice in her head. "I hear you." Besides, it had never been that much fun so this should only count as a little sin.

She caught her reflection in the mirror. She was blushing. She hated it. How could she go about her task with that darn telltale flush?

One glance at her watch and she swabbed on a little lipstick. Her clothes were not what she wanted, baggy pants and a thick sweater. But they were all she had.

Toreas walked into the pie shop with her knees knocking together and asked for a table for two. Before the hostess had a chance to seat her, Jared showed up beside her, tall, not quite dark, actually not dark at all, and handsome.

She watched as he smiled down at the waitress, then turned to acknowledge her. His eyes exuded warmth. She was surprised she had never noticed that before.

"Hello, Mr. Stone."

He stuck his hand out to her. "Can't we at least let go of the Mr. Stone? Please call me Jared." He smiled at her then. "I already have a table. By the way, may I call you Toreas?"

She felt the heat rising to her face and hated it. The man had only smiled at her. She didn't answer; instead, she followed him to a table where he had two cups of coffee waiting.

She remembered her mother always telling her never to leave a drink on the table and come back for it; someone could slip something in it.

Toreas looked at Jared, not quite trusting him, yet doubting he would go to such lengths. After all, the man wasn't a criminal, was he?

She glanced at the cup placed in front of the chair she took, and then at Jared. "Thanks for the coffee, but I prefer tea."

That was a lie. Toreas hated tea. But she hated even more that Jared had presumed to order for her. Besides, that nagging little thought continued to creep in on her. What if he had put something in it?

Her stomach was lurching as though there were acrobats doing a full routine in there. The man seated before her definitely had no need to drug the women he wanted.

"So, To..re..as."

He said her name slowly, making it feel like a caress and making her aware of how wholly inadequate she was at this seduction nonsense. Toreas wanted to call Jared's name and make it sound as sensuous as he'd made hers sound, but she wasn't any good at things like that.

"You may not believe me, but I truly had no idea that Derrick was bringing the crew to your meeting," Jared said and smiled.

When he reached for his coffee Toreas caught the slight tremble in his hand. She searched his eyes, sensing the nervousness in him that he was trying desperately to hide.   •

His dimples kept going in, then peeking out at her, as though they couldn't decide what to do. There was a half smile tugging at the corner of his bottom lip, but it wasn't reaching his eyes. It was then she knew with a certainty he was as unsure about the outcome of their meeting as she was.

Toreas sat back in her chair biting first her bottom lip, then her top, her head tilted at a forty-five degree angle observing him.

Jared picked up his cup and took a drink, at the same time signaling the waitress to the table. "Would you bring the lady a cup of tea please?" He glanced in Toreas's direction.

"Is there any type that you prefer?"

"Just plain tea." She was flustered with him watching her. Even though she wasn't a tea drinker, she could have been a little more sophisticated, asked for some herbal tea at least. Now what was he thinking? Plain tea for a plain woman?

Jared was nervous. He had been sitting in the restaurant for almost thirty minutes. Every five minutes he'd had the waitress bring fresh cups of coffee because he wanted to give the impression that he'd just arrived. She was annoyed over his insistence on clean cups each time, but that was a must. Refilled cups looked refilled to him.

The last time he'd re-ordered, he'd given the waitress a twenty and smiled at her. "I'm meeting someone I'm trying hard to impress."

He knew the right words to use on women. They loved a sensitive man. He knew the waitress would find cute the idea that he was going to so much trouble to impress a woman and stop hassling him.

Whatever it took. He could be charming when he chose to be and right now he chose to be.

The waitress had a smirk on her face when he ordered tea for Toreas, enough of one that Jared wanted to ask her to give him back the twenty. Maybe not quite, but the smirk irritated him. He was having enough trouble dealing with one woman. Two was one too many.

He was pretending not to watch Toreas's every move. She probably thought he'd not seen her wistful look at the cup of coffee. Liar. For whatever reason, she didn't want the one he'd had waiting. Probably thought he'd poisoned it.

He'd given her the quick once-over when he went to meet her at the front—baggy pants and thick bulky sweater, as usual. Neither garment did a thing for her appearance except to make her look washed out.

His eyes fell on her lips, her best feature. She was looking intently at him from thick full lashes. Ahh, he'd almost forgotten. Toreas Rose had remarkable brown eyes, eyes that told exactly what she was thinking, eyes that were constantly shooting sparks of fire in his direction.

He saw the faint splotch of color on her brown cheeks and wondered why she was blushing. He'd done or said nothing that anyone could construe as sexual.

It was obvious Toreas was uncomfortable with him. Jared wondered if she might perhaps be a virgin. He almost laughed. In this day and age…?

Her gaze was still fastened on him and now he was the one beginning to squirm. He wanted to bed this uptight prude who sat across from him, just once. Any more than that and she would be falling madly in love with him, clinging to him. And that he didn't want.

He'd never had a tiny woman and by no stretch of the imagination one who was not well versed in the pleasures of the flesh. Regardless, he could feel a growing hunger. He wouldn't be satisfied until he'd had her. Once.

"So, Mr. Stone." His raised eyebrow stopped her. "I'm sorry, Jared. Can we end this? Will you please cease your attack on me?"

He wanted to tell her yes, but their feud was bringing in big revenue to the station. He couldn't ask Derrick to give that up simply because Toreas Rose's lips tasted like strawberries and he wanted to see if the rest of her tasted the same way.

"My boss isn't ready for this to die out yet." Jared watched as Toreas's lips thinned in disapproval. "But I have thought of something that might help all of us."

She was eyeing him suspiciously, and with good reason. "Seriously. You could come on the show." He saw the look on her face.

"Hear me out. I'm sure your friend Kelle can show you some moves to use if I get out of hand." This time he was rewarded with a smile.

"Let's hear your proposal, Jared."

He arched his eyebrows at her, surprised how much he liked hearing his name coming from her mouth.

"Well," he smiled. "I was thinking of having you come on several shows and demonstrate a few self-defense moves."

"That's not my thing. I told you, I'm only learning. Kelle is the expert, not me."

"I don't want Kelle. I want you."

Toreas's hand moved toward the coffee cup before she remembered she'd told him she didn't like the stuff. He wasn't saying he wanted her in a sexual way, but just the same, she had felt a slight chill followed by amazing warmth spreading throughout her body.

"My coming back on your show would help your career and the station, is that what you're trying to tell me?"

"Yes, that's right."

"How is that going to help me, or my group, or ARW?"

"All publicity helps, trust me, good or bad. The public hears there's a fight or a banned book and right away they want it."

"How do you know this?"

"I was in advertising and public relations. I thought I'd told you that already. Never mind." Jared smiled. "Trust me, I know what I'm talking about. I'll bet the sales of romance novels have risen already."

"How do you know more people are reading romance because of, as you say, our little feud?"

"I know. It's the way the world works."

"I'm not sure about that. My chapter is about ready to kick me out if I don't call a halt to this."

"I'm asking you in a way to be my partner. We can script it."

"You mean lie to the public."

Jared looked at the woman in amazement. How was what he was asking of her any different from writing fiction. He decided to ask.

"Isn't that what you do, write fiction?"

"But I don't lie."

"Are you saying guys are as stupid as you writers make them out to be and that every woman is a heroine?"

Toreas was smiling and it was irritating the heck out of Jared. It appeared she was laughing at him and he didn't like it. "Why are you smiling?" he asked irritably.

"You're asking me if I think men are stupid. I can't believe you would ask me such a loaded question."

"What are you talking about?"

"Look at you, you're annoyed. You're frowning at me with your face scrunched up in concentration. Your expression looks like a petulant little boy's."

"So I'm stupid?"

"A smart man wouldn't ask me that question."

"Ms. Rose, are you by chance calling me stupid?"

"No, you did that yourself! You just said you were stupid. And I thought we were on a first name basis."

Jared could sense she was enjoying this. He was trying not to glare at the woman. After all, glaring at her would not get her in his bed. And now more than ever he was determined to wipe that smug look off her face.

When he finished with her, Toreas Rose wouldn't know what hit her. Jared definitely intended to make her shed that Quaker look. He didn't like the way she treated him as if he didn't matter. No woman had ever done that to him before. *What about Gina?* A little voice whispered. He'd almost forgotten his two-timing ex.

The women were as different as ice cream and yogurt. Gina was a knockout and Toreas... He glared again at her and thought, *This woman should be grateful that I even want her.* He tapped his fingers on the table and glared more fiercely, not surprised that it had no effect on her. But still, he wanted to put her in her place.

"Look, all men are not stupid and we're not put here for your amusement." He smirked then. "Neither are all women heroines. If a man has the balls..."

He caught her disapproving look. "If, in your book, some weenie by chance attempts to behave like a man you women go and lop them off."

Her disapproval had now turned into an all-out frown. She appeared to be studying him and her appraisal of him helped to fuel his next words. "Romance novels are forever having the man get knocked out and the woman saving him. He's shot, thrown from a horse, or about to be dragged across the plains."

He smiled then. "Different stories, same ending. Damsel in distress becomes the one to save the day." He looked over at her. She wasn't amused by his assessment.

Maybe a different approach would work better. "Why aren't any of your heroes fat?"

"Because women have fat husbands in real life. Why do we want to read about them?" Toreas turned toward the waitress thanking her for the tea, watching as she took away the coffee she could definitely use while having this conversation with Jared. She took several sips of the tea, trying not to make a face at the taste.

Jared placed his elbow on the table and cupped his chin with his hand. He leaned across the table drawing Toreas's eyes, wanting to kiss her.

"Do you really believe it's the women who rescue the men?"

"Of course. Look around you. Ask the women who run the household, pay the bills, keep up with the repairs, and the kids."

"And the workplace?" Jared asked.

"Of course in the workplace. Women may not earn the same pay but they are the ones who make sure the job gets done."

"Your opinion of men is very low. How did you ever become a romance writer?"

"As an avid romance reader I suppose I may have thought finding a hero would be easy. Since it wasn't, I decided to write, to create the hero that most men can never be."

Jared saw the small smile that played around Toreas's mouth and knew she was probably at least halfway kidding but he wasn't quite sure. He decided to switch again. "Does this apply to married couples or couples with commitments?"

"Most definitely to both. Married women are the ones who have to know where their husband's shoes are and give him the confidence to do his job and then listen to him gripe about it on a bad day and praise him on a good day. If the couple's in a committed relationship it's still the woman who's doing all the planning for their future. She's the one who knows where they're headed and she has to also make sure her man's confidence is built up."

"Isn't that what a relationship is all about?"

"Ha." Toreas pulled away from Jared's eyes. "Do you really think there is one man in the world who gives to a woman what she gives to him?"

"You sound as if you hate men, Toreas."

"I don't hate men," she answered when she could find her voice. She took another sip of the tea without thinking. "I'm realistic."

"Do you have a man?"

He was eyeing her, knowing his question was going to make her blush. *Good,* he thought as he watched her cheeks turn from a faint red to a deep rose. "Well, To..re..as, do you have a man?"

Toreas groaned. There he went again, making her name sound as if he were whispering it while making love to her. She backed even farther away, her mouth dry in spite of the pungent tea she had neglected to sweeten.

"Mr. Stone, what does any of this have to do with the reason we're here?"

Jared hesitated, then signaled for the waitress. "Would you like some pie or anything else to eat, drink or taste?" He smiled at her then, having intentionally made the offer sound suggestive.

"No, thank you," Toreas murmured, not even knowing if he heard. He was busy turning his charm on the waitress, or so she thought.

Jared still very much had his mind on Toreas Rose. It seemed her hatred of him went beyond the fact that he criticized romance writers. His whole gender was under attack. Now for the sake of the male gender he might have to have her twice. No more. There would be danger in more.

He waited until the waitress delivered his pie, aware that his companion was growing more uncomfortable and that he had better find a way to ease the tension.

"You come back on the show, we spar a little, I let up a little. Just a little back and forth good-natured ribbing. It will help both of our careers."

Toreas was watching Jared, his lips, his hands, his eyes, and wishing she weren't attracted to him. Oh, she almost forgot. She wasn't attracted to him, she just needed him for research.

"Do you call what you've been doing good-natured ribbing? I don't." At last some words had managed to come out of her mouth. It almost made Toreas proud.

"Ouch, that hurts." Jared tried grinning at her, but could tell that was having no effect. "I thought this meeting was to bury the past. That will take a little help here. I'm trying, you're resisting."

Toreas stared hard at Jared. This time she was the one in control. She sensed it and liked it. The tables were turned. She was not on his television show.

"If I help you with your show, will you do me a favor?"

I knew it. Enough charm and they all come around eventually. "Sure, Toreas. You help me get as much mileage out of this as we can and I'm at your disposal. What do you need?"

I need you to help me with research for my book."

Jared was smiling. "I'll be glad to. I've worked in several different fields so any questions you want to ask me I feel confident I can answer."

She imitated Jared's position by placing her own elbow on the table and leaning her chin into the palm of her hand. "It's not a question that I need answered, Mr. Stone."

Oh, oh. She was back to Mr. Stone. This didn't bode well. "Exactly what is it you do need, Toreas?" This time Jared knew precisely what to do. He leaned in to meet her. She was his. All he had to do was reel her in.

Look at her, he thought. *She's like a fish on a hook and I control her.* He was enjoying this. So he had something the woman wanted. Now they could deal.

"I want you to make love to me, Mr. Stone."

Jared was glad he had swallowed his last bite of pie or he surely would have sprayed it across the table. As it was, Toreas had backed away and was calmly wiping her face with her paper napkin. His saliva, no doubt.

"You want what?"

"I want you to make love to me. Once, Mr. Stone, and only for research.

8

Jared sat still, sure that he was in shock. He had to be or else he was losing his hearing. He mentally calculated his age. Thirty-four. Usually too young to lose one's hearing, but then again, maybe not.

He was now hearing a strange clackety-clack sound coming from under the table. He narrowed his eyes at Toreas who was sitting across from him. The most amazing thing of all, she wasn't blushing.

That proved it. His hearing was going. The woman blushed at the mention of an inconsequential kiss. If he'd heard what he thought he'd heard, she would be beet red.

He stared at her, still hearing the sounds coming from beneath the table. He looked at her lips and remembered the kiss. Inconsequential his behind. It was the taste of her lips that had him sitting across from her now wanting her so badly that he'd imagined she'd just given him the keys to the kingdom.

Jared could stand the sound no longer without investigating. "Excuse me," he said to Toreas and bent his head under the table to see what the racket was.

Her left leg was shaking at least forty miles an hour, he estimated, banging the table. Jared's mouth fell open as he watched her leg in wonder. She wasn't blushing but her leg was about to become unhinged. He wasn't losing his hearing. He'd heard her correctly.

He banged his head as he came up from under the table, scowling at his companion. In the short time he'd known her, the woman had caused several types of pain to different parts of his anatomy.

He drummed his fingers against the table faster and faster. He was hoping to unnerve her. It always worked on Derrick. Nothing. She sat across from him sipping her tea. If it wasn't for that infernal racket she was making with her leg, he would think she was kidding.

It was obvious she wasn't going to talk, so it was up to him. "You want me to do what?"

"I want you to make love to me, Mr. Stone. In return, I will go along with your milking this feud. I will return on your program."

"Lady, are you crazy? Or are you on something?"

She smiled at him then. A sweet angelic smile from those lips that had just issued a hellish proposal. He felt a pulling at his groin. Now he was the one who was crazy.

Okay, time for a little reality check. He decided to revert to their original formality, which in light of what they were discussing seemed stupid to him. But he couldn't call her Toreas without wanting her.

"Ms. Rose, are you asking me to be a male whore?" There now. Maybe that would shock some sense into her. He pulled his lips into what he hoped was a leer. He needed to scare some sense into her.

"Male whore? I never thought of that." Toreas almost grinned before stopping herself. "But I think I like the sound of it."

Jared was getting angry. Toreas was toying with him. "I thought you were serious. I thought we came here to discuss putting an end to this nonsense."

"We did. I listened to your proposal and you've listened to mine. That's the deal, Mr. Stone. Take it or leave it."

Okay, so she wants to play with me, does she? Jared allowed his eyes to travel over her body, undressing her as he went. The task was hard even for his vivid imagination. It was difficult for him to imagine what lay beneath the bulky sweater and baggy pants.

He was rewarded when he noticed the tinge of color finally coming to her cheeks. He smiled inwardly and continued his perusal, only more slowly. He noticed she was staring into her cup.

Just what I thought, a prude. "Okay, Ms. Rose, excuse me, Toreas. I think since I will be helping you-" He stopped and smiled. "I should at least continue calling you by your first name."

Good. Now the ball was back in his possession. This was his game. So she wanted to mess with his head, did she? *Well now, we'll just see who has the last laugh.*

"There's a motel a couple of doors down the street. We could go there if you like. That is, if you're finished with your tea."

He watched as she lifted her eyes to his and replaced her cup on the saucer.

"No, Mr. Stone. Not today."

He was enjoying this now. There was a slight tinge of fear in her voice. *So she wants to play chicken. Let's see who backs down first.* "Hey, my schedule is free," Jared declared. "Right now is as good a time as any."

He leaned back, grinning broadly at her. "That is, unless you're afraid, or just messing with my head. If you're serious, let's do this thing now."

"You must be crazy if you think I'd sleep with you without checking out your medical background."

Toreas's hand disappeared into her briefcase in the chair beside her. Jared glanced at it, then her, wondering why he'd not noticed it before.

He frowned as she pulled up at least a twenty page questionnaire and plopped it down in front of him.

"You need to fill this out. Also, I'll want to make an appointment with my own doctor for you to be tested."

"You're asking me to take an AIDS test?"

"Of course, but I also want you tested for venereal disease."

Jared glared at the woman. Now he truly was angry. She had proposed the most ridiculous thing he'd ever heard and now, this. "What about you, Toreas?" This time he did not caress her name.

"Well, I don't sleep around. But of course I'll make an appointment for both of us."

She was now glaring at him. *She's insulted*, he thought. *Well, I'll be. She asks me something like this but she's insulted that I ask her.* His anger before had been only on simmer. Now it was at the boiling point.

Who did she think she was with her holier than thou attitude? And to just assume he slept around. He was the one who should be insulted.

"I don't really know you and you're asking me for what exactly, Toreas, stud services? Well, who knows how many other men you've been with?"

The fingers of her right hand curled into a ball and Jared braced himself, waiting, not believing she had the nerve to be angry.

"I've never done this before," Toreas said softly. "I've never propositioned a man before.

"So am I to be your personal guinea pig? Every time you want to try something new, you'll call me? You want to try out a new punch you learn from Kelle and you'll call me to beat the hell out of me? Is that the way you see this thing going?"

Jared was furious. But there was something else. He'd never been this excited about a woman in his entire life. He continued glaring at her but he would give anything right now if she would take him up on his offer to find the nearest motel.

Stop that, Jared. What was he thinking? Of course he wasn't going to sleep with this woman, be her lab rat. He had some pride. Yet he couldn't deny the tightening of his loins, the irresistible urge to take her in his arms and kiss her, really kiss her just to see if she did taste like strawberries.

"Why me, Toreas? Have you been secretly lusting after me? Is that the real reason you called the station, so it could finally come down to this?"

He was hoping she'd get up and run. Her face couldn't be any redder if he'd colored it. He was amazed. He'd never seen any woman of any race as red as Toreas was at the moment. He had been right in his assessment before: Romance writers were pure evil, through and through.

Yet here she sat bundled up like Frosty the Snowman. In the midst of people eating around them, just as calmly as you please, she was asking him something no woman ever had. And part of him felt dirty.

Her opinion of him shouldn't matter, but for some nutty reason it did. Maybe she wanted revenge after the article in the morning paper. Possibly she only wanted to make him think he would get to sample her, then pull away. Perhaps they'd actually get to a motel one day and she'd cry rape and have him arrested.

She hadn't answered, so he asked again. "Why me?" She didn't look at him but at least this time she answered.

"I thought about what you said, about my research, and I decided it's conceivable that you're right. Perhaps I should do some field research. Like I said, I don't sleep around."

She was insulted and hurt. Why should she be hurt? Did she think because he was a man he wouldn't have any feelings? Jared glared at her again, knowing her low opinion of men, of him. It was possible she really did think that this would all be okay with him, like 'It's party time, let's go.'

"That still doesn't tell me why you chose me to be your field assignment." He wasn't going to let her off the hook on this one.

Toreas brought her eyes up to look directly into his. This time she didn't turn away. "That's easy. I can't stand you, I think you're despicable."

"So why would you want to sleep with me?" Jared was forcing himself to continue looking at her. That remark hurt.

"I'm in the middle of my book and my heroine is involved with a jerk. A jerk that, by the way, she sleeps with, one who makes her eyes roll to the back of her head. So I need to know what it's like to go to bed with a jerk. I need to know for myself the feelings my heroine has. I need to know if it's possible to have one's eyes roll to the back of their head."

"So your character's a slut?" Why should he be nice and polite when she wasn't? He was waiting for her to glare at him or to redden even more. She did neither.

"No, she's not a slut, just a woman looking for Mr. Right. On her journey she meets Mr. Wrong."

"The jerk?"

"Yes, the jerk."

Jared leaned back in his chair waiting for the desire he felt to wane. He was not going to be the pig she evidently thought he was. He watched her fiddle with the napkin, tearing it into piles and then sweeping the piles into her bag.

"I didn't mean to hurt your feelings," Toreas almost whispered.

He continued glaring at her. So she thought he had feelings after all? How nice.

"Well, exactly how did you mean it?" Jared asked. "Was I to feel honored by your request?" He noticed that at least now Toreas did have the good taste to appear contrite.

"I thought it would be easier to do this with you. You see, I'm not attracted to you and there would be no emotional attachment. I'm sorry about the way I blurted this out, but I just need to use you for research. Just once, Mr. Stone."

Jared bristled. "You've already said just once. I understand that." He lifted the lengthy questionnaire. "You want me to go through all of this and go to the doctor for just once?"

"I couldn't do it any other way."

"What if once is not enough?"

"It will have to be. I'm not looking to have an affair with you. I just want research—"

"Please don't use that word again. Tell me something. Are you a virgin?"

"Of course I'm not a virgin."

"Then why don't you just use your memory?"

"Because frankly, Jared, at the risk of hurting your feelings again, I've only slept with nice guys. My heroine is with a jerk and I find I'm stuck on exactly what he does differently."

She attempted to turn away but Jared caught her chin in his hand and held it, making her look at him. "Exactly what is it you think a jerk does differently from nice guys? Do you think I tie my women up, or maybe beat them?"

"I don't know. That's why I'm asking you to do this. Listen, you're going to get something out of this deal also. I'll even sign a contract with you saying I'll come on what, four, maybe five shows? That should make us even, don't you think?"

"I'm not sure. I don't know what the going rate for prostitution is nowadays."

"This isn't prostitution, Mr. Stone."

"What would you call it?"

"A business agreement between adults. No money will exchange hands."

He watched her as a horrified look crossed her face. Surely she wasn't thinking of saying what her eyes clearly told him she thought.

"Is that the problem? You want money?"

Before he could think about it Jared grabbed both of her hands and yanked her toward him, Kelle's teachings be damned. Her legs were pinned under the table and he had her hands, so he should be relatively safe.

He watched as her lips thinned again in disapproval. She had a way of looking at him like a schoolmarm, making him feel guilty. And this time he was the one in the right. Jared had honestly come wanting to make peace with her. Well, that and he had wanted to go to bed with her. Once.

So what's the problem, Jared? She's offering you exactly what you want. You can have her and never see her again. He knew what the problem was. She was beginning to worm her way under his skin. He didn't think having her only once would be enough.

"You are the most annoying woman I have ever met. You've punched me, and now you've insulted my very ethics. How dare you assume that I would just grab an opportunity to jump your bones?"

Jared was talking to Toreas through clenched teeth. "For your information, I'm not the least bit attracted to you either. I prefer women. You look more like a scared child."

He was aware he was being mean, but this mere slip of a woman was making him feel about as welcome as an ant at a picnic.

She was trying to pull away from him but he tightened his grip. "Not every man will accept sex just because it's offered. Who the hell do you think you are coming in here and saying you want to use me for research? I am not going to be part of your research.

"And whatever fancy word you want to use, it's still prostitution and the last I heard it was illegal. I could have you arrested for solicitation. Imagine if I put your proposition on the air."

He released her then. He saw the fear enter her eyes and something glistened. Oh hell, he hoped she wouldn't cry. Sure, he'd been hard on her. But she was treating him worse than a piece of meat. She was treating him like dirt.

Her lips were open slightly. She had a pleading look but he wasn't going to relieve her fears. He wouldn't deny the possibility of airing her proposal. If she thought that he was that big a jerk, then to hell with her. Let her think whatever she wanted.

Jared sat waiting for her to gather her things and run out of the restaurant. She gathered her things all right, but she didn't run. She turned toward him, her right hand extended.

"Thank you for meeting with me, Mr. Stone."

He continued to watch as she opened her purse and placed money on the table. He let her. He was relieved to see the slight tremble of her fingers.

For some strange reason he was relieved to know that she'd never asked another man to go to bed with her. He didn't doubt her honesty. She'd barely been able to ask him, and then only because she thought he was a jerk. True, it wasn't a compliment for him, but still he was glad.

Jared sat at the table alone, watching her as she made her exit. She was walking naturally, unhurried, but the trembling in her fingers had given her away. This was probably the hardest thing she'd ever done.

He knew he was right about her. There was something fierce inside of her that gave her a strength that he admired. With a groan, Jared closed his eyes, realizing how close he'd come to having her. He fingered the papers she'd left, smiling at his own bruised ego.

She'd offered exactly what he said he wanted. He should have been happy, but he wasn't. Suddenly it was important to Jared to prove to this woman, this tiny romance writer, that he was not a demon.

When I prove that to her, when she trusts me completely, then I'll have my fill of her. It won't be for research and it won't be once. No, Ms. Toreas Rose, I may be a jerk, but before I'm finished with you, you will be begging this jerk for more.

9

Toreas walked out the door of the restaurant counting slowly to herself. She wanted nothing more than to run but Jared was watching her. She'd already made a fool of herself. To run would be like slapping her own face.

Liz was right. He had turned her down. It wouldn't hurt so much if it was only the sex he didn't want. It was her he didn't want. He said she looked like a scared child. And he'd called her a pimp, or was it a john?

It didn't matter. He'd actually used neither of the words but he had told her she was soliciting. And he'd been angry. Why, she wondered, should he be so upset? It had been his suggestion that she get more experience.

Oh my God, she thought. *Liz*. She wished she had kept her big mouth shut. Then she wouldn't have to explain that he'd turned her down cold.

What if Jared made good on his threat and told his audience what she had said? *Stupid, stupid, stupid*. She'd forgotten who she was talking to. The man could have been taping every word she said.

All Toreas wanted to do was go home and curl into a ball and not come out. She wouldn't talk to Liz. She didn't want to lie, but she wasn't going to admit that the man had more or less told her flat out that he wouldn't sleep with her if she was the last woman on earth.

She felt a tiny twinge of conscience. She always told Liz the truth. What did it matter now? Liz wasn't the one critiquing her behavior.

Toreas lifted her eyes toward the heavens. "Back off," she yelled, ignoring the curious looks on the faces of passersby. "Can't I sin and be humiliated in peace? Do you always have to get in on the act?"

Toreas wished suddenly that she were Catholic. She could find a church, confess her sins, pray the rosary and be given absolution. That was the way to go.

But Baptists, nope, they had to milk sin and guilt to death. You sinned when you were three and you remembered that sin always and took it to the grave.

She had a whole pile of sins now, but in all her twenty-nine years she had never sworn. Not swearing was the one big thing her father had drummed into her head.

"Damn, damn, hell and ahh...shit." There, that should do it. She looked up again at the blue sky. *Now all I have to do is go and covet my neighbor's house and commit murder. That should take care of my breaking some more commandments.*

The next day Toreas forced herself to turn the television on to Jared's show. She had to know if he was going to mention their meeting.

She breathed a sigh of relief when she saw it wasn't Jared hosting the show but his boss, Derrick. She quickly turned up the sound, hoping that this meant Jared was fired.

What she heard instead was an edited version of her conversation with Jared Stone when she'd left her number for him to call her.

"How do you prepare for interviews? Most people take notes."

Toreas listened with disbelief to her voice answering, *"Kelle teaches us karate."*

She turned the set off in disgust, vowing never to watch Channel One again. Jared had told her he wasn't taping her. Liar. Now he'd completely twisted her conversation, making her seem violent and stupid. God, what a mess.

"Please Lord, help me out of this!" Toreas stopped in mid prayer. Hadn't she told God yesterday to stay out of her life? Wasn't that what this whole thing was about? She'd wanted a man who could finally upstage God and make him leave her alone.

She was tired of doing what was expected of her, saying what everyone thought she should say, doing what they thought she should do. And she was tired of God and her father being in her head, critiquing her life. Why on earth would she want Jared? The last thing she needed was another critic.

Toreas waited for the bolt of lighting to hit her. Surely it must be coming. Why was God involved in every aspect of her life that she didn't want him in?

She closed her eyes tightly, wondering why God was never there when she sent out manuscripts. He was never there when she received the numerous rejection slips that were vague, just "Sorry, we don't want this."

She could hear her father's answer as clearly as if he were standing there. "God doesn't answer foolish prayers."

"Why are my dreams foolish?"

"Because they don't edify the kingdom."

Damn, damn and double damn. She was tired of that phrase. Most normal people didn't have an idea what it meant. Then again, most normal people didn't have voices in their heads constantly talking to them.

Toreas laughed out loud then, because she'd found a group of people who heard voices. All writers were constantly having conversations with their characters. That aspect of course was normal. The characters weren't critics. It was the critics she'd had enough of.

She was tired of hearing those voices telling her she was doing wrong. She knew that. She wasn't stupid. She wanted to do wrong.

Only thing was, she had no one with whom to do wrong with. Even God couldn't think what she'd done with Fred was sinning; surely it wasn't even fornicating. Heck, if she couldn't remember it, maybe it never happened.

Toreas laughed once more. Didn't she get the chance to commit at least one big, delicious sin, enjoy it totally and completely and then be forgiven for it?

For the next ten days she stayed in her apartment, not answering the phone or going near her computer. There were tons of emails all wanting her to explain her actions. So she avoided all links with the outside world. She couldn't write and the callers only wanted to yell at her. Via email or phone, yelling was yelling.

Maybe it was time she resigned from her chapter. Forget writing, become a missionary. That would please her father, wouldn't it?

She gave herself every conceivable reason for not going to her writers' group. Her head ached, she didn't feel like going out, maybe she was coming down with something and was contagious. None of the excuses worked. She wasn't a quitter. She would go and face the music.

Having made the decision to go, Toreas went to her car and drove to the meeting before she could find an excuse that she would accept. She took in a deep breath before entering the room, allowing it to fill every cell. Then she expelled it and entered.

Glancing around the room, she quickly found an empty seat and sat down and waited. There was a definite chill in the room. Kelle was not looking at her, neither was Liz. Toreas sat quietly looking at nothing but her own notepad, hoping to not draw attention to herself.

She looked up and focused on Becca when she began to speak. Scowling, Becca glanced in Toreas's direction.

"We've received a letter from ARW. They've taken out an ad saying that American Romance Writers does not condone violence of any sort."

Toreas sat stunned. All eyes were on her and she knew it. "They're also having their attorneys check whether a member can be suspended for committing such an act."

Toreas rolled her eyes. She didn't believe it. *Thanks a lot, God. This was one mess where I could have used Your help. Sure, I said I was thinking of resigning, but I didn't mean it. These women are my family.*

Her eyes on Becca, Toreas couldn't help thinking how her life had become parallel to a romance novel. If this were mere fiction, however, the door would open and Jared would enter.

Her head did a quick turn in the direction of the door and she watched the knob in anticipation. Nothing. She could breathe again. The last thing she needed was to see him. She took in a breath and waited. When the door handle still didn't turn she wondered if she was finally catching a break. Could it be possible that her prayers were going to be answered?

For once it seemed God was on her side. Maybe her life was not going according to any pre-written script. She could exhale, thankful that this was her life and not some story she'd wandered into accidentally.

Her attention returned to Becca. This she could handle. This was something she could argue and plead. This was real. Toreas almost felt relief hearing she was about to be kicked out of ARW and her local chapter. It meant her life wasn't just some random scene.

A minor disturbance sounded outside the room. Her eyes went to the door handle, all at once knowing what was about to happen. It was becoming apparent to Toreas that God was having fun with her. The door opened and Jared Stone strode into the room as though he owned it and the women in it.

"Mr. Stone," Becca began. "You're not allowed to disrupt our meeting."

"I'm joining." He walked toward Toreas and stopped directly in front of her. "Ms. Rose has been selling me on what a good, forgiving group of women you are. Isn't that right, Toreas?"

Toreas didn't answer him. How could she with all eyes on her? The only thing she wanted was what had gotten her in trouble in the first place. She wanted to slug Jared.

Okay, so ARW didn't believe in violence, her chapter didn't believe in violence, God didn't believe in violence and neither did her father.

But none of them were her. Right this moment Toreas believed in it with all her might. But for now, all she could do was sit like a bump on a log watching as Jared reached into his wallet and walked toward

Becca.

"You have no legitimate reason to keep me out, so here's my money."

Toreas watched as Jared smiled at Becca. Toreas absolutely hated the man, now more than ever. She wished that Becca would kick him out on his wonderfully firm behind. Instead, what she heard was anything but that.

"You have to join ARW," Becca informed Jared.

"Not a problem," he answered. "Sign me up."

Toreas watched him, noting the smug, arrogant look on his face. Why was he here? Evidently to torture her or maybe he was her punishment for sinning.

If Jared had wanted to make an entrance and disrupt the meeting he had managed to do just that. At least she could be grateful that there was someone sitting on either side of her. The only chairs left were stacked against the back wall.

She and thirty other women all held one collective breath as he circled the room, then finally headed in the direction of the stacked chairs.

She closed her eyes for a moment against his image. He was a sight to behold. He walked slowly, moving with long graceful strides toward the stacked chairs. He lifted the top one off with ease before turning and looking in Toreas's direction. As his eyes found hers, she saw all the women looking first at Jared, then at her.

Where the heck did he think he was going to put that chair? She watched him walking purposefully toward her. He was going to do it. He sat directly behind her and there was nothing she could do. He was a bona fide member.

Not attracted to him. Wasn't that what she'd told him? Every nerve in her body was singing from his nearness. She still remembered when he'd held her hands tightly in his, telling her that he didn't want her. It had been all she could do not to kiss him. She'd sure wanted to.

Jared stretched, his long legs bumping into Toreas's chair. It was an accident but he was glad to be sitting behind her. He'd unnerved her with his presence but of course she'd never show it.

She was angry with him. He could tell from the stillness with which she held her body. What did she have to be angry about? He was the one out of work.

He kicked her chair again, this time deliberately. He wondered if she even knew he was no longer on the show. After Derrick had aired his doctored-up conversation with her, Jared had slugged him and walked out.

Romance writers had ruined his life twice, first with Gina, and now it was their fault he no longer had a job. Correction, it was the fault of Toreas Rose.

He moved his chair even closer, wanting to tantalize his senses with a hint of her perfume. Nothing. He couldn't believe she didn't wear something so essential.

He was trying to pay at least partial attention to what was being said, but Toreas was proving to be as much of a distraction for him as he'd intended to be for her. Yeah, it was her fault that he'd slugged his friend and quit his job. It was her fault for making him want her, not just her body, but her respect. And it was her fault that he sat behind her, wanting her, and hating that she didn't want him. The moment he began to believe that this mess was really Toreas's fault he'd believe again in the Easter bunny.

Jared could keep neither his mind or his eyes off her. Every time she moved the slightest bit, his eyes followed her. He was trying to envision what she was hiding behind yet another baggy and this time god-awful-ugly outfit. The woman needed help all right, in more ways than one. She needed a fashion consultant.

The women began moving around, startling Jared out of his daydreams. At first he thought the meeting was over but that couldn't be. He'd only been in the room, what? He looked at his watch. About twenty minutes.

"Jared, you're in group two. You're a new member so you shouldn't give your opinions until after at least sitting in on several critiques."

He looked up into smiling eyes. At least they were friendly and the woman wasn't glaring at him. He should have been paying attention but knew it wouldn't matter. The women would forgive him. They always did,

"And where might group two be?" he asked her, smiling at her in a way that he knew she would take to mean something else. He was thinking of using his considerable charm on all the women. Why be shy? He knew the women found him appealing.

"Group two's over here at this table with me."

Jared glanced around the room to find the table Toreas was now sitting at. He would have to work this with finesse and all his charm.

He smiled up into the pleasant blue eyes and lowered his voice seductively. He pointed toward Toreas's table. "Do you mind if I sit over there? If I stay here, you beautiful ladies will prove too much of a distraction."

The woman giggled and asked someone else from Toreas's table to switch with Jared. There, that was easy. He took the vacated seat, dismissing the idea of asking the woman seated next to Toreas to move. He was already pushing it.

He watched Toreas's frantic gestures to the other women. It appeared she had given them something and now wanted it back. *It's her work*, he thought with lightning speed. *She's being critiqued and she doesn't want me to read it.*

But the women were refusing. In fact, the one to his right handed him a copy and Jared smiled while reading her name badge. "Thanks, Dianne." He read Toreas's chapter in between watching her reactions.

She was trying to appear nonchalant but not pulling it off. She was staring off into space. Then he noticed her pretending to read. He could tell she was pretending because every time he looked up she was staring at him.

He listened to the different comments the women gave on her chapter. He was going to be a good boy, not say a word. Some of the things they said made no sense to him. They were little things, he thought, picky things, and he wondered why they even mentioned them.

He was given another chapter from one of the writers and again he sat and listened to the comments. He watched the woman's eyes as she bravely tried to mask her feelings as her friends ripped into her work.

He wondered why they, not they, but Toreas, had gotten so upset with his critiques. It seemed to him they did the same thing to each other that he'd done. At least he'd never pretended to be helping. Some of the comments were downright mean.

Jared was given a third chapter to read from someone else. He was beginning to notice a pattern here. All the women wrote the same.

"Your stories are the same," he blurted out.

"You're not supposed to give your opinion." Toreas glared at him, then down at the chapter in front of her. "Besides, they're all very different."

"Page two, boy meets girl." He returned her look. "Your words might be different but the premise is the same. No variation. I know exactly what's going to happen in each story."

"You can't know that. We don't even know what's going to happen yet and we're the writers."

"Maybe that's why you can't see it. You're too involved. Why can't they meet on page three, or in the middle of the book?"

"That's not the way it's done."

"Why not?" Jared turned from Toreas to the woman who'd answered him.

"The reader wants to know immediately who the hero is or she'll stop reading. They expect a certain thing."

Jared turned back toward Toreas. "Do you really believe this diverse group of intelligent women you told me about would not be able to read a book if it's not plotted out like every other book they've ever read?"

"You're twisting our words, Jared. There is a certain order to things. A certain way the editors want them. They tell us the readers want this, and that's what we do."

He looked around the room. "So you're all a bunch of automated robots and you don't give your readers credit for having an attention span longer than that of a two-year-old?" He smiled at her then.

"And you ladies think I'm the one who was condescending to you and your readership. Aren't any of you brave enough to venture out, try something new, something that's not the norm?"

Toreas was glaring at him. "Jared, you're not a writer and you're not a romance reader, so you know absolutely nothing about what we do."

"Well, To…re…as." He purposefully caressed her name. "I know all of your stories are boring and they lack any realism."

"That's why they're called fiction, Jared. They're not supposed to be real." She lowered her voice after being shushed by several women from other tables.

Oh, he was enjoying this. "I don't see a woman falling for a man the moment she looks at him. But maybe you can help me out on this. Has it ever happened to you?"

He watched as Toreas stared down at the paper, determined not to look at him. "Have any of you ever had a one night stand simply for the sake of research?"

Jared looked slowly around the table at the open mouths and shocked expressions on the women's faces. Toreas was blushing prettily as he had known she would be.

"I'm sorry, ladies. That was perhaps a little crass of me. Let me put this a different way. Let's say you have your character, your heroine, right? Let's say you have her sleep with a man for research. How would she go about it?"

"That depends. Is your heroine a virgin?"

"Ah, at last, a woman brave enough to speak up." Jared smiled at the woman. No, she's not a virgin."

"Then why would she need to do that?"

"She feels she needs to, because, though she's not a virgin, she's also not very experienced."

"That's pretty weak. For one thing she should need better motivation than that. Is there any other motivation? Like could she secretly be in love with the man?"

For a moment Jared smiled, resisting the temptation to turn in

Toreas's direction. "Let's say she's not in love with the guy. In fact she can't stand him." This time he did glance briefly at Toreas before continuing. "Her motivation is simply that she wants to know what it's like to sleep with a jerk."

This time he was gentleman enough not to look at Toreas. He didn't have to. But she deserved this. He knew she didn't dare leave. That would be giving away her secret.

Dianne answered him this time. "That's dumb. We would never write about such a weak or stupid woman."

"That's my point exactly. Why can't the woman be weak or stupid?"

"That's not romance, Jared. It doesn't sell."

"Why? Don't stupid people fall in love and marry and have stupid kids?"

"I don't necessarily see the heroine as stupid if she decided to see what she's…"

"What she's been missing," Jared finished for Toreas. "Would you ever proposition a man for sex, Ms. Rose?" This time he didn't look away but then again neither did she.

"Mr. Stone, this is a critique session. It's not a time for confessions." Toreas looked down her nose at him. "By the way, you don't happen to look like a member of any clergy that I'm familiar with."

"I'm sorry if I offended you, Ms. Rose. Of course I'm sure your friends know you would never do anything like that. Look at the way you're dressed. You're much too proper for that."

He watched as Toreas's blush became deeper. "Besides, I think you would be much too considerate a person to ever judge another human being on what you think their morals are. And you'd have to be making a judgment to assume a man would go along with such a proposal."

He listened to the women laughing. He turned from one to the other, glancing briefly back at Toreas. "Why are you ladies laughing?"

"A man turn down sex? You've got to be kidding." This time it was the woman across from him, but he could tell they were all of the same opinion.

"Is that what all of you think about men?" A big resounding "yes," brought more shushing from the other tables.

Jared's mouth was now the one open in surprise. "Let me get this straight. You women think your readers have absolutely no attention span, that they have to have a formula to read by, and that men are big stupid bodies waiting around for sex."

This time the laughter was so loud that the other women didn't shush them but asked what they were talking about.

"Well," Toreas began, "our newest member thinks we don't have much regard for our readers, or for men, neither of which is true. Just some men." She looked toward Jared and their eyes connected for a long moment before he answered.

"I know I'm not supposed to voice an opinion at this meeting, but I had a legitimate question that led to a discussion," Jared said as sweetly as he knew how. He looked back at Toreas.

"If the rest of you ladies would like in on this maybe you can be of some help to me." Jared smiled as the women readjusted their seats in order to face him.

"I can answer that question you had before about why I hate romance novels. They're all the same."

There was a loud roaring, all the women clamoring at once. If he weren't now a member they undoubtedly would have kicked him out again.

"Ladies, I'm really not trying to be insulting. I'm trying to be helpful. Don't any of you ever break out, take chances, switch point of view because you want to, or not have exactly twenty five lines to a page or ten pages to a chapter?"

He stood then. "I bet you have to have a precise number of sentences to every paragraph. You women are so rigid. I've been sitting here listening to all of the comments and they all revolve around these issues. I think the issues are stupid."

"Jared, the publisher and the editors set the guidelines for what they want. We don't have any control over it. We can't just write anything we please. There are only a few romance authors who can get away with that. And they're the really big names."

Jared was watching Becca and the other women. He really had no intention of offending them, but their work was the same. He wondered how they could stand being boxed in.

"Are you women happy writing like this? I mean, to use one of your favorite words, what's your motivation?"

"We write because we enjoy it." Becca's voice was loud and the other women cheered her on.

"That's bull." Jared began pacing around the room. "You write because you want to be published. You want your books in a library, in the bookstores, you want to be told that you're a great storyteller."

He was beginning to feel as if he were again in enemy camp. "Ladies, lighten up. I know someone somewhere gave you that spiel about being happy just writing, but that probably came from someone with a ton of books sitting in book stores.

"Think about it. The haves are always telling the have nots how much better not having it is. They're always saying what a burden having money brings. Do you see them giving away their money? Ladies, I was in advertising. I can sell anything to anyone even if they don't want it. You can do the same."

"Jared, it's different for writers, especially romance writers. We're hemmed in because of the rules. If we wrote mainstream we could get away with a little more."

"Then why don't you do that?" He was surprised that Toreas had spoken up and without a hint of anger.

"Because we like romance," she answered. "We like the idea of a strong woman knowing what she wants and going after it, and we like that in the end she finds love and happiness."

He looked at her, this time really looked at her. God, she was beautiful. Whatever had made him think she was mousy? She was anything but.

"Real life's not like that," he answered her. "There are bumps along the road. Sometimes the people don't end up together, they maybe just find a way to annoy each other until one gives up and leaves."

This time it was Becca who answered him. "That's the point. Real life sucks at times. Our novels give women a chance to escape from the crying children, the dirty dishes and the demanding husband. Do you really think women want to read about that after dealing with it all day?"

He thought for a moment. "That's a good answer. I like it." He smiled at Becca, then the other women in turn, his eyes coming to rest on Toreas.

"Maybe you'll be willing to help me understand the need for such rigid structure." He saw the hesitation and the 'no' in her eyes. "That is what the group is about, isn't it, helping each other?"

"She'll help you," Becca answered for her. "I'm sure that'll go a long way in getting headquarters off our backs."

"Excuse me?" Jared turned toward Becca again, having never heard them mention headquarters.

"I'm sorry," she answered him. "We sometimes refer to ARW by HD or headquarters. They've been concerned because of what's been happening with you and Toreas. Actually I think your joining our group might help us," Becca finished with a wistful note in her voice.

"Are you serious about being a part of our group, Jared?"

He remembered Liz. "Sure, I'm serious. Anyone can write a romance. It shouldn't take me longer than two or three weeks."

The room burst into laughter, laughter Jared knew was directed at him. He dared a glance at Toreas and saw she was smiling. He'd never seen her smile. The action lit up her entire face. He wondered if she knew it.

Not attracted to her, he'd told her. Man, what a lie. Since meeting her everything about his life had revolved around her and the writers he professed to hate. Now instead of avoiding them, he joined them. Jared smiled at the women. He was beginning to believe the women really did possess magical powers. He couldn't wait to find out what happened next.

Jared gave into his urges and smiled at Toreas. Not attracted to her, his behind. This woman was making him break all his rules. She was too tiny. She was a bossy little loudmouth. She was a prude, and the worst thing of all, she was a romance writer.

And he wanted her. God help him, he wanted her.

10

Toreas woke with one of the worst headaches she could ever remember having. She looked at her alarm clock and groaned. How had she managed to sleep until ten?

Jared Stone. That's how. After invading the meeting and becoming a member, he'd had the audacity to follow them to the restaurant they went to after each meeting.

Of course nothing would do but for him to sit right next to her, holding court. All the women had started listening to him, liking his ideas for their books.

Toreas didn't know if his ideas were any good or not. She'd been unable to pay attention. His hand had kept brushing her thigh. He kept saying sorry, but somehow Toreas didn't think it was a mistake.

She felt humiliated. He'd told her to her face he didn't want her, yet she found herself hoping he'd touch her again.

She'd been unable to eat her mozzarella sticks. The hard breading had caught in her throat and she'd coughed. Jared had smiled at her and held out her glass of water.

When she could take it no longer, she got up abruptly, scraping her chair against the hardwood floor in her haste. Jared stood and she looked at him. Before she had a chance to say a word he gave not only a reasonable but plausible explanation.

"Toreas, it's late and even though Kelle has taught you how to defend yourself, you shouldn't leave alone. I'll walk you to your car."

What could she say? It made sense and besides, Becca was frowning at her. If allowing Jared to walk her to her car would get her back in their good graces then she'd go along with it.

Toreas swung her legs over the side of the bed. "Liar," she said to the wall. She couldn't deny enjoying the feel of Jared's hand on her arm as they'd left together.

He'd stood as her sentry while she unlocked the car door. When she turned to get in, brushing against him, he was staring down at her as if he wanted to kiss her as much as she wanted him to.

It must have had something to do with the full moon that had been shining down on them. He wasn't attracted to her. He'd said so. And she wasn't attracted to him. She only wanted him for research.

Still, she couldn't deny the quickening of her pulse when he looked into her eyes. She'd barely mumbled a thank you, wondering how she would actually get into her car without touching him again. He was standing that close.

At the last instant Jared moved slightly, just enough so that she could enter the vehicle. "Good night, Toreas. I'll see you soon." He'd managed to make it seem like they'd had a date. Darn him for making her want him. If only she hadn't come up with that crazy proposal.

She got in her car and was about to say goodnight when she stopped. Jared was cocking his head sideways, observing her with a critical eye.

"That's a really ugly outfit you have on." He'd smiled then and walked back into the restaurant.

And that's why Toreas had woken with a headache. Jared was right. What was she supposed to do now? She would be seeing him often. All her clothes looked the same. Would this be what she had to look forward to at every meeting, not only a critique of her work but a critique of her clothes?

She needed some coffee. She'd put it on, then go brush her teeth and take a shower. Then maybe she could cope with the morning and her memories of last night.

Just as she finished filling the pot with water, there was a knock on her door. It had to be one of her neighbors. Her building was secure and no one could get in without first being buzzed in. She went to the door intending to open it just a crack.

Toreas reached for the doorknob and stopped, checking the peephole instead. It couldn't be. Jared Stone. What was he doing at her house and how the heck did he know where she lived? How did he get in?

Her thoughts were coming in a jumble. She hadn't even brushed her teeth, she couldn't let him in.

"Good morning, Toreas, is that your eye I see peeping out at me?"

She turned from the door and fell against it. "Why are you here?"

"I need your help with my book."

"Your book? When did you start a book?"

"Last night when I went home." He was touching the door, peeping back at her. "Can't we talk about this inside? I feel rather silly talking to you through this door."

He was right. She was feeling a bit silly herself. She opened the door and stepped way back into the room, backing as far from Jared as she could get.

"Listen, I haven't showered. I just got out of bed a few minutes ago."

He arched an eyebrow in her direction. "Are you naked under there?" He watched as she blushed. "After our discussion on sleeping together, I don't think my comment inappropriate. Do you?"

He had the nerve to be smiling at her in that sexy way he had about him. His brown eyes, if she didn't know better, were tinged with desire, but that couldn't be. He didn't want her. Toreas decided to ignore his comment. "I'll be out in ten minutes."

"Take your time," Jared answered. "Mind if I have a cup of coffee?"

"Why didn't you have your coffee before you came here?" Toreas mumbled over her shoulder as she headed for her bedroom and the shower. Her answer was anything but polite. She almost stopped in her tracks in disbelief at her actions. She who'd been raised to always show Southern hospitality. Even after she moved to Chicago she'd held on to those Southern traditions. She stopped in her tracks before turning to face Jared. She hunched her shoulder and tried for a smile. "I'm sorry, Jared. I tend to be evil before I've had my morning coffee. Sure, as soon as it's ready, feel free to help yourself."

There were a dozen questions Toreas wanted to ask Jared, but he had her at an extreme disadvantage. He'd shown up on her doorstep clean and sexy and, she, why she looked worst than usual.

Toreas brushed her teeth while adjusting the shower. Her body and hair were squeaky clean in under five minutes. Her head was crowded now with not only the voices of God and her father but the entire congregation and the hallelujah choir to boot. And for what? Letting Jared in?

Toreas hastily pushed the clothes aside in her closet. Jared's comment from the night before was still stinging. She looked over her clothes and groaned. She didn't own anything pretty.

Since her parents and her meager savings were financing her two years to give her as yet unsuccessful writing career a try, she had been extremely frugal with money.

Toreas looked at the torn and faded jeans at the very back of her closet. She used those for working around the house. Another glance at her clothes and the torn jeans looked better. She didn't want Jared to tell her again her clothes were ugly. She was already aware of what he thought of her.

Toreas walked back into her kitchen feeling uncomfortable in her own apartment as she noticed Jared had made himself quite at home.

He was drinking coffee and had several pieces of paper spread out in front of him.

She planted herself in front of him. "Why are you here, Jared?"

He looked her over, noticing her still wet hair. There were ebony ringlets curling around her ears and forehead. He liked knowing that she'd not bothered to use a dryer. He liked the way the droplets of water sparkled on hair that had grown at least two inches in the month since he'd first met her.

"I already told you." He pointed down at the papers on the table. "I started my romance novel last night. I want you to read it."

He saw her eyes straying toward the table despite the frown on her face. He knew she was curious. "Becca said you would help. Remember?"

"Listen, Jared, Becca's not the one you've been constantly lying to and humiliating on your show. You said you weren't taping our conversation." Her frown deepened as she looked at the clock.

"Shouldn't you be at work? Or is that the reason? You're here to spy on me for your show?"

He looked at her hard, his eyes narrowing, and she thought she saw a tiny spark of anger in them and wondered why.

He took another sip of his coffee, then raised his body to reach the pot for a refill. "I no longer have a job."

Toreas found herself staring at him. "Why?" She didn't dare hope that it had anything to do with her. She closed her palm and waited.

"I didn't lie to you about taping our conversation. And I wasn't the one who aired it."

"You said you were on your cell phone." She was not going to believe him this easily. "How could they tape a cell phone?"

"I don't know. Josh once asked to use my phone. I don't know if he inserted a bug. I don't know how it was done. I just want you to know this time I kept my promise to you."

Jared brought his eyes up to meet hers. He could feel his heart pounding. Why was it important that she think well of him? He watched the emotions flashing across her face and knew she still didn't trust him, not fully.

"You can search me." He stood and moved toward her, his arms raised in the air in a gesture of surrender. "I have nothing to hide. You've won, Toreas Rose. You beat me."

He was only inches from her face. Her lips were trembling. He could see that easily and she must have put something that smelled amazingly like wildflowers in her hair.

At least she uses scented shampoo, he thought, resisting the urge to kiss her, wanting to focus on something trivial.

"I don't want to search you, Jared," Toreas whispered softly. She wanted to, and she wanted to back away from him at the same time. He was making her crazy. "Why are you saying I won?"

"You wanted me gone from the station. I slugged my boss and walked out."

His eyes were holding hers and this time there was desire hidden beneath the smoke. "You did this because of me?" Toreas asked.

"I did this because of me." Jared tilted his head and smiled at her. "And because of my promise to you. I don't give promises easily. When I do I try to the best of my ability to keep them." He smiled again.

"Had I known about your proposition in advance I might not have been so hasty. Our ratings would have shot through the roof."

He backed away from her. If he didn't, he would ravish her then and there without her permission and definitely without her silly questionnaire. No, they were both safer if he moved.

Jared saw Toreas smiling, and he could tell she was trying not to. But for once he had done something to please her. An unexpected jolt of pure joy hit him in the chest.

He went back to his seat at the table. He only wanted to bed the woman once, maybe twice. Okay, make it three or four times, no more.

Jared groaned inwardly as he stared at Toreas. Why was she becoming his obsession? When he'd imagined himself in love with Gina he'd never felt this tremendous lightness that he felt just being in Toreas's presence. He didn't know what it was with this obnoxious, annoying little woman, but she was sure managing to keep him hotter than hell.

He watched her as she sat and gingerly picked up one of the papers with his handwritten scrawl and began to read.

Last night I met the most annoying woman
with dark brown eyes that shoot fire. She
was nothing to look at, well, at least at
first glance, with the exception of her
eyes and her soft, luscious lips. And she
was rude as hell, but for some unfathomable
reason I've become irretrievably intrigued
by her.

Toreas put down the paper, trying not to blush, not knowing if Jared meant the words on the paper for her or if he was merely teasing, not knowing if the words were an insult or a compliment.

"So how is it?" Jared asked. "Do you think I show promise as a writer?"

Toreas couldn't help smiling back at Jared. He was smiling at her in such a seductive manner that he was making her breathless with wanting. She glanced again at his paper.

If he were talking about her, he had again insulted her. He didn't want her, he'd told her so himself. He thought her clothes were ugly and now he thought she was nothing to look at. Why on God's green earth would she want him?

"It's fine, Jared. You've got a good beginning, but you need more than a paragraph to make a book." She smiled at him again. "Writing bad reviews and trashing a writer's work in public is one thing. There are thousands of critics who think they can do any book better than the author who wrote it. I believe you're going to find it's a lot harder to write an entire novel than you think. I'm glad you're going to try. At least if it does nothing else, you'll soon find out this isn't an easy job."

He didn't answer immediately. Instead, he sat watching her. "Can I read one of your love scenes?" She was about to say no and he sensed it. "Won't you show me how it's done?"

Toreas sighed loudly, getting up from the table. Her mind was on a love scene all right, but not the one she'd written. Darn Becca anyway. And darn ARW for not believing in violence.

She snatched the last page from her printer bed knowing it contained her most erotic scene to date. She slid into the chair and handed the paper over.

> The pads of his fingers touched the
> back of her hand and she drew away
> feeling that delicious shiver she'd
> longed for. And now she was afraid
> of what would come next. She'd given
> up on the idea of seducing him. Or
> rather, he'd rejected it out of hand.

Toreas listened to Jared's husky voice reading her words. *"He kissed her and she melted."*

Jared laid the paper back on the table and looked into the brown eyes that faced him. "You're right. You do need help." He saw her flush with embarrassment.

"Toreas, let me ask you a question. Have you ever melted from a man's kisses?"

"Why are you asking me that, Jared? It's none of your business. I thought you came here because you wanted my help."

"I do. I'm not trying to insult you, but you'll have to admit, that scene is kind of boring. It shows no passion. You can't relay what you've never felt."

"You don't know what I've experienced," Toreas snapped at him. "Besides, my work is fiction."

Jared noticed her haughty tone. If she thought she was putting him in his place, she had another thought coming. "At least what I wrote, I've experienced and I've only been a romance writer since last night."

Strangle him, that's what she'd do. Then she'd hide the body. ARW would never have to find out. She could say that she didn't believe in violence. Jared would be dead. He would not be able to dispute her.

Jared noticed that strange gleam in Toreas's eyes and put his hands up playfully. "I'm willing to help you, so calm down and stop looking at me like that."

"Just how are you willing to help me?"

He stood and walked away from her, a safe distance, she noticed. "How are you planning to help me, Jared?" The mischievous smile on his face indicated his help would be of a sexual nature.

This time she would not blush. "If you're talking about what I said, forget it."

"I'm not offering to sleep with you. As I said, I'm not a whore. Besides, that contract you talked about, well, it would be of no interest now. I no longer have a job."

"And you have no interest in me," she said quietly. "I remember."

Jared stared at her for a long moment. "And you have no interest in me. Right? If I'm not mistaken, you loathe me." He tilted his head to the side and studied her briefly. "Are those your feelings?"

"Yes."

"Good." He smiled at her again. "Then we shouldn't have any problems. I was proposing to help you with the kiss. Come here, Toreas." When she didn't move he speared her with a look.

"Come here, To…re…as," he called, once again caressing her name. He waited, wanting to run to her but he wouldn't. She would come to him.

"Now," he commanded, and in utter disbelief he watched her come to him.

"I'm going to kiss you and you're going to record the sensations. Take note." She turned slightly from him, her eyes landing on the pad and pen on the table and he put out an arm to stop her. "Mental notes, Toreas. Just remember this is only for your research and we'll only do it one time."

She was watching him intently. "Close your eyes and feel what I'm doing, what I'm going to do," he commanded her. Once more he was stunned to see her obey.

He kept his own eyes open. He wanted to see what his touches did to her. First he placed the palms of both hands on the soft skin of her cheeks. Then he bent his massive frame over her and kissed her softly on the lips.

Hmmm, he thought. He was not going to rush this. He'd been waiting too long. He ran his tongue slowly across her lips, back and forth, back and forth, touching her chin, tickling the soft flesh of her cheeks peeking out between the pads of his fingers.

"What do you feel, Toreas?"

She didn't answer but he could feel her trembling in his arms. *Like hell she doesn't want me*, he thought and began lightly nipping at her lips, moving to her neck, pushing away the heavy material of her sweater.

Her smell was clean and feminine. Nothing to tickle his nose like the scent of perfume that he'd thought she should wear. She smelled natural. The scent was all Toreas Rose, and it tantalized his senses.

He used his tongue like a battering ram, gently of course, to force her lips apart. He found her tongue and began a gentle sucking which he abandoned only to examine the interior of her mouth.

The taste of her was magnificent. He lingered, taking his time, pulling her in closer, noticing her arms remained slack at her side, her own tongue inactive.

She was determined to show no emotion. Did she not know he could feel the need rising in her as it was in him? The heat from her mouth was because of him. He knew it.

He sucked gently on her tongue again, then without warning plunged deeper and deeper, reveling in the taste of Toreas Rose.

In the instant when he knew for sure that if he kissed her a second longer he would be willing to fill out her silly papers, Jared drew away and gently pushed her from him.

As Toreas opened her eyes he looked at her with amusement. "Just imagine what it would be like if we were attracted to each other."

11

Toreas stood with her back to Jared trying to compose herself. There were as many things happening inside her head as there were in her body.

For the first time in her entire life, guilt was being shoved out by a stronger emotion. Desire. She'd never felt anything this strongly before, but knew it for what it surely had to be.

Her father's voice was quelled to a slight whisper. She could barely hear the choir. Toreas stood for a long moment enjoying the sensations coursing through her body.

One kiss? Was Jared mad? She had to have another, even at the risk of him rejecting her again. If necessary, she would use the same lame excuse that he had, for the good of her writing. If that didn't work, she'd remind him that they were sisters, sort of.

"Jared." She spoke to him without turning. It would be easier to take a no that way.

"Yes, Toreas?"

"I don't think you got that kiss quite right. I can't visualize it well enough to recreate it on paper. You must have done something wrong."

She smiled to herself when she heard the scrape of the chair and his footsteps coming toward her.

"Then by all means let's do it again."

He turned her to face him before she could even blink. She took a long look at him. He wasn't even trying to mask his desire. That knowledge pleased her.

He was smiling at her and she wanted so much to believe his smile. Even if the smile was insincere she would accept the kiss.

"Why don't you participate this time?" Jared asked. "It might make the kiss work a little bit better."

Before she could answer or protest, he was kissing her and she was drowning in him, wanting him for her very own. The heat of his body penetrated through her thick sweater and she worried that she would faint of heat exhaustion.

Toreas gave herself over completely to his kiss, her tongue battling his. She was hungry, so very hungry for him. She gave herself permission to enjoy him, to explore the texture of his mouth, the feelings he produced in her body.

Like magic her head was cleared of all the past intrusions. The only voice screaming out in her brain was his. With one, no, two kisses he'd done it. He'd pushed all of the guilt aside and she was reveling in the wonder when she felt herself floating upward.

Oh my God, she thought to herself. *This can't be happening. I can't possibly be floating.* But she was. She kicked her feet and sure enough they were not on the ground. She circled her arms around his broad shoulders, pulling him tighter, not wondering how she could reach him.

It didn't matter, she'd floated right into his arms and that's where she wanted to be. She heard the sound of bells so clearly that she opened her eyes to look around.

Jared was holding her up off the ground, a good two feet in the air. She hadn't floated at all. He'd merely lifted her up. She looked into his eyes, wondering when he'd done it. She hadn't felt him lift her, just that wonderful floating sensation.

"Was that better?" he asked. She did notice that his voice was thick and he was still holding onto her.

"I think that should do it," Toreas managed to squeak as she kept her attention on Jared. He slid her body slowly downward, keeping her in contact with him. She wanted to groan, to wrap her legs around him and refuse to move as she felt his hardness pressing into her belly.

He sat her down. Her feet now on the floor, she was fighting to hold on to her dignity and not grovel for yet another kiss. She turned her head toward the table, then back toward him, bringing her eyes to his.

"You were right, Jared. That was pretty good for two people who aren't attracted to each other." She walked away from him this time as he had done to her after the last kiss.

For several hours they worked together, mostly on his story. Toreas couldn't help noticing it seemed to be about her. But she didn't ask and he didn't say.

They worked that way until a grumble from Jared's stomach forced Toreas to look at the clock. He was probably hungry. She knew she was. She hadn't eaten breakfast and now it was time to eat again.

"It's lunch time," she said to Jared, but didn't bother offering him anything. She wanted to, but the way he was watching her, she felt suddenly afraid of what she really wanted to offer him.

They had been together long enough. She might not be the most experienced person in the world, but she knew sometimes things could happen when people were confined together. Feelings they didn't really have could confuse things. She couldn't let that happen.

"I suppose I should leave." He spoke softly as though his statement were meant to be taken as a question. His eyes riveted her in place.

Toreas barely heard Jared. She was too busy looking at him and wondering how she had the strength to let him go.

"I could go out and get us some lunch," Jared offered, "unless of course you're too busy and have other things to do."

He was looking hopeful. That she hadn't missed. But he'd given her an out and she needed to take it. She needed to return to reality.

She'd gotten caught up in what they were creating. None of it was real, not the kiss and not the feelings she was beginning to have.

They were playing a game, both wanting to win. The lines were blurring and Toreas was no longer sure just how much she still loathed him, if at all.

But she had to resist him and keep her defenses up partially or she would become consumed by him as she never had been by another living soul. When a man like Jared decided to walk out of her life, she knew without a doubt he would break her heart.

Toreas mentally calculated what she had in her fridge to make lunch. She had enough for two. She sighed and shook her head to clear her emotions. She couldn't make Jared lunch, and she couldn't allow him to bring it back, not yet anyway.

"Yeah, you're right, I am busy. I almost forgot that I have an appointment." Toreas's voice was unconvincing but she'd be darned if she'd admit the truth. She couldn't bring her eyes up to meet his.

She'd done that once too often already, and each time he'd been staring at her with some look she couldn't quite explain. All she knew for sure was that his look was making her melt. She remembered Jared's earlier question to her asking if a man's kisses had ever made her melt and the answer was yes, yes. His kisses had made her melt. His kisses had given her the ability to float.

"Jared, are you going to be okay?"

His eyebrow quirked upward and it was plain to see he had no idea what she was talking about.

"I mean your job, Jared. I didn't want you to lose your job." He stared at her until she felt the heat coming to her cheeks. "Well, it's not something I should have wanted, and I'm sorry about that. So are you going to be okay financially?"

He smiled then. "I'll be okay, Toreas."

"If you'd like, until you find another job, I could make dinner for you. I always cook enough for two."

She slapped her left hand over her open mouth, then her right hand over her left, shocked. She couldn't make him lunch, but she could offer to make him dinner every night. Jared was laughing at her reaction. Then he was a gentleman about her offer.

"Would you like to take your offer back?"

He grinned that darn sexy grin of his and Toreas felt wetness in her panties. Before she could take another breath, she felt the liquid cascading down her thigh, making her doubly glad she'd thrown on the worn pair of jeans. At least her embarrassment would be kept private.

"I can see that you spoke without thinking." Jared grinned again.

Here was her opportunity, she could pull back. Toreas was arranging the words in her head to tell Jared she was sorry, but what she heard coming out of her mouth was something entirely different.

"You're more than welcome to come for dinner, Jared. That is what our chapter is all about. We're there for each other."

"So this is just a writers' thing?"

"Yes," she lied.

He was smiling down at her. "Then tell me what time and I'll be back." He waited, watching her.

"Six," Toreas whispered, then cleared her throat. "Come back at six. I always eat at that time."

"One more thing. We're not romantically attracted to each other, so do you think it would be possible to be friends?"

"We can try." She stepped back from him. What had she been expecting, for him to kiss her goodbye? He'd just repeated he didn't want her. She wrapped her arms around her waist to keep her body from shaking. Then he decided to speak again.

"I was wondering how it was that you first came to be watching my program?"

"I watched you for weeks." Too late Toreas realized what she'd said. She was pinching her hand trying her best not to allow the telltale flush of color to give her away.

"So, you were my fourth fan." Jared smiled, then headed for the door. "I'll see you at six," he said without even turning around.

He was gone and Toreas was left to ponder what she'd admitted to him. He didn't know that she'd started watching him with the sound muted because she found him so darn handsome and his eyes had called to her.

No one must ever know she'd had a secret crush on Jared. That is, until she'd un-muted the television and started listening to the nonsense he spouted.

After his attack on the romance genre and its readers, her little infatuation had quickly turned to loathing. And now what was it between them? She was at a loss to explain it.

But whatever it was, Toreas was grateful to Jared for ridding her of her unwanted feelings of guilt. She owed him a few dinners for lifting that monumental weight from her.

☞

Jared left Toreas's apartment thinking he shouldn't return. There was something happening between them that he didn't want and didn't need.

What had started out as a little innocent revenge and harmless fun had escalated into... What? He wasn't sure. What he was sure of was that he liked kissing her. He really, really liked it. So much that he wished he were back in her apartment. If he wasn't kissing her, he could look at her lips and remember as he'd done all morning. He could make her blush when she caught him looking, and he could write his feelings down on paper. He knew what he was writing wasn't good, but it was making her smile, and her smile was making him write.

He had to stop thinking so much about kissing her and seriously think how he was going to support himself. He'd been touched by her asking about his finances.

In truth, he hadn't given it much thought. He supposed he could always return to California and resume his old job but he wasn't of a mind to. And it had nothing to do with Gina or her model boyfriend.

It had more to do with a short feisty woman with dripping wet hair that dried naturally, framing her face in a rapidly expanding afro. The style suited her. And like it or not, Jared was forced to admit that his not wanting to return to his job at either the advertising agency or the PR firm had to do with the way Toreas had responded to his kisses.

No woman had ever so opened herself up to him. He had felt her vulnerability and her fear. Both made him want to protect her, to claim her. He never wanted her to let go like that with anyone else. He would feel like a pig to say it, but it was what he was feeling so he saw no harm in thinking it. Jared could tell from the feel of her body in his arms that no man had ever made her feel the things he had.

He was proud of that. He had been right about him having to teach her. But he'd been wrong about her being a prude. He'd sensed the sensuous woman she'd done her best to bury under mountains of ugly, baggy clothes, and a quiet demeanor.

There was a raging fire inside Toreas and if his guess was right, he'd lit the match. He couldn't help wondering why she attempted to kill that side of herself. It didn't matter. He'd resurrected it.

Jared was aware he was taking too much credit for Toreas's strength. He smiled, remembering when she'd asked him to sleep with her. That had taken a lot of courage.

Even last night, he thought, she'd faced him and had not backed down. It was mean of him to throw her offer in her face, but she'd taken it and answered him.

Oh yes, there was indeed something about the lovely Ms. Toreas Rose that had Jared wanting to peel away her layers until he found the woman she was meant to be.

For a moment his chest puffed with pride. He was the one who'd discovered the treasure long buried. And he would be the one to taste the fruits.

An unexpected tinge of jealousy hit him as he imagined another man with his arms around her. He had never felt jealous of Gina's new lover, just angry at her and hurt that she thought she needed to turn to books.

He'd make sure that Toreas wouldn't turn to books unless it was his loving that gave her inspiration.

Jared was brought up short. *Wow*, he thought to himself. *I'm beginning to sound as if I'm falling in love with her.*

12

Jared sat on his sofa munching on his burger and wondering how he'd managed to allow his feelings to get so out of control over a romance writer.

If he returned to L.A. now, he could safely put Toreas out of his mind. More importantly, she would not become a part of his heart.

He'd only goaded her into helping him with his excuse for a book just to irritate her further. And his joining her romance chapter was something he'd thought up on the spur of the moment and gone with.

He didn't really blame Toreas for being upset on hearing the edited tape of their conversation. Still, he didn't like the way she'd automatically assumed he'd betrayed her again and taped her.

When Jared thought about it, there was a long list of things he didn't like about her, starting with the fact that she acted as though she were morally superior to him.

He glanced at her twenty-page list of questions that he'd brought home and tossed on the coffee table weeks ago. He didn't know why he'd kept it. The sight of the document irritated him.

She'd had the gall to ask him to sleep with her for research without any regard for his feelings. *Oh that's right, Jared. None of the women think men have any feelings.* He'd almost forgotten the women laughing at him last night.

He picked the questionnaire up and began looking it over. This was the most insulting thing of all, her assuming he was a depraved pig.

He noted the way she worded her questions. 'How many hookers have you been with?' Not, 'Have you ever been with a hooker?'

Yes, Jared, old boy, she has a pretty low opinion of you.

So why do you want her? He knew it was so much more than the kiss, but he didn't know the word for it. Something about her very essence captured his imagination.

He took another bite of his burger. If he didn't stop thinking about

Toreas and concentrate on finding another job he might actually have to eat dinner with her out of need. He only had enough money in his bank account to tide him over for a few months.

The flashing red light on his answering machine drew Jared's attention and he wondered why he hadn't noticed it before. He walked over and pushed the button, wondering if Toreas had left a message for him not to come.

Instead he heard Derrick's voice. "Jared, if you're over your little temper tantrum, call me. It's time to come back to work."

He closed his eyes and whispered, "Thank you." He wouldn't have to leave Chicago. He wouldn't have to leave Toreas. She wouldn't have to feel sorry for him and cook him dinner. But he wanted her to.

The idea of having dinner with her every night was doing magical things to his libido. Jared dialed Derrick's number. *I'll tell her*, he thought. *Just not tonight.*

✍

Toreas took a quick inventory of her freezer and cabinet, remembering her bold statement. Sure, she cooked enough for two people. Herself. She always made her dinners stretch for two nights and sometimes even a third.

She really couldn't afford to feed Jared more than a few dinners. Every penny was budgeted and the idea of going to her father for extra money didn't appeal to her at all.

Still, she felt she owed Jared. She didn't want to smile but she did. She felt like royalty, as though he had fought a duel over her honor. Maybe she had misjudged him after all.

Of course she would be lying if she didn't admit that the thought of kissing Jared again was in her mind. His ability to still all the critics in her head telling her no was nothing less than a miracle.

Toreas almost laughed that it had taken a critic to get rid of all her internal critics.

She'd spent practically her entire life trying to find a way to turn off those inner sensors. Now she'd found it. Jared. There must be something magical about him.

She gave herself a mental pat on the back. Her idea to use him for research was working. She was indeed inspired. Toreas smiled while removing her last two steaks from the freezer.

Her plan before inviting Jared had been to make a pot of spaghetti. That would usually last her for four days. But she didn't want to give Jared spaghetti for his first dinner. His first dinner. The thought made her tingle just thinking of it.

Promptly at six, her bell rang. She had taken another shower and had changed into an old shift she'd stopped wearing because it fit her curves too closely. There was no denying she had it on because of Jared's comments about her clothes. Toreas reached out her hand to open the door and noticed the slight shaking. *Stop that*, she scolded herself. *This is not a date.*

Jared was loaded down with two bags filled with food. And that smile of his...

"Hello." Jared grinned and walked into the apartment.

"Hi, why the food?"

He pushed the door closed with his foot. "I'm not broke yet, so I wanted to pitch in and buy some groceries since you're going to be doing the cooking."

Toreas watched him as he made his way into her kitchen with ease. He started putting things away as though he belonged there. It felt right.

"You've bought enough food to last a month. It won't take you that long to find another job." She was smiling at him, hoping her words gave him some encouragement.

Jared didn't turn from the freezer. Now was the time to tell her he had his old job back. But her comment only reiterated that she was going to allow him to come only as long as he was out of work.

He was trying desperately to convince himself that he was doing nothing wrong. He would tell her eventually. It wasn't like he was going to eat her food under false pretenses. He'd bought the food with the exception of whatever it was they were having tonight.

"Something smells good," he said, changing the subject.

"Jared, it's okay to be nervous about finding another job, but you're good at what you do. Someone will snap you up in no time."

Okay, he thought, *now she's gone and done it. Now he was beginning to feel just a little guilty.*

"Toreas, don't worry about it." He desperately needed a new topic. "How do you make it?" He spread his hand expansively. "You don't appear to be independently wealthy."

"I'm not." She smiled at him. "When I made this decision to write I worked like a maniac for six months, saving every dime to give myself two years to try."

"You made enough money in six months to carry you for two years?" Jared couldn't help noticing the tiny spots of color that dotted her cheeks.

"No way. I made a deal with my parents. They're helping me out. If after two years I haven't made a dent that counts, then I'm to give up..." Toreas paused and looked at him.

"Those are their words, not mine. If I don't make it in two years, I'll stop writing romance, reading romance, thinking about romance and dedicate my life to a more useful endeavor."

"Wow." Jared looked at her, seeing a faint light in her eyes and hearing the despair in her voice. "How much time do you have left?"

"Five months," she answered.

"What are you going to do if it doesn't happen?"

"Like you, I'll find a job. Life goes on. Now, enough of this. Lets have dinner."

&

For two weeks Jared showed up on Toreas's doorstep promptly at six. Each night he brought either dessert or wine. He ignored her scolding him about spending his money when he didn't have a job. He still hadn't told her.

He hated himself for accepting her pity and concern under false pretenses but he didn't want it to end. He hadn't kissed her again but he was content just being around her.

They had developed an easy comfort with each other. She'd slowly confided in him about the turmoil that raged inside of her. That told him he'd been right about her hiding her sensual nature. The fact that she'd played the part of her daddy's good little girl all her life and had not really given in to her desires touched him. It was probably her feelings of guilt that had not allowed her to enjoy her first experiences.

There had been no need for Toreas to fill him in on the strong religious influences. It was there in everything she did and said. It was obvious she didn't agree with everything she'd been taught or she wouldn't have become a romance writer. It was also obvious to Jared that Toreas felt guilty for doing so. That guilt, he believed, stopped her flow of passion on the written page and in every aspect of her life.

Jared found himself liking the woman. He'd readily admit he wanted to be the one to help her release her passionate nature. But beyond that, he liked her.

And the more he liked her, the more Jared was sure he was falling in love with her. He didn't want to. Love with a woman like Toreas Rose meant marriage. Right now the most he could give her was sex. Granted great sex, but no more than that.

There was one other thing he could give her and was giving her. Friendship. He could see a slight change in her writing. She wasn't exactly writing erotically, but then again, she was adding a little spice.

He was pulling for her to make her dreams happen. Maybe then when she found out the truth she'd forgive him. He'd gone back to work for good reasons, first because he needed a paycheck, and second, because Derrick believed he needed him to help make his own dream come true.

But the most important reason he'd taken his old job back was that he didn't want to leave Toreas, not yet. Of course he hadn't told her, not with words anyway.

But then again she was still pretending to herself and to him that she wasn't attracted to him. He was afraid that if he told her how he really felt she would turn tail and run, her puritanical upbringing getting the better of her.

He knew part of the reason she'd been able to let go of the guilt about the two of them spending so much time alone together in her apartment was that she'd managed to convince herself that there was nothing going on between them.

That was the biggest lie either of them had ever told. The air sizzled between them. Since his days were spent at the station, Jared had little chance to write until he spent time after dinner with Toreas. Then he'd rack his brain for something to write, anything to make Toreas smile.

He regretted the lies between them. His plan to have her trust him was quickly giving way to an abundance of lies. He'd told her he couldn't work on his book with her during the day because he was job hunting. He still found time to eat dinner with her each night.

He felt guilty about the lies, not about the writing. His writing was for one purpose and one purpose only. He was writing only love scenes now, trying to tempt Toreas into another kiss.

He was amused when one of the members of the group would call and she would shush him, not wanting them to know he was at her house.

It delighted him that a romance writer couldn't see what was happening in front of her nose. She never mentioned the fact that at the meetings everyone saved the spot next to her for him.

Even at the restaurant afterwards, the women would look at Toreas and ask where she was sitting, then move down one seat from her, making sure Jared was positioned on her left.

And for once Jared was not betraying Toreas by talking. He didn't mention the private time they spent together, but knew every member understood there was more happening than the two of them writing together.

The only time they weren't together during the meetings was on critique night. Jared had started taking whichever group he was assigned to. He found himself enjoying the women. He loved being able to get a rise out of them with his off-the-wall comments. He also enjoyed it when he could get them to make changes, which happened quite frequently.

Jared had been back on the job a little over a month. After dinner tonight he'd thought it made sense since he and Toreas were already together and going to the same place to go together, but she'd insisted they go alone. He'd finally made up his mind. This would be the night he told her the truth. And hopefully he could convince her that he was no longer attacking the writers.

That in itself would be hard to do since he still was, only now it was only taking up a smaller segment of his show. Derrick was insisting that he bring it back as his lead in. So far, Jared had managed to avoid making the writers the main focus of attack. Since the ratings were still high, Derrick had merely grumbled and accepted it passively.

Jared was sitting in his small group reading the women's chapters when something they said caught his attention.

"I'm thinking of entering The Purple Plum," Liz announced.

Jared could feel himself frowning. The women were encouraging Liz as though what she said was of tremendous importance.

"What's The Purple Plum?" he asked.

For a moment they looked at him and he felt like an outsider again. Then they smiled and Liz answered.

"The Purple Plum is like the academy awards for romance writers who haven't been published."

He glanced over toward Toreas's group. "Can anyone enter?"

"Any member in good standing with a completed manuscript."

His eyes strayed again toward Toreas. He was wondering if he could convince her to enter the contest. Her manuscript wasn't finished and to tell the truth, he didn't think it was good enough for her to win. But he wanted to give her some encouragement, as she had done for him. Her time of financial support from her parents was drawing to a close and he believed she was closer than ever to releasing her passion and allowing it to flow freely onto the paper.

If Jared could help Toreas gather her courage to enter something like that, he wouldn't mind her wrath when she found out that he was working. It was decided. He would remain quiet until he helped her.

Jared returned his attention to the women at his own table and listened patiently as they told him about the Bard, the award given for published authors.

He watched the women's faces as they talked about different conventions, from nationals to the many local ones held throughout the country. He listened with interest as they told him of an upcoming convention they were all planning to attend.

He wondered if Toreas had ever gone to one of the conventions. These women were talking with such passion that he was convinced Toreas had never gone. Jared wanted to give this to her. He would pester Toreas to finish her manuscript and to go the convention. He could put off telling her he was back at the station for awhile.

He would tell her tonight that he'd found another job in television, just so she'd stop worrying about him and making him feel guilty. He would just not tell her where. Just a little white lie. Who would it hurt? None of the women watched his program anyway.

13

"Toreas, why don't you enter The Purple Plum?" Jared stared at her over the rim of the coffee mug. She was watching him, her brown eyes giving him the once-over.

"How did you find out about that?"

"Tonight at the critique. Liz is going to enter. I was thinking maybe you should." He smiled at her.

Instead of smiling back, she got up, removing their coffee cups in the process. Her subtle hint that he'd stayed long enough.

"Liz's a fantastic writer."

Jared noticed the awe in her voice. It made him want to wrap his arms around her. Not giving himself time to think, he walked behind her and put his hand tentatively around her shoulder.

He felt the pace of her breathing change. "I found a job," Jared said softly and felt her tense. "There's no need for me to come over every night...unless you want me to."

Toreas was feeling flushed. This close to Jared she was again wanting things she'd denied wanting.

"That's good. I knew you wouldn't be without a job too long." What the heck was she talking about? She was already feeling his loss.

She did want him to find a job, didn't she? She couldn't answer that one. It had been so much fun cooking for him, eating with him, writing with him, and pretending. Toreas didn't want it to end.

"Tell me about your job. Is it still in television or is it something else?"

"It's doing pretty much what I was doing before."

"Trashing romances writers?"

Jared hesitated a second, knowing that that was indeed what Derrick was hoping he'd do. "Toreas, I'll make you a promise. I have no plans on going back to trashing what you and the other romance writers do. I know what you do is important to you."

"So what are you going to be doing?"

"I'm not sure yet," Jared answered, trying not to squirm. He could see from the way Toreas was watching him that she still didn't quite trust him not to hurt her or her romance group. He'd also noticed that she'd conveniently not answered about his continuing to have dinner with her. He was disappointed but it wasn't altogether unexpected. If he continued to come for dinner he could just imagine the guilt that would entail for her. Right now she could salve her conscience with the thought that she was helping him out. It was time to change the subject of his job.

"Let's forget about the job. It's just something to do for right now." He smiled. "Tell me, are you going to enter the contest for The Purple Plum?"

"Are you thinking about entering, Jared?" Toreas asked. She was stalling to avoid answering whether she wanted him to come over. How could she be sure he still wanted to come?

She turned to face him. His eyes were again filled with desire and he was watching her intently in the oddest way.

She closed her eyes and waited for the intrusion of voices but they didn't come. She stopped breathing, wondering if she looked like an idiot standing there with her eyes closed in expectancy.

Then his lips came down over hers, softly, and his arms closed about her.

The kiss was hard for her to explain. It was brief and so different from the other two they'd shared. There was an intense hunger on both parts but they were both keeping it in check.

"How did you know I needed something for the scene I'm working on?" Toreas asked.

"You're using what just happened for a scene?"

Jared arched his eyebrows and his eyes clouded over. Toreas wanted to push him away from her but she couldn't move. She was stuck where she was.

She shivered as he ran one hand down the side of her cheek. "Am I still just a research project to you?"

She wasn't going to get caught like that. "What am I to you, Jared? Am I just an unfinished story?"

"You don't trust me, do you?"

His lips came down to cover hers, then stopped but a kiss away. She was sharing his breath, the need to cling to him overcoming her good sense. His muscles rippled beneath the fabric of his shirt.

Toreas could feel the evidence of his desire as he lowered his lips the last fraction of an inch and kissed her, melting away her doubts, replacing them with a hunger that frightened her.

"Trust me, Toreas," he moaned into her ear. "I could fall in love with you very easily if I'm given the slightest bit of encouragement."

God, how she wanted to believe him. She smiled up at him, resisting the pull of lust in his eyes. She had to try to inject some humor, anything to get them away from discussing their feelings. "You're a reporter. A critic." She tried her feet; they could move now. She walked away from him and back to the safety of her overstuffed chair.

She had expected him to follow and tease her but he didn't. He stood his ground, staring after her, a half frown on his face. His look was making her nervous.

"I haven't said a demeaning word about romance writers in weeks. Still you don't trust me."

She saw he was serious. "Jared, you haven't had a job in weeks. You haven't had an opportunity to attack us." She was half joking with him but he wasn't smiling. Instead, his frown deepened.

She realized her remark could be construed as insensitive. "Jared, I was only joking. I'm sorry."

Only then did he make a step toward her. "Do you believe that's the only reason I've stopped my attacks? I thought things had changed between us."

She didn't like the way he was gazing at her. He was making her believe in magic, in love. She couldn't hold out that hope. The kiss in the kitchen was an ending because of the month they'd shared. She couldn't think it meant anything more than that to him.

Toreas wanted light, she wanted to chase away the sudden thickness of the charged air. He was descending on her, his eyes all over her at once.

She looked away from him to think. "Well, something has changed, Jared. You don't call my clothes ugly anymore."

He stopped and laughed. She breathed easier, knowing she had accomplished what she wanted.

"But they still are atrocious," he answered her. "Why do you buy things that look like this?"

He was standing in front of her, his hand touching the well worn fabric of the heavy cotton shirt she had on. This shirt she thought was pretty. There were flowers and beads covering it in different patterns.

"Are you trying to hide from the world so no one sees you?"

She felt the warmth crawling over her body. "I buy things I can afford, Jared."

"But why do they have to be so big and look so awful? If I didn't know better I would think all of your clothes came from a thrift shop."

Toreas laughed and touched her shirt. "I thought this was nice." She laughed even harder as the shock of truth hit Jared.

"I don't believe it. Why? And don't tell me again you do this to save money."

"Being wasteful is a sin," she scolded.

"Even if the clothes are three sizes too large and look like this?"

He was pointing at her, sputtering, unable to say what he really thought and she knew he was trying hard not to be mean.

She didn't care. Jared Stone talking about her wardrobe she could take. Him looking at her with his eyes turning smoky with desire she couldn't handle.

He sat in the chair opposite her, scratching the tip of his nose with his left index finger. "You do that very well."

"What?"

"Distract me. We started out with me asking you to enter The Purple Plum. Now we're talking fashion."

"I didn't know that I was doing that."

"Of course you knew it."

Toreas laughed. "Okay. Guilty."

Something happened then and they both felt it. Jared stood with a question in his eyes, watching as Toreas licked her lips, her eyes never leaving his face, giving him silent permission. Her breath was coming out in little pants. A look of total lust filled her eyes before fear obliterated it. He was losing her. He had to think of something fast.

"Toreas, I think it's time for another lesson. I know you have the kiss down pat but there's more." He stood in front of her. "Are you ready to learn?"

Before she could answer, Jared dipped his head down and captured her trembling lips in his own. He heard her moan and swallowed it. "To…re…as," he said, intentionally caressing her name. "Are you ready?" Moving closer, he nipped her ear, allowing his hands to roam over her body. She wasn't talking, just breathing hard.

Jared could feel his flesh swell and harden. His erection was pushing against her and she attempted to move away but he held her in place playing with her behind. He twirled his tongue into her ear, licked the perspiration from her neck, the scent of her becoming a part of him. He groaned and bent to lift her into his arms.

"Jared?"

"We're just going to take it to the next level, Toreas. Anytime you want me to stop all you have to do is say so. I promise I will stop."

God, if she said the word *stop*, he didn't know what he would do, because stopping wasn't in his plans. Jared wanted to make love to Toreas. The thought of being buried deep in her wetness made the flesh in his pants jerk.

He had to be careful, she was skittish, that much he knew. Her head was buried in his neck and he could feel her body heat. But the heat from her face was different. He didn't have to look at her to know she was embarrassed as hell. He walked toward what he was praying was her bedroom and knew immediately that it was when her hand went out to the door jamb to block his entry.

"Jared," Toreas moaned, "I don't think we should."

"We haven't done anything yet. Come on, I have something I want you to experience. You told me you'd never had your eyes to roll back in your head. Have you ever had an orgasm?" Jared tightened his arms to keep her from jumping out of them. "Toreas," he said softly, "I don't have to do the deed to make you come."

"Jared?"

"Jared what," he teased. "You think I'm too vulgar?"

"A little."

"Then I guess I shouldn't tell you that right about now I want to lick you all over and have you scream out my name. I'll tell you what, I'll get your pad and paper and you can write down your sensations. What do you think?" He stopped a step away from entering the bedroom, dropped his head down to hers and kissed the top of her head before exploring her ear with his tongue again. "Do you want me to take you back to get your pad?" he whispered hoarsely.

"No, I think I can remember."

"If you can't I can always do it again." This time he was barely able to get the words out. He was choking, barely able to breathe over the delicious delicacy he held in his arms. God, he could come right there just from holding her, but he had to do this right. He had to give her time to adjust. He had to make her believe that he was falling in love with her.

Damn. Jared took a step toward her bed and another. Her eyes opened finally and her head raised to look at him. Her brown eyes held his and the look slayed him. "I'm not going to hurt you, Toreas."

"Jared, I feel so…turn out the light."

"I want to look at you, Toreas, you need me to. How are you going to write about the lust you see in my eyes if you don't see it?"

He laid her gently on the bed, afraid that once he did she would kick him from the bedroom but she didn't. She did, however, try to scoot as far away from him as she could get.

Jared grinned. He loved a challenge. He blinked. The miles and miles of clothing she had on would indeed prove to be a challenge. At least it was only the oversized shirt that he had to worry about.

"What are you going to do, Jared?"

"I'm going to show you the proper way to write a love scene."

"I thought you said it was trash?"

"Trash done right is glorious." He grinned again at her.

"Do I have to participate?"

Now that stumped him. Jared narrowed his eyes and took a good look at her. Surely she had to be joking. But she wasn't. *Do I want her to participate?* His eyes closed as he imagined her hands on him, touching him, caressing him, her fingers running up and down over his too hot flesh…

"Jared?"

He blinked as he opened his eyes. Another beautiful image shot to hell and back. He wanted to laugh but more than anything he wanted to fall on his knees and thank God that this woman he was falling in love with was so inexperienced. He'd have to amend how many times he wanted her. It was beginning to feel like he'd want her for a lifetime.

"Jared, have you changed your mind?"

"God," he groaned, and made his way toward her on his knees. *Kisses*, he decided. He'd start with kisses. Toreas needed to relax and Jared needed to taste her. He slid upward, lay beside her and stretched his legs out in front of him, knowing she was watching. He adjusted his head on her pillow and sighed, reaching for her hand. "Let's talk, Toreas. You said you're not a virgin, right?"

"Right, I'm not."

"Have you ever actually touched a man?"

"Of course."

"I don't mean his face or his chest. I mean have you ever helped a man to achieve an arousal, have you brought him to orgasm with your beautiful fingers?" he asked, playing with her fingers.

The fear was creeping back into her eyes. "Have you ever used those beautiful soft lips of yours and made a man see heaven?" To his surprise Toreas laughed.

"How do you know whether I could make a man see heaven?"

"Because you have done nothing but run from me and already I'm so damn near heaven I could burst. I want you."

"But, Jared…"

"I know."

"Did you mean it? If I ask, you'll stop at any point?"

"Oh yes, but if I do my job correctly you won't say stop."

"Your job?"

"Let me tutor you."

Toreas couldn't help being a little disappointed. So he wanted to tutor her, did he? His hand was sliding underneath her blouse, his fingers cool and making her shiver. Toreas felt wetness pooling between her thighs and wondered if it were truly the cool touch or the hot fever Jared produced in her body. Her breath hitched and she squirmed. What she wanted to do was throw off all her clothes and attack Jared, but she didn't want to appear too eager. Toreas laughed softly in embarrassment.

"Are you laughing at my efforts?" Jared asked.

"I'm laughing that you're pretending this is for either of our books."

"Oh, you think I'm lying, Toreas? I do plan to write about this. Now if you don't want to have this experience then let me know." He pretended to pull away. "But I bet it will make you a better writer."

"What about my imagination?"

"Hmm, let's see." Before Toreas could stop him he'd lifted up her blouse and was blowing kisses on her abdomen a moment before his tongue dipped deep inside her belly button and a moan filled with lust escaped her pretty mouth. "So tell me, Toreas, does your imagination compare with this? Would you like for me to stop?"

Stop? Was the man kidding. "No, Jared, don't stop," Toreas said, feeling a physical ache for the first time in her entire life. She was in need of the things this man was doing to her. Jared was making her feel things she'd never felt and she wanted more.

A snap of her pants brought her out of her reverie. "Jared, we agreed."

"We agreed that when you wanted me to stop, you would tell me and I would do it. Do you want me to stop so soon?"

His voice dropped several octaves. "Toreas, please," he moaned. "I just want to touch you. Listen," he said, trying hard to talk. "I need help with my scene too. Can't you help me?" He saw her lips curl into a smile. She didn't believe it, but she wanted a way out of saying no, a way to soothe her conscience and he'd just handed it to her on a silver platter.

"Okay, if you really need my help."

Her voice was husky, filled with desire and lust. Jared dared to glance at her. Her brown eyes were alive with fire.

Oh God, he thought, how had this delicious treasure been overlooked? How could any man have had her and not allowed her to enjoy it. *A damn shame*, he thought, then smiled. But the shame of the man who'd taken Toreas's virginity and hadn't known what to do with it was Jared's good fortune. He knew exactly with to do with Toreas and her desires.

Make him stop? Hell no, Jared thought. She would be begging for more and so would he. He was already imagining being buried deep inside her. A shiver claimed him and he rocked his erection against the side of Toreas's leg. He bit his lips to retain control. His hand slid inside the band of Toreas's jeans and down a coupled of inches. She refused to budge.

"Toreas, you need to lift your hips so I can take your pants off."

"I'm not taking my pants off."

"Then how am I going to give you what I have for you?"

"I'm not taking my pants off."

Jared leaned on an elbow and looked at her. "Okay, but can we pull them down a little more? There is so much of you I want to see. I want to see what you're hiding in the vee of your thighs. I want to see your panties. Are they cotton, Toreas? Is that the reason you don't want me to see them? Are they some god-awful thrift store seconds?"

He watched while her toasty brown skin reddened and she became angry.

"My underwear is my business." Toreas said, her voice dripping with sarcasm.

"But it's cotton, isn't it?"

"Jared, let's stop."

"I'm sorry, I like cotton. My briefs are the tittie whitties. They're cotton so I shouldn't talk. Would you like me to show you what I'm wearing?"

Before Toreas could answer Jared sprang from the bed and took off his pants. He smiled proudly at the way his underwear tented. And then some vague knowing pulled at him and had him thinking, *Oh Oh. Think quick, Jared, you're going to lose her.* "I'm sorry about that, Toreas, you have that effect me, but it's nothing to worry about." He swallowed. She wasn't buying. She was closing her eyes, determined to end this game, but he hoped not yet. There were so many things Jared had to show her.

Toreas felt as though she were drowning. She was doing things with Jared she'd never done with her two boyfriends and Jared wasn't a boyfriend. He wasn't even a date or a one night stand. Heck, she didn't know what he was, only that she was falling in love with him. That wasn't right. She wasn't falling, she was already there. Toreas loved the way they were together when they were alone. She was beginning to trust him with her feelings, her work…now her body. She shivered. He was talking dirty to her and prude that she was, she hoped to God he never stopped.

Toreas stared at Jared. His underwear was tented. She knew she should stop gawking but couldn't. She'd had sex a total of eleven and a half times. Four times with the guy she'd given her virginity to at the age of twenty-four, just to see if it was worth all the fuss. It wasn't. After the fourth try neither of them had been satisfied. She'd done the deed, but she'd refused to allow him to touch her in her private area. In fact, she'd thought he was downright nasty, especially when he expected her to put her mouth on him. Toreas had thought good riddance and he'd come right out and said it.

Then there was Fred two years later. At least they'd had a relationship of sorts. One of her brothers had set them up. How they'd ever had sex in the first place was still a mystery. It was after that last half time, the one where Fred was done before he'd even entered her, that he'd proposed and they'd skipped their happy time behinds to the courthouse. It was at the courthouse that some sense came to Toreas. She didn't want to spend a lifetime of half getting there. She didn't care if her brothers kicked her behind and Fred's. Toreas had half suspected that Fred's reason for asking her to marry him was so as not to get his butt kicked by her brothers. Even if it wasn't the reason, her running away like an imbecile from the courthouse gave Fred his out on a silver platter. Since they were both still alive, it was safe to say Fred had not blabbed.

In the eleven and a half times she'd had sex it had been in the dark so no, Toreas had never seen anyone standing there with their underwear tented. It had been three years since Fred.

Toreas wasn't sure if her natural urges had finally kicked in, urges she'd thought she didn't have. Or maybe it was Jared, or that since she'd begun trying to write romance she'd suddenly turned slutty.

"Toreas, what's wrong?"

Toreas blinked and looked at Jared. What the heck did he think he was doing? He was moving forward much too fast. This had started out as a game, and now he'd turned it into something more. Who the heck did he think she was?

"Put your pants back on."

"I...I..."

"I...I...nothing, put your pants back on."

"I only took them off so you could see my underwear, its cotton," Jared finished lamely.

"I don't care what it is, put your pants back on." She reached for the pillow behind her head and threw it at him. "What did you think we were doing here, Jared?"

"We were having fun," he said, hopping on one foot as he dodged another pillow. "I'll have to tell you, Toreas, this is definitely not how to write a love scene."

"You're crazy. Get out of my bedroom now," Toreas said, then burst out laughing. "Jared, you're too much." He turned toward her and she hopped quickly from the bed. "Thanks for the lesson."

"You're welcome," Jared groaned, wishing he'd waited a little longer, not pushed so quickly. He took in the image Toreas projected as she marched back into the safety of her living room. One of these days he would see what she kept hidden behind all of the dowdy clothes.

✍

Fire ran rampant through her veins
and she breathed as though each breath
would be her last. She was falling in
love with him and he was clueless. What
did one do with a clueless man, she wondered?

Jared smiled a little as he laid Toreas's paper on the table. "That's very good, Toreas, a lot better than the stuff you wrote a couple of months ago. Do you want to read mine?" he asked and handed over his paper. For a moment she hesitated and Jared wondered if she would take the paper. He found himself suddenly hoping that she would.

Strawberries, that's what she
smelled like, fresh luscious
strawberries. He'd had a taste
of her lips and could still taste
her on his tongue. He wondered
what would happen when she let down her
defenses, when he moved over her body
the way that he wanted. He wondered
if all of her tasted like fresh strawberries.
He was taking it slow, waiting for permission.
It had begun as a game but now it was much
more. He wondered if she knew he was falling
for her. He wondered if he told her if she'd
think it was a line.

Jared watched Toreas as she read and saw the moment she knew it was about her. Her skin warmed with the heat of her embarrassment and she swiped at her luscious lips. He'd be willing to bet liquid was pooling in her nether regions. What he wouldn't give to find out. But he'd learned his lesson. He would take it slower, he'd wait until she was ready to admit that things had changed.

"Toreas," Jared called softly and waited for her to turn toward him. He saw the desire in her eyes, the hope that flared and died only to be replaced by fear. She still didn't trust him or his motives. He decided to steer them both to safer ground. "How was it?" he asked.

"I liked it very much. I think you show a lot of promise." Toreas looked down. "Your scene is a lot better than mine. Maybe we should change places. Maybe I should become the critic."

"Are you going to enter the contest?" Jared asked, gazing tenderly at her, not wanting to revisit the days of him tearing into her group. Not wanting her to ask about his job.

"I'm not ready, Jared. Besides, that's fifty bucks I don't have."

"If that's the only thing stopping you…" He reached for his wallet."

For the first time in a month Toreas's head became crowded with voices. The choir was singing its head off.

"Don't, Jared." She wondered how he could not know a Baptist girl taking money from a man she wasn't married to was practically a mortal sin.

He was staring at her in that way he had that told her he was laughing at her. She knew he thought her a prude in ugly clothing. A prude he didn't mind kissing because he was forced into it by their nearness, but a prude he wasn't attracted to.

She looked away from him. He had a way of making her divulge secrets about herself. The man already knew more about her feelings than she'd ever intended. She sighed loudly. "If I can finish my book in time, I'll enter."

"Why should I trust you?"

"Because I keep my word." She wished she had said that differently. Okay, so she couldn't blame him for not finding her attractive in oversized thrift store apparel and now she was back to attacking his morals.

She noticed he sank back into the chair before he spoke. "Honesty's a big deal with you, isn't it?"

"Yes," Toreas answered without hesitation. "Shouldn't it be?"

"Well, I was wondering, you say you only kiss me to help you with a scene, I say you're lying. I say your feelings for me have changed into something else."

"We weren't talking about my feelings, Jared."

"No, we were talking about honesty. Tell me something. Is it okay for you to lie to me, but I'm not to lie to you?" He stood then.

"I haven't lied to you, Jared."

"You're lying now."

Toreas pushed her behind into the cushion of the couch. Jared was towering over her. His nearness was making her feel vulnerable. "Fair warning, Jared, Kelle taught me several new moves."

He remained where he was for several seconds longer, then walked away. "I think I should say good night."

He walked over the threshold before turning around. "Just so you know this, Ms. Rose, even with your hideous clothes, I find you very attractive. In fact, I think you're beautiful."

Then Jared was gone, leaving Toreas to doubt the sincerity of his words. Just because he said he found her attractive didn't mean he was attracted to her.

He was right about one thing: She *was* being a hypocrite. She was more than attracted to him. Toreas wondered why it was so hard for her to just have told him that she didn't want him to stop coming over for dinner.

That wouldn't have caused a cataclysmic eruption in the Bible Belt. She wished she knew why being with Jared was so much harder than being with her last two boyfriends. And she had been with them in the biblical sense.

Toreas stood staring at the door. She had hit on the problem. Jared wasn't her boyfriend. But he was the only man who'd come close to making her feel that loving wasn't a sin.

I'm not just falling in love with Jared, *I love him*, she acknowledged once again. She hugged her arms close to her body, feeling the tremors of excitement course through her.

I can't believe this. Romance writer falls in love with romance critic. Pure hogwash. That happens only in fiction and badly written fiction at that, she thought.

Ten minutes later Toreas was still trying her best to talk herself out of what she had known for weeks. She was in love with Jared Stone, and the knowledge both thrilled and terrified her.

What about Jared? He looked at her with desire but that didn't mean he had any feelings for her. She'd hate to look like a fool in front of him again.

He would have to be the first one to say that he loved her. She was feeling stubborn. If Jared wanted to continue eating with her he could ask. Until he did, she would keep her feelings to herself as she'd always done. Keeping her emotions bottled up tightly was nothing new for her.

Only this time Toreas felt a sense of urgency. She wanted Jared to speak before she became so desperate she had to resort to her toys.

✐

Jared walked away from Toreas's door angry with her and himself. Neither of them had the guts to say that things had changed.

Yeah, he fumed to himself. *All she had to do was tell me she enjoyed my coming over, that she didn't want it to stop.* Jared ignored the fact that he could have as easily told her he wanted to continue.

How the heck had things escalated to the point where Toreas was once again saying she didn't trust him? His plan was to tell her, but somehow he'd gotten sidetracked.

His male pride had been wounded once again when she questioned his motives and ethics. Never mind that he was lying to her. He wanted Toreas to trust him.

Jared shook his head. *I'm in love with her*, he thought and waited for the urge to flee to overtake him. It didn't happen. Sure, he knew what it meant. He'd known it all along. Love with a woman like Toreas Rose meant two things: commitment and marriage.

Jared grinned. He wanted to be committed to Toreas. He could imagine fighting with her for the rest of his life. In fact, he wanted to marry her.

Maybe as soon as his brain could become adjusted to that bit of information Jared could tell Toreas how much his feelings for her had changed.

Right now, though, she deserved to not know. If she thought he could kiss her in that manner and have it not mean a thing, she needed more training than he'd originally thought.

14

For the next two weeks Jared found himself busy with a format change at the station. He called Toreas several times to ask what she was doing for dinner.

Each time she answered that she'd eaten already. He knew she was lying. After a month of having dinner with her every night the one thing he knew about her was that she was a stickler for routine. Dinner precisely at six. He could call at three P.M. and she'd give the same answer. "I've eaten."

Everything she did was timed. He was annoyed that she never gave him an opportunity to invite her out, or that she didn't invite him over.

The most he could do was give her encouragement on her writing. Regardless of what happened between them, he wanted her to make it as a writer.

Jared had thought of a way to help repair some of the damage he had done earlier to Toreas and to the group, and by doing so he was hoping she would forgive him for lying to her.

With only minor resistance from Derrick, Jared had developed a series of episodes featuring romance writers in a positive light. He had already taped several shows with members of different chapters and romance writers who didn't belong to any organization. He was planning on doing the same with his own chapter.

That was still a hard concept. Jared Stone, a member of American Romance Writers. He didn't dare breathe a word to anyone at work. Derrick would have laughed in his face.

The thought of dropping out of the group was in the back of his mind. He'd never been serious when he'd challenged the women, telling them he would write a book in three weeks.

Well, they'd had a good laugh on him, but then again he hadn't really tried. He'd been too busy writing scenes that would make Toreas blush, hoping the heat from his words would fire her passion for him.

If nothing else, he had a new respect for the writers. Reluctantly at first, he had been forced to admit they worked hard. He also admitted to himself that they'd had nothing do with Gina's leaving. And Gina had had nothing to do with his not being able to keep the promise he'd made to his mother. He knew in his heart that his mother would never have wanted him to marry a woman he didn't truly love in order to keep a promise to her. He smiled, wondering if his mother was watching over him, knowing she would approve of the woman he'd fallen in love with. A grin spread across Jared's face. He owed Gina big time for leaving him.

If she had never left he would have never come to Chicago and he would have never met Toreas Rose, or Liz, or Kelle or any of the other women. So Jared was now over being dumped.

Jared thought about Toreas, not realizing until now that his fear of being dumped was why he'd not told her how he felt. Enough games. He hadn't seen her and he wanted to, badly. If Mohammed wouldn't go to the mountain then the mountain was darn sure going to go to Mohammad. He sighed, wondering if she'd give in this time. He dialed her number and waited.

"Toreas," he said, when she picked up and didn't bother to say hello. Of course he knew she knew it was him. Another thing about her he'd noted was that she always checked the caller ID before picking up the phone. She was beginning to irritate him by her silence.

"Toreas, you know it's me. Why aren't you saying anything?"

"You called me," she answered.

He couldn't help grinning. Oil and water and damn if he didn't still want her.

"I want to take you out. Will you go?" Jared asked.

"You mean on a date?"

So this was the way it was going to go. "When a man asks you out, what does he usually mean by it?"

"You're not just any man, Jared."

If it had been any other woman he would have taken that as a compliment but not with Toreas Rose. No, with her there was always something hidden underneath. He rose to the challenge. "You're right, I'm not just any man. I'm a jerk, right?" Jared tapped his foot impatiently, waiting for Toreas to say that wasn't what she'd meant, or that he wasn't a jerk.

"When do you want to go out?" Toreas asked at last.

So she was going to leave him hanging on that one. At least she hadn't flat out refused him.

"How about Sunday morning?"

"Why?"

"There's something special I want to take you to."

"No, I didn't mean that. I meant why do you want to date me?"

"Why do men usually want to date you?"

"To get in my pants, or more accurately, to get me out of my pants. At least that seems to be what you're after."

She laughed, the sound of it a husky breeze that touched his soul and gave him an instant erection. Jared clenched his teeth, wanting to throttle her.

"Do you really mean you have no idea why I would want to date you?" Jared asked patiently.

"Nope, none."

"Are you kidding me?"

"Don't think so."

"Do you want me to tell you over the phone?"

"I can take it," Toreas laughed.

"You're a true contradiction. You know that, don't you? One moment you're this naïve, almost virginal mousy writer, and the next you're this wanton vamp who teases me and leaves me…" he paused, then whispered softly, "breathless." He heard the catch of her breath on the other end, Toreas hadn't expected that. "So will you go out with me?" he continued.

"Yes, Jared. Where are we going? You said it was something special?"

"The Parrot Cage on South Shore at the South Shore Cultural Center. There's a launch party there and I thought you might like to go."

"What kind of launch party?"

Jared found himself squirming. "A romance writer, all right. Don't you dare laugh," he warned, knowing that Toreas was going to ignore the warning.

"Who's the writer, and how on earth did you hear about it?"

"Some woman named Barbara something. I saw her picture. She had on these red, thigh high leather boots. *Hot*, he remembered but didn't share that information with Toreas. He shook his head to dislodge the image. "She was being carried on a chair by four burly firemen. If nothing else it should give me something to write about."

"You didn't say how you found out about it."

And he wasn't going to. In actuality Derrick had found the flyer and practically ordered Jared to go and cover the event for the station. As long as she wasn't someone Toreas knew, he didn't see the harm. Besides, Jared thought Toreas might like it and the food, he'd been told, was wonderful.

"Jared, I'm waiting. What are you doing, making up an answer?"

"I'm wondering why it should matter. I've never been quizzed before when I've asked a woman out on a date."

"But you've never asked me, Jared."

"You're right. I have a confession. I really enjoy being with you, spending time with you. I want to see if we can enjoy ourselves the same way in public. I'd like to try."

"So would I," Toreas admitted before her voice went soft. "Jared, I enjoy spending time with you also." She gave a nervous laugh. "I think it'll be fun." She laughed again, the excitement coming through.

He felt that all the way to his soul. She'd staked him, bagged him and claimed him and now she was determined to make him work for her love. This should be fun; he'd see if she'd crack first. The moment Toreas admitted she cared he'd tell her he was in love with her. Hell, he'd even drop on his knees and make a commitment. But not until she let go of every bit of nonsense that she'd clung to.

Jared wanted the Toreas Rose she was meant to be, not the uptight woman who hid her sexuality away as though it were something to be ashamed of. He was determined that he would taste the forbidden fruit and make her eyes roll back in her head as she'd asked him to do. Hell, by the time he was done with her she might just be the one on her knee proposing to him.

"Is it a date, Toreas?"

"Yes."

"Was it really that hard?"

"You have no idea."

Thing was, he did have an idea. "Okay then, Toreas, I'll pick you up at nine, and come prepared to eat." He said a hasty goodbye before she could change her mind.

For the next two days Jared kept waiting for a call. He didn't call Toreas because he didn't want to make it easy for her to tell him something had come up. Another thing he'd uncovered: She was more than a bit of a loner, preferring to stay home rather than venture out.

That was more than likely part of the reason some man hadn't found her and discovered just how truly glorious she really was. "Thank God," he muttered again. She was all his.

✍

Jared knocked on Toreas's door, wondering now that the weather had finally turned chilly what she would have on. She'd worn bulky sweaters the entire summer. Now that it was almost the end of September he couldn't begin to imagine her look. He did know she wouldn't do anything special to make herself look more appealing to him.

When the door opened, Jared's mouth opened wide in shock and he blinked, then laughed. "Wow," he exclaimed. "You clean up nicely." He took her hand and turned her around for a better view of the body fitting dark green sweater and olive pants. He took a step back. Lipstick. He couldn't believe she had on lipstick. He laughed. "Toreas, I do believe you're trying to make an impression on me."

"Think again, Jared," Toreas denied. "I just thought this would be nice to wear today."

"You know you might get cool. What are you going to do?" He smiled and tilted his head, hoping she'd say he could keep her warm. Ha, no such luck. He should have known.

Toreas immediately went to the closet, grabbed a huge sweater and threw it to Jared. He caught it and brought it to his nose and sniffed. Soap. He shook his head slightly, knowing he'd been searching for the scent of fresh strawberries. Now he knew, only her hair and her skin smelled of the fruit. He caught her gaze and held it, glad that her skin was not only scented, but tasted like strawberries. At least as much of her skin as he'd gotten a chance to taste.

"Are you smelling my sweater?"

"Yes," Jared admitted. "Do you mind?"

"Knock yourself out. I think you have some strange habits. I worry about you, Jared. Maybe you should go back to the television show. Your trying to write romance is bringing out some kooky things."

Jared cringed inwardly. This would be a good time to come clean, but of course he wouldn't, not yet. Toreas wouldn't go out with him if he did. He struck a pose, imitating the way she'd stood when she'd given him that karate punch. "Are you questioning my manhood, Ms. Rose?" She laughed. They were back on safe ground. *I'll tell her soon*, he thought, *just give us a chance to have one date.*

Driving down Lake Shore Drive, Toreas joked with him easily, touching him, occasionally laughing when he'd glance in her direction. He wished he'd thought to do this sooner. When he pulled into the red brick entrance of the South Shore Cultural Center, Jared heard Toreas's sharp intake of breath.

"What's wrong?"

"It's beautiful."

"You've never been here before?" Jared asked in amazement.

"Yes, I've been. It's just been a long time and I'm always amazed how beautiful it is." She smiled. "This was a good idea."

Jared felt as though he'd won a prize. He could feel his chest expanding with pride. She was smiling, she was happy, and it was because of him.

"Will we have time to look around?" Toreas asked as Jared parked.

She glanced up at him, looked away, then back. The look he was giving her was so filled with lust that she was embarrassed and happy at the same time.

"Stop that," she said softly. "If Michael or Billy ever caught you looking at me like that, they'd beat the crap out of you."

"Who are Michael and Billy?"

"My brothers."

"Do you really want me to stop looking at you the way that I am and to stop thinking the things that I'm thinking?"

Toreas tilted her head back and stared at Jared.

"Not really, but maybe tone it down a notch in public."

Jared couldn't believe her, she really was something. He took her hand and, laughing, walked with her to the entrance. "What kind of look did I have, Toreas?"

"One that was melting the skin off my bones."

"Did it do anything to melt your resolve?"

"More than you know." She gave his fingers a squeeze. "This is a first date, Jared, try remembering that."

"Then you see a second and a third…and a…"

Jared's arms went around Toreas's waist and he pulled her close. He couldn't help feeling protective toward her, she was so damn tiny. But of course if he told her that, she'd probably want to stop snuggling next to him and give him a karate chop or some such nonsense. He heard her sigh of pleasure and laughed softly. They were a couple whether either of them admitted it or not.

Two hours later, after a lavish buffet of grits, fried potatoes with onions, chicken, mac and cheese and the world's most delicious bread pudding, they were stuffed. They'd both met and talked with Barbara Keaton and Jared had bought them each a copy of her book, Blaze. Now he understood the red boots and the firemen. *What a terrific marketing strategy*, he thought. He'd have to share that with the other writers. Ideas were coming fast and furiously as he gazed down on Toreas. Now he'd have to think of other things for them to do.

A bit before they were going to leave, Chef Ricky Moore came out and poured complimentary glasses of elder flower water, a sparkling water for those who didn't drink alcohol. It looked like champagne and was having the same effect. Toreas was giving him the same lustful looks he knew he'd given her.

And he could only sit like a fool across from her and grin, almost unable to talk. She was everything he hadn't wanted in the beginning. But now she was exactly what he needed. Thank God Gina ran off with a cover model or he would have never found Toreas.

As they left the center, Jared held onto Toreas's hand and they walked together for a closer view of Lake Michigan. She was trembling. Perfect, he thought. "Are you cold?" he asked.

"A little."

"Good," he whispered in her ear. "I was hoping for a chance to keep you warm." Jared pulled her in close, tilted her chin and kissed her, tasting her sweetness as he sucked on her tongue, wanting so much more than he could have right now in public. A shudder ripped through him. Yep, roped and hogtied. He was down for the count. "I like this," Jared whispered into her hair. "The two of us dating." He laughed. "This is so surreal I can't believe it."

"Thanks," Toreas grinned. "This was very nice, the book signing, the launch party, the whole thing. And what better place to have it than here."

"Yeah, what better use for what was once a restricted club than to host so many African American oriented events," Jared sighed. "But it's a shame the place is so underused so much of the time. The programs are really good and a lot of them are free." He hunched his shoulders. "I'd like to get the word out, get more people to come and take a look."

"For someone who's pretty new to Chicago you sound like you're a part of this place," Toreas stopped walking and gazed up into Jared's eyes.

"I am, I'm a member." He saw pride fill Toreas's eyes and decided to come clean. "It's a tax write-off," Jared said, thinking it would change the glow in her eyes, but it didn't. She squeezed his hand.

"You're a contradiction, Jared. You trashed my profession and now you're a member of our group, though I still don't believe a serious member, and you have stopped attacking us. Thank you."

A lump was beginning to form in the pit of Jared's abdomen. He knew he didn't deserve Toreas's thanks, or her pride in him, not yet anyway. He still had to tell her about his job, and he still had to do the story on Barbara Keaton. Derrick was counting on it.

"Toreas, do you believe all publicity is good publicity? I mean, for instance, if someone wrote about this event today and said some maybe not nice things, wouldn't the publicity still help Barbara? She would probably sell more books."

Toreas dropped Jared's hand as though it were hot. "Are you serious? Of course it's not the same. If you truly had any idea how hard we all work to make our stories good, only to have critics rip us apart, you'd know what it does to us."

"But, Toreas, it comes with the territory."

"That doesn't mean that it doesn't hurt, Jared."

"But it hasn't happened to you. Why are you getting so upset?"

"Listen, it's happened to my friends. If you think getting rejection letters is bad, just try having your dream come true only to have someone print a nasty review on Amazon for the entire world to see. It hurts."

"People are allowed their opinions…freedom of speech."

"Jared, after being with us do you really think it's that simple? It's so much more than freedom of speech or opinions. You've seen how hard we all work to get better at our craft, you know we're all nice people. I don't think one of us could be as mean as the people who take potshots at us."

"Do you mean me?" Jared asked around the lump that had now risen to his throat.

Toreas looked directly at him. "Yes, Jared, I mean you." She smiled. "When you were doing it, that is. Thank God you're no longer working for the station. I don't think I could date you if you were. I'd be too afraid you'd be dating me to dig up dirt. Even this nice day, this book launch, I'd be afraid you were trying to find an angle to use, something to tear the author apart."

Toreas gave Jared a smile meant to convey she believed he'd changed. The smile widened into a full grin. "But you're not working for Derrick, so Barbara is safe." Toreas looped her hand through Jared's arms. "In case you're wondering why I was thanking you, that's the reason. You've changed and so have I. We're no longer the same people we were a few months ago."

"No, we're not," Jared said, and groaned silently. He was worse than he was a few months ago. He was now deceiving her and now he knew for sure it would not be taken as a prank.

Jared felt Toreas's soft hand in his and knew he'd have to wait until she was as committed to him as he was to her. It was wrong and he knew it. But he was in love with her. He didn't want to lose her at this stage of the game. He kissed her again, smiling inwardly when she took control of the kiss and sucked his tongue into her mouth, pulling on his very essence. A band of desire filled him each time she pulled. He groaned, not wanting her to stop, but knowing that here was not the place.

"Want to go?" he asked as his hands circled her waist.

"Yes, but not home. I want to go to Navy Pier."

Jared attempted to stare her down. "After a kiss like that you want to go to Navy Pier?"

"Yeah, I think we both need to cool down."

"I thought where we were headed was a good place to be, only to finish we need some privacy."

"This is a first date, Jared, remember?"

"What were the last two months?"

"Practice."

Jared couldn't have prevented the laugh if he'd tried. He'd give her Navy Pier and anything else she might want. He thought of the story he had to do for Derrick. Yes, he'd even do that for her as well. He'd find a way to put a positive slant on the story even if that wasn't what Derrick wanted, even if he found himself out of a job again.

🖎

She wrapped her arms around his neck, meeting the thrust of his tongue with the trust of her own. Liquid heat surged inside her pooling in her womb. Toreas moaned. Oh God! She was so pliable. This man had turned her to butter and she was melting.

Toreas felt the clenching between her thighs, felt the pulse of want bearing down on her. She wanted him but she'd never asked any man to make love to her. How could she now? "Jared." She found her voice but before she could say more he was kissing her, pulling on her tongue and she was drowning in need.

Jared could feel Toreas's entire body trembling with need, with desire for him. Her shudders were wreaking havoc with his body, his desire for her increasing moment by moment.

His face was buried in her neck. He breathed in her scent, sending a wave of urgent throbbing to his penis. His arousal was painful; he had to have her. Now. No more imagining the feel of being buried in her wetness. He kissed his way from her neck to her luscious mouth, suckling her tongue, drawing on her essence. God, if he could only hold out until he entered her, until he'd given her pleasure.

"Are you on the pill?"

"Of course not." Toreas stopped and looked at Jared. "Why should I need them?"

His hand stilled. "Do you have any condoms I could use?"

"Again, should I?"

Jared stopped what was he was doing. "Toreas, how long has it been for you?" He narrowed his eyes as he waited for an answer. She was pulling back but this time he didn't attempt to stop her. He stared at her. "Toreas, how long?"

"How long has it been for you?" she asked, turning the question around as he'd known she would do.

"A few months, "Jared answered, watching her. "And you?" He could see her calculating the time. He thought of that questionnaire she'd given him months ago and groaned. No way in hell were they having sex tonight. Damn.

If only he'd brought the damn condoms but nooo, he'd wanted to pretend that he'd not come to her home to make love to her, that he'd not taken her out for the day with repayment on his mind. Having a ready condom at his disposal said he'd planned it, didn't it?

Toreas took a good look at Jared. She was no longer filled with lust. Now it was the way it had been in the courthouse, when she'd stood before the judge to marry Fred. Common sense had returned as she calculated the risks she'd be putting herself in by having unprotected sex.

"Jared, when was your last physical?" Toreas asked, moving farther away.

"Why," he asked suspiciously, knowing what she was getting at.

"I don't sleep around, Jared, my relationships have always been serious."

"And mine weren't?"

Toreas shrugged her shoulder. "I'm not sleeping with you. I don't know what I was thinking about, not without…"

He stood and glared at her, daring her to say the words. That damn dictionary, that's what she was referring to. She wanted his life history on paper. He didn't believe her.

"I thought we'd passed that. We've been dating for over a month now. Making love is a part of dating."

"But making love isn't worth dying for," Toreas retorted.

"Have you ever had unprotected sex, Toreas?"

"Of course not," she spat indignantly.

"But you believe I have?"

"If you haven't, it should be easy enough to prove."

Jared was glaring, the thought of making love to Toreas forgotten. "I think I'll require proof that should I touch you, I won't catch anything," Jared said through clenched teeth, allowing the anger he was feeling to take control.

"I've never had unprotected sex." Toreas returned Jared's glare, hating that her emotions could so easily be viewed by others. She was Black, she had no business blushing but she did all the time. And now she could feel the heat rushing quickly through her body as the blush colored her entire face and for the billionth time Toreas was happy she wasn't high yellow, like her cousin Latanya. Still, she was aware that people could tell when she blushed. "I'm not getting checked," she said, holding Jared's gaze.

"Are you exempt?" he asked.

"I know what I've done."

"And I know what I've done."

Jared shook his head. "Toreas, you are without a doubt the most exasperating woman I've ever known. Why I keep trying to make love to you is a mystery to me."

He saw her chin tilt, saw her eyes flash, watched as the flutter stayed at the base of her throat for a moment too long. She was angry and he didn't give a damn if she were.

"You want to make love to me, Jared, because it's not easy. If it were, you wouldn't want to."

Jared cocked his head and laughed. Pissed wasn't a strong enough word for how he felt. He decided to throw back a little of her medicine at her. "I don't think I want to anymore anyway. I just thought you expected it. I mean, all day long you've been all over me."

Jared narrowed his eyes and glared at her. "If you remember, Ms. Rose, you were the one who first propositioned me. If you really want me to make you feel the things you say you do, then you need to tell me. I don't have the energy to keep trying with you. You're locked up tighter than Fort Knox. It would take an army to get through your barricades. I just don't have the patience for it. If you don't mind, Ms. Rose, I think we can both safely say this date is now officially over."

15

"Jared, you've gone way too soft. I should have known your being involved with the Rose woman and the writing group was going to warp your thinking. Come on, Jared, snap out of it, get that old killer instinct back. For the first time we're making money here at the station, not just covering our budget. Do you have any idea how hard it is to get people to watch and how much harder it is to get them to advertise? They're buying advertising on your program, Jared, because they love the fighting. Now you want me to back off. I don't think so. We'll run the story without you if we have to. We'll use your pictures from the event and Stella can do the piece."

"Derrick, as a favor to me, don't do it. Yes, I owed you, but my debt has been paid. Like you said, you're actually making money and it's because of me. So just this one time give me a break."

Derrick stared for a long moment in disbelief at Jared before he spoke. "You might as well put a ring on that woman's finger, because she sure as hell has one through your nose."

Jared laughed. "I plan to do just that." At Derrick's snort of disgust, a wide grin graced Jared's face. "I'll tell you what. Stop glaring at me and I'll hook you up with Barbara Keaton. She's agreed to come on the show, and she's hot and single. I think the two of you would hit it off."

"What if she won't date me?"

"I'm not a pimp. I can only give you an introduction and talk you up to her. The rest is on you."

"So you say she's hot?"

"Very."

"Is she a diva?"

"Nope."

"Then go ahead, give the writers a break, but after that the next ten shows I want you to go back to your old ways. I've already changed the time of the show for you. Since you're still dating her I can only assume that your lady love isn't any the wiser."

"Knowing Toreas I'm sure she'd have said something if she knew about it." Jared thought about it for a moment. He was being sneaky and deceitful. He needed just a little more time to get Toreas to stop fighting her feelings for him.

"Derrick, about changing the name of the show, you said you'd consider it. What's the verdict? Are we going with a new name?"

"Can't do that, Jared. A lot of the advertisers like the name of the show. Our viewers like it. Look, I've already bent over backward because you're a friend. I should have kept the show in the same time slot instead of changing it. Now that's it. You keep pushing me and you're going back in your old time slot. That's the deal, take it or leave it."

Jared thought of Toreas's habits, six P.M. dinner, then she did the dishes and called her parents. She didn't even turn her television on in the evening until nine to watch the evening news. Sometimes she'd watch a movie at eight but that was rare. He tried not to think about the real possibility of one of the other women from the romance group possibly tuning it.

"Keep it six," Jared answered at last, sticking his hand out. "As long as you're not expecting me to go back to trashing the writers we have a deal."

"Jared, I said I wanted you to do ten shows in your old style."

"This is my deal. I'll not push on the name change but I'm not going back to my old format, not even for one show. Now the ball's in your court. Take it or leave it."

For a moment Jared wondered if Derrick would hold out. When he grudgingly stuck his hand out Jared smiled and shook it, hoping his luck would hold out a little longer.

A little voice was warning him that he'd get caught but the memory of Toreas's kisses reminded him that he'd not had enough of her and she had not yet admitted to how she felt. He needed more time.

✍

The man had a face that scared small
children and some adults. His wife's wasn't
much better, but there was something about the
two of them, especially when they were in the
presence of each other that changed all of that.
They were in love and love transformed them.

Toreas held Jared's most recent try between the tips of her fingers. He really was pretty good. "I like this," she said, looking at him.

"I thought you would. Like I said, all heroes and heroines don't have to be good looking or tall. Look at me. I prefer a short, mouthy, opinionated woman. Who'd thunk it?" He laughed and tried to kiss her but Toreas held up her hand.

"Here, read mine."

> *He touched her and she burned. The*
> *craving for him touching her soul and*
> *making her his. It didn't matter that*
> *he was a foot shorter, or bald and*
> *fifty pounds overweight with a more*
> *than noticeable paunch. No, the only thing*
> *that mattered to her was the look in his*
> *eyes. He adored her and in return she*
> *adored him. He'd laid claim to her love*
> *and her soul had followed suit.*

Jared shook his head. "I have to admit I'm impressed. But I do think the fact that we've been officially dating now for over a month has something to do with the change in your writing. I'm influencing you." He grinned. "And you're influencing me. You're loosening up. Now are you really going to put this in your book, or is this just for my benefit?"

"This is just for you. I see your point, Jared. When love happens it doesn't matter if the people are short, bald, stupid or fat." Toreas hunched her shoulder. "But still, it isn't done that way. Women want to lose themselves in the possibility of what ifs."

"I think we need to change their perception of love."

"You mean give them rose-colored glasses?"

Jared smiled at her. "No, I mean take away the tinted lenses and learn to appreciate true beauty. After all, beauty is in the eyes of the beholder."

"Tell me, Jared, what do you see when you look at me?"

"Are you fishing?"

"Yes."

"There is no need. I see a passionate and beautiful woman with eyes that make me weak in the knees and lips that taste of fresh strawberries." He grinned. "When I've tasted more, I can better tell you what the rest of you tastes like. Don't you want to know if you taste like strawberries all over?"

"Maybe, Jared, in time."

"When? When I fill out that damn questionnaire?"

At this Toreas didn't get angry, just gave him a look. "When I think enough time has passed, and when I'm ready."

Jared was gazing down at Toreas, at her nipples, pebbled and pushing hard against the rough material of yet another overly large and ugly shirt. "Baby, you're ready, you just don't want to admit it."

For the next hour or so Jared and Toreas kissed and teased and wrote in between. And all would have been fine if Toreas hadn't whispered to him as he was leaving.

"Jared, no one has ever defended my honor the way that you have, well, no one who wasn't my brother or my father. Thank you," she'd whispered and kissed him lightly. "I know it was hard leaving the station and Derrick, but I do appreciate that you did it for me." She hugged him close. "Your leaving is what brought us together, what made us possible. I have to admit that I didn't know if I should believe you," she said shyly. "I kept checking your old time to see if you were really gone." And then she'd done the unthinkable: She'd looked into his eyes and uttered the words that had killed him.

"I trust you, Jared. I trust you enough that I'm ready to share our secret with the rest of the chapter."

She'd kissed him then like she never wanted to let him go, and that time it had been Jared who'd pulled away. The guilt had overwhelmed him and he was praying all the way home that she'd forgive him. Now here it was two weeks later and every time Jared had been with Toreas since that night, it'd only gotten harder. He'd made more excuses in the last two weeks to cut his visit and their dates short than she'd done in their entire relationship. The guilt was eating Jared alive; he had to tell her. She trusted him, just what he'd wanted, but now the fact that she did was killing him. Tonight after the meeting he would tell her.

Several hours later Jared walked into the meeting room at the library where their group met for their meetings and took his usual place next to Toreas. He blinked as he stared at her. Damn, she really was changing. He watched as her eyes lit up when she looked at him and he groaned. This was going to be harder than he thought. She had on form-fitting slacks and a pretty blouse. Her hair was no longer in the afro that she'd worn since he'd met her but straight and shiny, emphasizing the jet black coloring. She had a sassy cut that suited her face almost as well as the afro he loved. It was obvious she'd hot combed her hair for the news they were going to share with the group. Later he'd have to tell her that she shouldn't have bothered. He still preferred her afro. His gaze remained on her and he smiled.

"Jared, I finished my book. I'm going to enter the contest. Would you like to skip the restaurant and come over and help me celebrate?"

Her smile was huge as she whispered to him. He smiled back at her. He'd received the message loud and clear. Her eyes were sparkling and she looked beautiful. Tonight she was ready to make love to him. His stomach lurched. He sure hoped she'd want to after he revealed his secret. He could only pray that she would still give him that look of adoration. And that she would still trust him.

"Jared, what's wrong? Why aren't you answering me? Don't you want to come and help me celebrate?"

"Yes, of course I want to, but there's something important I have to tell you so let's not stay for the entire meeting tonight. I want to tell you this as soon as possible."

Jared saw Toreas smile at him and wondered if he'd actually said the words out loud or merely thought them. He couldn't be sure but if he'd said them, he had probably raised her suspicions.

"I thought you wanted me to tell everyone about us?"

"I do...and we will...it's just that what I have to tell you tonight is more important. I really need to talk to you, okay?" Jared could see the questioning in her eyes, the fears. He smiled, answering the unasked question. "We're okay, Toreas, don't worry and don't imagine anything. Just wait until I have a chance to tell you things that I need to.

"You're making this sound so mysterious but if you want to be alone I'm more than ready for that and, Jared, this time I've prepared."

Toreas grinned while Jared sucked in his breath and smiled at her in return. The last thing Jared felt like doing was smiling. He had a lot of atoning to do.

Taking a seat next to Toreas was the hardest thing Jared had ever had to do. He was aware deceiving her had gone on for too long. Now all he wanted to do was tell her and get it over with. He tried not to focus on her but that was an impossible task. Hell, she'd let him know then and there that they were finally going to make love. Damn, he should just go for it, make love to her and then tell her. Jared groaned. He'd deceived her long enough. He would not take this last gift from her without her knowing everything. He sighed and groaned again.

He could barely keep his mind focused on the meeting or the guest speaker. His thoughts kept straying to what he would say to Toreas.

Jared could tell she was having as hard a time as he on keeping her mind on the business at hand. She kept looking at him as if she knew a secret and was finally ready to let him in on it.

The feelings that flooded his entire being he had never experienced before. Now he knew for sure he'd never loved Gina. He'd never felt like this. The very idea that a woman would ever make him go weak in the knees was unthinkable. But this short, annoying romance writer had done exactly that. She'd won his heart.

The speaker was done and Jared had barely heard her. He couldn't wait until he could escape with Toreas. Then all the lies would cease.

"Jared, I caught your show last night. It was very good. Even that segment at the end, the one with the woman who came in here pushing a microphone in our faces. Even she did good last night."

He felt Toreas turn toward him. He glanced at her. She hadn't moved but yet she had. She was waiting for him to answer Liz.

"Thanks," was all he said.

"We heard from Suburban East that you had them on the show. They thought you were terrific," Becca chimed in.

Jared rubbed his hand roughly over his face. *One more hour and this would have been over. I would have been the one to tell her.*

The change in her was subtle but he noticed. She was no longer stealing glances at him, smiling with a promise in her eyes and on her lips. Only inches apart and he no longer felt her heat.

Toreas sat as still as she possibly could. *Stupid, stupid, stupid*, she scolded herself. Her eyes skimmed over her new outfit.

She now regretted the money she'd spent on the clothes. Sure, she'd bought them at Wal-Mart, the only place she could afford, but they were new and they fit. She'd done this for a man who'd lied to her yet again.

Toreas was having a difficult time keeping the tears from her eyes. She heard Jared whispering to her but she tuned him out.

He touched the underside of her arm and she snatched away from him so viciously that she knocked both of their satchels from the table.

She picked them up and looked into his golden brown eyes. "Stay away from me," she hissed at him before returning to her upright position.

She could barely wait for the meeting to end. Her feet took the steps two at a time. She had to get away from him.

He was calling her name but she ignored him as she hurried to her car. She wanted to run but didn't want him to know she felt hurt or betrayed.

"Toreas, wait, let me explain."

He was directly behind her now. She felt the weight of her bag leave her arms and head for the ground. In that instant she was aware of what she was about to do.

She attempted an uppercut to the jaw only to have him capture her arm. Then with the right she tried a hammer fist. She looked at him in surprise.

"Kelle's been teaching me too."

If she weren't so furious, she would have found the whole thing hilarious. The thought vanished almost as quickly as it came.

Jared was standing closer to her than before. To top it off, Kelle had taught Jared how to deflect her punches. She was doubly betrayed.

For a moment she felt a bit like a woman in an historical who runs away screaming from the man she loves only to have him tower over her and kiss her, overpowering her with his love.

Well, Jared was towering over her but he was making no move to kiss her. Luckily for him, she thought. Toreas closed her eyes for a scant moment as she flexed the fingers of both hands.

"Toreas, you need to give me a chance to explain."

"What you mean is I need to give you time to think of another lie." Toreas blinked away the tears that threatened to come. "Jared, I should have known all long that you were lying, that this was all a part of some story you were probably doing. You must really think I'm stupid."

"As a matter of fact at this moment I do think you're behaving as though you're stupid. How could you even begin to believe that nonsense, that I'm working on a story by being with you. We're dating. We've been dating for three months now. We're a couple, Toreas, we're in a relationship. This is not how a relationship work, not one of us jumping to conclusions and not allowing the other a chance to explain."

"Now you're a relationship expert?"

"Well, I'm more of one than you are. At least I've had a relationship in the last decade. And by that, yes, I mean I've had a physical relationship and I've never had to beg for it. Do you think I've been putting up with your nonsense just to get into your pants? Listen, if all I wanted from you were sex I could have had that long ago and don't give me that look. I could have. We haven't made love because I've respected your wishes. I've taken it slow so you would trust me. I wanted you to know this was more than sex for me."

"And the trust, Jared, do you still want that?"

"Yes, Toreas, I not only want it I demand it. If we're going to have a relationship I demand that you trust me."

"After what you've done, you want me to trust you?"

"Do I even get a trial, Toreas? Or are you just going to execute me because of all the horrible things you think I've done? Listen, if you're that damn determined not to have a life then I don't think I want to be with you anyway. You're still an uptight, snooty little morals policewoman who thinks she's better than anyone else. You think it makes you sanctimonious to not make love when you're hornier than hell. You're a liar. You lie to yourself and you lie to me. And I don't call you on that do I?" He was scowling. "This is your call. You tell me what it is you want."

A couple of seconds was all that it would take for her to regain her focus. That much she knew, she'd used the technique her entire life to blot out hurt, anger, disappointment and pain. She used it now and as always, it worked.

"Excuse me, Jared," Toreas said in a voice so calm that she amazed herself. There was not a trace of emotion anywhere. No, that she would keep buried until later. What she wanted was not to be made a fool of once again, not to have everyone in the chapter know that Jared was still more than likely taking potshot at the writers. She groaned. "What I want, Jared, is for you to get out of my sight, my chapter and my life. Leave me alone."

As Jared moved away she retrieved her bag, opened the door to her car, got in and drove away. And she did it all without looking at him.

So what would come next? she wondered. *If this were merely fiction, it would be time for the dark moment, when everything looks as if it's within my reach only to be snatched away.*

For the last few months her life had been going according to some script that someone somewhere in the universe must have written.

If this were a story Toreas wouldn't be surprised to find Jared waiting for her when she reached home. Only she wasn't ready to play this part. Besides, she knew Jared was not going to come to her crawling on his hands and knees. That was not his way and she knew it. But just in case, maybe she'd find someplace to go and maybe she'd stay for a couple of hours. She'd almost had that elusive something that she'd sought. It had been within reach. But how could any relationship survive on lies? She frowned into the darkness of her car. Jared had called her a liar. But her lying about her desires didn't come close to his lie to her.

But a lie is a lie. Damn him, she thought as Jared's voice droned in her head. Would she now have to hear Jared's voice in her head as one of her internal critics.

☜

Jared looked at Toreas's car. He wasn't in the mood to chase after her, not tonight. Besides, they would only end up where they had begun. He was angry with himself for deceiving her. He loved her and, damn it, she loved him. He clenched his teeth. Loving this woman was going to cause harm to one of them, he was sure. By now he thought he had to have an ulcer. His stomach was burning like crazy. Of course he'd known what he was doing was wrong and of course he'd known Toreas would be pissed, but still he hadn't been prepared for the ice in her eyes, for her to write him off without giving him a chance to explain. He wasn't prepared for her to take away her trust.

He looked back toward the building at the rest of the women coming out. Someone called out to him asking if he was going to the restaurant.

He waved a hand and shouted back, "No." He couldn't sit with the women tonight. They were happy about his new approach to romance writers. If he had to name the one thing he was proud of, it was that.

Toreas paced in front of her door for over an hour when she finally returned home. She was annoyed that she was still waiting for Jared to ring her bell so she could buzz him up and slam the door in his face. He never showed.

Doesn't he understand the way this thing is supposed to work? Toreas fumed silently. *You'd think the least he could do since he had the gall to join the group was to read a few novels.*

Then he would at least know he should be at her house groveling, begging her to forgive him for lying to her, for sponging off her for over a month, for breaking bread under false pretenses. For making her believe in him and in them, for starting a relationship with her while deceiving her. For dating her for over three months without saying a word. As angry as she was with Jared, she wanted him there explaining and she wanted him to have a darn good explanation.

She glared at the door in anger. It was obvious Jared wasn't going to show. Now Toreas was angry for a different reason. Tonight had been the night she was going to give in to her desires. She'd thought it time to take the lid off the cookie jar. She thought about the package of condoms she'd bought and tucked into the side table next to her bed. She was ready. A shiver raced down her spine. She was more than ready.

Toreas replayed the evening in her mind. The strange look in Jared's eyes when she'd told him to come over, the slight sadness and worry that she'd spotted. Could it have anything at all to do with this mess? Then she remembered his words: "I have something important to tell you."

What was it he'd wanted to say? She glanced toward the phone, wishing now she'd given him a chance to explain. He'd promised to tell her something important. *Darn him anyway.* She stalked through her apartment snapping off the lights. *He should be here begging me to forgive him.*

✍

Anger was burning in him so hot that he needed something cold to douse the fire. Jared grabbed a cold beer and downed it, hoping to extinguish the anger that burned in his gut. No such luck. He crumpled the can and reached for another, wondering how many more it would take to cool the fires of his anger. It sure as hell would take a lot more than two to cool his passion.

Jared brought the can close to his face and examined it. There was nothing in there that would even begin to make the hunger he was feeling recede into the background. Just the thought of Toreas made Jared angry all over again. He didn't like that she'd taken control over his life and emotions so completely. He didn't like it one little bit.

He turned his head to glare at the phone. The silence was mocking him. She wouldn't call and he knew it. She was too damn stubborn. Despite what his common sense told him, Jared automatically checked for the flash of the answering machine beside it.

There was no blinking red light to give him hope that this time Toreas had called to say she was sorry, to ask for his forgiveness.

He wouldn't be the one to call her. *To hell with her and to hell with loving her.* Now he was glad that he hadn't told her that he loved her. If Toreas couldn't trust him enough to wait for his explanation, then he didn't need her.

Jared downed the second beer and reached for a third, feeling the ache in his groin calling him a liar. He could not help conjuring up a picture of the way Toreas had looked tonight. Beautiful. And for only the third time since he'd met her, her clothes fit.

The smile on her lips and in her eyes was beckoning to him still. They should be celebrating.

Together.

Instead they were both angry.

And alone.

Jared took another sip of the cold beer, knowing it would take a lot more than that to put out the fire he was feeling.

16

Toreas awoke cranky and unfulfilled. Last night was supposed to have been magical. She had no idea who was writing the script for her life, but she sure wanted to edit it. There needed to be some big changes.

She'd given Jared's kisses too much power. All because she'd floated, all because she'd fallen in love with Jared, something she'd thought she was too smart to do. Enough of that nonsense.

There was one person who could talk her out of her funk and hopefully bring her back to planet Earth. She waited impatiently for Liz to answer. The memories of Jared's taste, his smell, his touch were driving her to distraction. "God, Liz, answer the phone."

"Hello. Ryan, stop that," Liz yelled at her youngest son. "Can't you see I'm on the phone?"

Toreas smiled to herself. This was more like it. Her friend reprimanding her son was normal, natural and familiar. This was her world. This part of her life Toreas could understand. "Hey, how are you?" she inquired of Liz.

"Don't give me that. What's going on with you and Jared? I saw the look you shot him when I mentioned his show."

"What look?"

"The look that said you wished he was dead. Come on, what gives?"

Toreas didn't want to tell her, but she wanted to talk about it and there was no better person to do it with than Liz. "I...oh never mind. It doesn't matter."

"What doesn't matter?"

Toreas pulled a stray hair strand into her mouth and pulled on it with her teeth, thinking how she'd cut it and hot combed it to look nice for Jared. As soon as she showered and washed her hair it would be back to her afro. What was she doing anyway? She had no hold on Jared, yet she felt betrayed. Liz would probably think she was acting childish if she told her.

"Toreas, come on, spit it out. What are friends for if you can't tell them your troubles?"

"It's just that he…" Toreas closed her eyes and took a deep breath. Telling Liz would be admitting she cared for Jared. "He told me he had quit the show a few months ago. He lied to me."

Toreas bit her lip, wanting Liz to volunteer more information but when she didn't, she was forced into asking, "Was Jared ever off the air at Channel One?"

"I don't know. I only tuned in because one of the women from Southeast called and said she was on his show. I hadn't known anything about him quitting. Hold on a minute. Ryan, cut it out"

A smile tugged at the corners of Toreas's lips. She sent a silent thank you to Ryan for giving her a moment to calm her jittery nerves. There was a slight pause. Toreas was aware she was putting more questions in Liz's mind. She could practically see her taking out her pen and beginning chapter two.

"Why did Jared tell you he quit?"

She was almost too embarrassed to answer. "It was after they aired the tape of me saying Kelle taught us karate to debate him."

"Oh that. Still, it doesn't make any sense. That was mild compared with some of the things Jared said on the air."

Toreas closed her eyes, willing the pain of betrayal away from her mind and her heart. "It's just that Jared promised me he wasn't taping our conversation."

"Conversation? What conversation?"

Toreas didn't blame Liz for being confused. "I called him to finally put an end to our feud. It was before he joined our group, before I started helping him." She caught herself before admitting it was also before she fell hopelessly in love with him.

"That was what, four or five months ago?"

"About." Toreas could answer her to the very second, but Liz didn't need to know that. Just as she didn't need to know about her actually asking Jared to sleep with her. What a fool she'd been.

She'd thought she was smart, that she was going into this thing with her eyes open. She had never intended to fall in love with him. God, she was stupid. Her life was an exact duplicate of the novels Jared despised.

"Liz, I forgot to ask you. Did you mail your manuscript off to the contest?" Toreas had to change the direction of the conversation. She was feeling too wounded to have Liz pick the scabs off her heart today.

"This morning, how about you?"

"Yesterday." Toreas breathed easier, knowing she'd successfully turned her friend's attention away from her interest in Jared.

"You know, I'm thinking of going to the *Autumn Authors'* Conference in Lisle. Are you going?"

"One hundred twenty-five dollars is a lot of money. I don't know." Toreas hesitated. She sighed, wanting for once to splurge. She could hear the excitement in Liz's voice and wanted to go to the conference. It would only take a little coaxing.

"Come on, Toreas, you're right down the street from the hotel, not even five minutes away. You don't even have to stay at the hotel. You can go home at night."

She glanced down at the brochure in her hand that she'd picked up only moments ago. She wondered if Jared was thinking of going. After all, he lived in Chicago and it would take him two hours to travel back and forth each day of the conference. Until this moment Toreas would have never dreamt of spending that kind of money on a conference. Now it didn't matter. In two months she was giving up her dream anyway.

She had made her decision sometime during the night. She was going to return to Georgia and give up all this nonsense. She would marry the first man her father shoved in her face. That was probably how the script was written anyway.

"Are you even listening to me?"

"Of course I am," Toreas answered, wondering what Liz had said.

"Then tell me what I said."

"This is childish. I'm not going to play this game with you."

"That's because you weren't listening. You know, if I didn't know better I would think you'd fallen for Jared. Nah, he's much too flashy for you and too big. You like small men, don't you?"

Liz was beginning to annoy her, making Toreas wish she'd never called. "What do you mean, I like small men?"

"No offense, but you're short. What would you ever do with a man like Jared? I can't even picture the two of you kissing. My God, the man would have to break his back to bend down to you."

"Or I could simply float up into his arms."

"What? What are you talking about?"

"Never mind." Toreas's ego was bruised. What she heard Liz saying was that Jared would never be interested in her. And that she knew already.

She did have to clear up one little point before she stopped talking to Liz, maybe forever. "I don't like my men small, thank you very much."

Liz was laughing on the other end. Now Toreas was quickly going from annoyed to angry. "Why are you laughing?"

"Because you're such a liar. Why don't you just admit you have the hots for Jared. I promise the world will not come to an end."

"I do not have the hots for him. And your thinking you know me so well is getting on my nerves," Toreas finished rather testily.

"It's not just me." Liz was still laughing. "Everyone knows it, except maybe the two of you. You can't keep your eyes off each other.

"Besides," Liz continued, "we've been critique partners for a long time and you never wrote like this before Jared. I'd say he's helped to loosen you up."

There was silence for a long moment. Toreas knew what was coming.

"Have you…?"

"Have I what?"

"You know what I'm talking about. Have you and Jared communed with nature?"

"None of your business. Liz, you're filthy."

"Why? Jeez, you've got me talking in such a stupid metaphor that my seven-year-old could listen to this conversation. You need to lighten up. If my son weren't here listening to me I'd tell you what you really need. But since he is, I'll just say you need communing bad."

Toreas didn't know if she hung up on Liz or vice versa. She just knew their conversation was severed. Was physical pleasure all that was ever on anyone's mind? But oh how she wanted to take a dip in that pool with Jared.

She glared at the phone before glimpsing her reflection in the mirror. She was pitiful. Even home alone she thought in terms of metaphors. Why couldn't she just say the word sex?

She walked closer to the mirror. "*I wanted to have sex with Jared last night.*" Toreas stood still while her face turned red. She waited for her internal critics to make her feel ashamed.

She thought of Jared and it was not shame that filled her but something else. Sex wasn't what she wanted from Jared, at least, not the main thing. Toreas didn't want to lie to herself any longer about her feelings for Jared. Even if she never told him she wouldn't deny it any longer. She wanted to be with Jared, to have him hold her, to touch her, to caress her, and finally to join with her. She wanted to fly to the heavens with him. Darn it, she wanted to knock some boots.

If she still thought in terms of metaphors then so be it. What she felt for Jared was so far removed from the crudity that three letter word, *sex* implied. She thought of the last kiss they'd shared.

It had been filled with such longing and hunger. All the emotions she'd managed to keep bottled up had been released in that one kiss. In that instant she'd known what she wanted, what he wanted. But they were both too stubborn to admit to their need.

✍🏻

Toreas was lonely. For the first time in her life she dared to admit it to herself. With her manuscript in the mail she was at loose ends. She knew she should start working on something else but she couldn't. Her mind kept straying to Jared, destroying her focus. The same as it had since the last meeting. She'd been ready to at least listen to Jared a week ago. But as more time passed she convinced herself that he couldn't care about her, couldn't be falling in love with her as she was with him, or he would not possibly have allowed so much time to pass without a word, not a note or a call. He certainly hadn't bothered to come over. That wasn't the way one went about proving their innocence. No, his actions were more those of a guilty man. And it definitely wasn't the way a man behaved who wanted a woman.

She couldn't believe how quickly time had passed. Each day she'd thought Jared would call or come over to explain and when he did neither she felt foolish.

For one instant she'd been tempted to watch his show just for a glimpse of him, but that was foolish. She'd used up her allotment of stupidity for this lifetime and was now working on the next. No, if there was anything between them he would have called. She decided to skip her writers' meeting to avoid seeing him.

✍🏻

Jared locked his office door behind him, then double checked it. The lock was one he'd installed himself after coming back. He valued his privacy and didn't intend for Derrick to either steal or tape him without his knowledge again.

He'd declined Derrick's and Josh's offer to stop and have a beer. He was going to his writers' meeting if for no other reason than to scowl at Toreas.

How dare she not call him? As far as he knew, she'd made no attempt to contact him. He was tired of the control she had over his life. Since she'd stormed out of the last meeting he'd neither seen nor heard from her and he was ready to confront her, to make her realize this time she would have to issue a genuine apology.

He stomped into the half empty room pretending not to look for her. It didn't work. Liz was on him the moment he sat down.

"She's not coming, you know."

"Who's not coming?"

"Not you too?"

Jared watched as Liz rolled her eyes. "Why don't the two of you just get over your little problems and admit you have a thing for each other, before it's too late?"

Toreas wasn't there for him to glare at so he glared at Liz. "I don't know what you're talking about."

"I'm talking about Toreas."

"You mean that opinionated little morals policewoman?" He glared again at Liz. "I don't have a thing for her," he spat out.

"You're right, you don't feel anything for Toreas. You always get this angry when I talk to you."

They stared at each other for a long moment, Jared not wanting to admit anything to Toreas's friend. "Did she mail off her manuscript?"

"Yes."

"Is she going to the conference?"

"You're sure asking a lot of questions about someone you don't care about."

For the first time in months Jared was thinking about doing a show on stubborn, nosy and pigheaded women. This time he wouldn't single out romance writers and readers. He'd take on the whole darn gender. Not one of them could ever answer a straight question without trying to play Perry Mason.

He sighed loudly, hoping Liz would get the hint. When she still did nothing but continue to stare at him, he was forced to explain.

"Liz, I was curious, that's all."

"Are you planning on going and ruining it for her? Because if you are, I'm going to tell my husband Mike to kick your butt. Or maybe I'll just have Kelle do it."

For the first time in two weeks Jared felt like smiling. "Don't worry, I'm not out to hurt her." When he saw that doubt remained on in Liz's eyes, he shook his head and gave her the peace sign. "I promise."

"Then why are you so angry with her? What did she do?"

She didn't trust me. He smiled at Liz, wishing he could tell her what he was thinking but it wouldn't be fair to Toreas. "I'm not angry with her, Liz, and I'm not going to hurt her. I just want to know if she's going to the conference."

"Yes, she's going and you'd better keep your word. Why are you always lying to her? Why did you tell her you quit your job? Are you still working on using our group for a story?"

He smiled, then laughed out loud. "That's an awfully lot of questions." He glanced at his watch. "I'll only answer one, the last one," he said pointedly. "I'm not using the group for a story."

He walked away then before Liz could have a chance to question him further. Now he knew why he wasn't married. Women could talk you to death. So why did he want Toreas Rose? He must be crazy. Perhaps he should volunteer for a complete lobotomy while it was still his choice.

The rest of the week before the conference seemed to crawl by. Jared attempted to talk himself out of going to the conference; the excuse that Lisle was almost an hour from Chicago was flimsy at best. Besides, he knew he wanted to go if for nothing more than to see Toreas. By the Friday night of the conference Jared felt as if he were dancing on hot coals. He was determined that this weekend, things would get settled between him and Toreas, regardless of the outcome.

He stood in the Lisle Hyatt at the bottom of the stairs near the table where the attendees checked in. He spotted her immediately because of the bulky coat.

Jared felt his heart skip a beat. The coat made her seem small and defenseless. He had the feeling she was trying to hide from the world. The second week of November and she was outfitted for a trek through the Andes. She flipped the scarf from her hair and it was once again straight. He'd have to tell her how he thought she looked even more beautiful when she washed her hair and allowed it to dry into an afro. His eyes slid down her body, noting she had returned to the bulky thrift store look. Brown cords two sizes too large topped by a man's tan sweater. This one, the both of them could have worn and easily fit in an extra person.

When she turned toward him, their eyes connected and nothing else mattered. He wanted her. His body was tingling strangely. Jared looked steadily at Toreas. She was the reason for his tingling.

"Hi, Toreas."

"Hello, Jared."

Her voice was stiff and polite. He smiled at her, hoping to prompt her into smiling in return. Nothing.

Toreas bit her lip and counted silently to ten. She had known he was coming. Liz had called on Wednesday to warn her. Too bad she'd been unable to warn her how she would feel seeing him.

"Can we talk?"

"Sure." She looked over his head. "We're friends, remember?"

Jared ignored her sarcastic comment as he slid his hand under her right elbow and turned her toward a quieter corner.

"I didn't lie to you." Her eyes bored into him, causing him to amend his statement. "I did quit, but Derrick asked me to come back. I was going to tell you."

"When did you get your job back?"

He hesitated, not wanting to say it out loud. "Will you promise to hear me out?"

Silence.

"Toreas, give me a chance here." Nothing. He knew what she

wanted. "When I went home the first day I had dinner with you, I found a message from Derrick. I called and got my old job back."

"Why didn't you just tell me the truth?" She smacked her hand lightly against the side of her head. "Truth, I'm sorry, I forgot you don't know the meaning of that word."

He'd promised himself he wasn't going to get angry, but she had a way of making him do things he would never have conceived of doing before she entered his life.

In one swift movement he had a firm grasp of her right hand in his own and pulled her to him. Before she had a chance to protest he was kissing her, tasting what had been denied him.

He felt her attempting to pull away at first. Then she stopped struggling and he felt her arms tightening around his middle.

He had won. Then and there he knew all he had to say was that he wanted her and she'd be in his hotel room before he finished the sentence. Damn her anyway. Why couldn't she just admit that she wanted him as much as he wanted her, that she was as in love with him as he was with her? But she wasn't going to say it and Jared was damned if he would say the words only to have her throw them back in his face. Two could play Toreas's game. He could be just as stubborn as she could. It would serve her right. *But it's punishing me*, he thought as he felt the quick jerk of his flesh in his pants. Still, it was time he took control of this situation.

It actually surprised Jared that instead of wooing Toreas he was scolding her when the kiss ended. "Truth. Toreas Rose, it seems as if I'm not the only one who doesn't know the meaning of the word. Why can't you admit that you care? Your kiss just now told me that you care. Why don't you just tell me how you feel about me? You're a little hypocrite who wants to beat me over the head with everything I say to you, dissecting it to see if it's true."

"What makes you think I care?" Toreas was glancing over his shoulder. She spotted Liz and Wendy watching her and knew they'd seen the kiss.

"I kiss men all the time, Jared. This kiss was nothing special." She walked away from him, grateful to run into one of the highest paid male cover models, John Cain, who was also a friend.

Toreas squealed as John picked her up and squeezed her in a bear hug. Usually when he would attempt to pick her up Toreas would stop him with a stern look and a finger or two wagged in his face.

Now with Jared watching she allowed John to hold her close to his body. His lips were all over her neck and face. When she felt the blush of embarrassment creeping up on her, Toreas ducked her head into John's massive chest, trying to prevent Jared from seeing she was uncomfortable.

Jared closed his eyes trying, to remember how to swallow. For a moment he flashed back and it was Gina he saw in the arms of a hunky male model. He tried to walk away but his legs refused to follow the commands of his brain.

He was face to face with the man, breathing in the strong scent of garlic emanating from his mouth. How could Toreas stay in his arms?

"Put her down. Now." He waited two seconds for him to comply, then forcibly removed Toreas from his arms and placed her on the floor behind him. "The lady is with me," Jared growled, blocking Toreas's body with his own, waiting for the man to complain.

When the cover model looked at him and grinned, Jared frowned and flexed his muscles. "Do you have any problems with me?" Jared flexed his muscles again and rolled his neck forward preparing to defend what was his. Whether she knew it or not, Toreas was his.

When the man smiled a crooked smile in his direction and walked off, Jared stared after him for a second. The guy probably didn't want to mess up his pretty face. With fierce possessiveness, Jared continued watching the man until he'd turned the corner of the lobby and was no longer visible.

Then Jared turned his attention to Toreas who wasn't looking in the least bit intimated. "What the hell was that all about?" he asked.

"You mean John? He's a friend, same as you." She attempted to walk away but Jared's strong hand held her in place.

"Toreas, I'm too old to play these juvenile games. I want you." Jared looked at her knowing what she wanted to hear, but he was still too angry with her to give it. "I'm attracted to you. There, now are you satisfied?"

"Sure, Jared. What woman wouldn't be with a compliment like that? How could I not be flattered?"

She was smiling at him. One of those smug smiles that made him want to kiss her senseless. She was patronizing him, baiting him, and he could feel the blood rushing through him, filling him with desire.

"Let's get through this conference. Then we need to do some serious talking. If we're going to be in a relationship then we need to set some ground rules. No more lying and no more of you allowing guys to paw all over you in a public place.

"Should I allow them to do it in private?"

"Not unless it's me. Look, I want to be in a relationship with you. We can figure out later if it will work. If not, we cut our losses and run. At least we would have tried. Anyway, when this damn conference is over the two of us are going to finish what we started months ago.

Make no mistake about that."

"Exactly what are you talking about?" Toreas asked sternly.

"Stop that nonsense, Toreas, and stop glaring at me. You can't frighten me away. When this is over I'm going to make love to you until we both are so tired that we can do nothing but sleep."

"And if I don't want to?"

"Liar," he said softly. "Would you like for me to show you how much you don't want to?" He glanced at her lips, then allowed his eyes to travel over her body until the telltale blush of red showed through her brown skin and obliterated the pigments. "Admit it, Toreas, you're a liar. You still want me to make your eyes roll back in your head. And I still want to taste you to find out if everything about you tastes like strawberries. I plan to make sure that you have several orgasms our first time out." She was blushing but not telling him to stop. He had his answer. And darn it he was even going to give her the answers that she'd demanded. He was leaving nothing to chance. When he made love to her, she would be ready completely. No silly barriers or unanswered questions would keep them apart this time. He'd taken care of everything. It was time for Toreas Rose to know that she belonged to him and no other, just as he belonged to her.

"Jared, you sound like some small time pimp. You can't give me orders and have me obey them. Are you crazy? Look, this isn't a romance story. This is my life, my real life. And I don't take orders from anyone, especially a man. Get that straight."

Jared lifted her chin with his finger and looked into her eyes. "Would you like for me to pick you up right now in this hotel lobby and carry you away to my room?"

Toreas was flushed. *Of course she did, that was exactly what she wanted.* Her eyes closed as she attempted to get her rapidly beating heart back under control. "Go away, Jared."

"Forever?" he asked quietly.

"No, definitely not forever." Toreas stared at him. "But for long enough to allow me to regain some self-control." She glanced at him, her eyes falling downward to the massive budge. "It seems like I'm not the only one affected by our kisses."

"Did I ever say our kisses didn't affect me?"

"I believe you did, Mr. Stone."

"Then I stand corrected, Ms. Rose. It appears we're both liars. I'll admit your kisses have the power to drive me insane. In fact I think they have because I've never done anything so crazy in my entire life. Everything I've done since I've met you is so out of character for me. You're a witch but a witch I want in my bed." This time he kissed her lightly on the lips. "You'd better join your friends, they're standing there in shock watching us. I'd say you no longer have to worry about telling anyone about us. I'd say the secret is out."

"Jared, you're behaving as if I have no choice in this."

"You do have a choice, To…re…as. I can make love to you here this weekend in my room where your friends will see you disappear behind my door and never see you again until this damn conference is over, or we could be a little more discreet and wait until the conference is over for me to ravage you. Then I will come to your home and make love to you until…," he grinned, "until I can no longer perform. Which do you prefer?"

"Privacy," she almost whispered.

"Good. Then go to your friends."

He waved at Liz and Wendy, not caring that they'd witnessed the little scene. "Your friends are waiting for you."

When Toreas attempted to brush past him, Jared put his hand out and stopped her. "No more stunts."

He stood watching her walk toward her friends. Every cell in his body was humming. He couldn't believe what he'd done. Not the challenging part, but the reason. No woman had ever before meant enough to Jared to make him put forth even the most minute effort to keep her.

He continued gazing at Toreas's bulky body in amazement, wondering how this tackily dressed woman was changing him from a rational adult male into a hormone-driven moron. There was still time to back away, to call a halt, but he knew he didn't want to. He wanted her in the worst way possible. And if he didn't stop looking at her and imagining what he would do to her later at her home he would embarrass himself.

He didn't have to look down for the evidence. He could feel it. Boy, could he feel it. For a moment his mind wandered to Gina. He'd never thought of fighting to keep her. He had been angry that she'd chosen someone else over him, but truth be told, he'd not been so terribly angry with her until his mom's death and the guilt over his unfulfilled promise to her. With Toreas it was different. Even now the thought of John's lips on her made him angry. There was no way he intended for anyone to ever touch her again but himself. Yep, roped and hogtied and that was just fine by him.

17

Toreas walked away from Jared, forcing herself not to look back at him. She was grateful to him for rescuing her from John. One more second of having to endure the smell of garlic and the hair she'd spent an hour hot combing would have curled from the fumes.

Toreas could tell Liz was nearly busting a gut trying not to laugh and Toreas wanted to think of some smart comment to make to wipe the look off her face but could think of none.

"So there's nothing going on with you and Jared, huh?"

"No, there isn't."

"Try telling him that. He's just standing there watching you. Besides, we saw the kiss and we saw what happened with John."

Toreas decided to just ignore Liz. Why deny something the women had seen with their own eyes? "Let's go upstairs and see who's here."

"Aren't you going to look at him?"

"No. Why?"

She walked up the stairs with her friends, resisting the urge to turn around until she touched the top step. Toreas turned her head slowly, to see if Jared was still there.

He was and he was looking at her, the look in his eyes smoky with desire. She gave him a half smile before closing her eyes. If she continued looking at him she would be running down the steps to fling herself in his arms.

She'd made enough of a spectacle of herself for one night. She knew the story would spread until at least twenty different authors would have it written in their next book. If she was lucky, they would make the woman something other than a romance writer. That would be too hokey. Toreas was glad of one other thing, that this was real life. If she'd ever written that scene she would have been attacked by every romance reader south of the North Pole. They would have derided her, saying her heroine was weak and shouldn't allow a man to order her around as Jared had just done.

Toreas took another peek in Jared's direction. Yes, but romance novels were fictional. This was real and it was her life. And she wanted Jared like she'd never wanted anything before. She wanted all the things he'd promised to do to her. And yes, God help her, she loved his caveman routine. The memory of him taking charge like that made her horny. She wanted him and she didn't care who thought she was being silly or weak. All she knew was that when all was said and done she'd have the satisfaction of having made love to Jared. And the ones who thought she was weak would never know the feelings she was having. She didn't believe another man could be capable of producing in another woman the exact same feelings which Jared produced in her. If it were possible, then all women would be acting as goofy as she was. Toreas laughed out loud and shook her head. He'd made her float and now he was making her skip.

Her skin was on fire. She was wishing she had booked a room. Right now she needed a cold shower. A real cold one. At least since she didn't have a room she wouldn't have to get stuck inviting Jared to her room.

Then it hit her. In both of their conditions she very much doubted they would wait until the conference was over. Toreas wanted it to be special, not more fodder for her friends to include in their stories. As much as she wanted Jared she wanted her time with him to remain private even more. She didn't want to be the object of gossip no matter how it was played. No, she'd much rather enjoy Jared without the snickers, real or imagined, that would come from her friends.

She was glad Jared had warned her he had a room. She should have thought of that. And she would have if she'd known before Wednesday that he was coming to the conference. She hadn't bothered getting a room because she lived five minutes away in Woodridge. Frankly, that knowledge alone had made her not want to splurge on yet another unnecessary expense. It seemed way too decadent.

A shiver of desire claimed her as she thought of the look in Jared's eyes when he'd offered to take her to his room and make love to her. Naturally Jared had a room. His finances weren't as bad as hers. She shivered again as she thought of him and her and his room, and what they could do there. At the moment she lacked the will power to fight him. She closed her eyes and ran her tongue across her lips, tasting Jared on them.

"Liz." Her voice was hoarse and low. Liz hadn't heard her. "Liz," she screamed, not realizing she had done so until several women turned to stare at her.

Liz was looking at her as if she thought she had lost her mind and Toreas couldn't blame her. They would deal with that later. For now she needed help.

"What's wrong with you? Why are you screeching at me at the top of your lungs?"

"Jared."

"Jared. What about Jared?"

"He's staying here. I need your help." Toreas was aware she wasn't making any sense. "Don't leave me alone with him."

"What are you talking about? Jared's downstairs."

"I mean later tonight, and for the rest of the weekend. I can't be alone with him, especially in his room."

"Then go home."

Liz was beginning to annoy her with her practicality. She sighed loudly, puffing out both cheeks, then expelling the air a number of times before she spoke again.

"I don't want to go home."

"You don't have a room."

"I know." She turned pleading eyes on her friend. "Let me bunk with you. I'll share the cost of the room."

"Kelle's sharing my room."

"I'll sleep on the floor."

"What is wrong with you? You don't want to be around Jared but you don't want to leave."

Toreas could feel the blush coming up her neck and working its way to her face. "I can't leave…" She looked away, then back at Liz. I don't want to leave Jared here…without me. Not with…all these women." There, she'd said it.

She watched the look of satisfaction slide across her friend's face. Liz thought she knew her so well. Disgust was slowly replacing her blush. She wished to God she didn't blush so easily.

"So there is something going on between you and Jared?"

"I think there might be, but right now I'm not sure what."

"Then why don't you share the room with him?"

Okay, now she was truly irritated. Her friend was being thick-headed. She looked sharply at Liz knowing Liz was going to force her to explain the entire situation to her. She knew Liz was enjoying this and doing it deliberately, probably because she'd lied to her about being attracted to Jared.

"Liz, I can't stay in Jared's room. Number one, he didn't ask me. Number two, it's too soon. Besides, Liz, what if he's pretending? What if he's only pursuing me to make a fool out of me, to air the entire thing?"

She had known that would elicit sympathy, but it annoyed her just how fast it did, as if Liz was already thinking that Jared must be crazy to want her.

"Okay, you can stay if it's all right with Kelle. And you don't have to sleep on the floor. You can bunk on the couch." Then Liz frowned at her, scrutinizing her clothes. "What are you going to do for clothes? You didn't bring anything."

"I'll go home and pack a few things."

"You've got it bad, don't you?"

"Don't tell anyone."

"I won't have to. I wasn't the only one standing in the lobby when he kissed you. There must have been thirty people walking around. Then when he took you out of John's arms everyone stopped. The security guards were on their way over there. We all thought Jared was going to deck him."

"Are you serious?"

"Didn't you see his face?"

Toreas smiled at Liz. Her body was tingling and she felt warm. "I was afraid to look. Nothing like this has ever happened to me before."

"I'll tell you my opinion. From what happened, I don't think he's after a story."

"Maybe not, but I don't want to be a one night stand for him either."

"That's what you wanted a few months ago, remember?"

It's just like Liz to bring that up, Toreas thought testily. Well, she was now her host, so she'd keep her mouth shut. At least she'd do her best not to blow up.

"It's not what I want now." She hugged Liz, stopping her friend's comeback. She didn't need Liz to remind her of her brash plan. She was only happy that Liz didn't know she'd attempted to put that plan into action and had been turned down.

As they hugged, Toreas couldn't help worrying if Jared was wooing her as some form of payback. He had been angry and insulted that she'd asked him to sleep with her. She had to be careful.

"Thanks, Liz. Just remember, no matter what, don't let me be alone with Jared. He's beginning to wear me down," she admitted. "And here in this hotel, I don't know if I can resist him on my own."

Toreas went with Liz in search of other members of their chapter. She tried to pretend that her mind wasn't on Jared as she smiled and talked to the other women. Even when they walked into the buffet for dinner she was still pretending Jared wasn't on her mind.

"To..re..as."

Toreas turned toward Jared. *There he goes caressing my name.* He hadn't done that in weeks. *Okay calm down*, she scolded herself.

You've got an entire weekend. Pace your lust. Just when she'd convinced her legs to move, Jared came alongside her, taking her plate from her hand.

She followed him before he could call her again. There was just so much a proper Baptist girl could take before she voluntarily turned into a pagan. He'd only brushed the back of her hand, but her entire body was on fire. She scanned the room quickly, looking for Liz.

They sat alone at a table meant for ten. She was getting nervous. Her eyes were drawn to his lips. She wanted to plant one on him. So far he'd been the aggressor. Now she wanted to shock those cute tight jeans off his cute tight butt.

"Are you listening to me?"

Toreas shook her head. "I'm sorry, I was thinking about something."

"What?"

"I was wondering what's happening with us. Tell me the truth now, Jared. If you're doing this for a joke I won't get angry with you, promise."

She felt his hand touch her cheek and she moved toward him. But he didn't kiss her. He was talking again and though she watched his lips move she couldn't hear his words. She was too busy thinking of kissing him, of touching him, him touching her. This was the second time he'd played the part of knight for her. Well, the first time she still wasn't so sure about. She had no proof that he'd actually quit his job. She wanted to believe him. For the sake of her heart she needed to believe him. She couldn't take much more disappointment where Jared was concerned.

"I need you to listen to me."

He was talking to her, his brown eyes boring into hers and honestly she was doing her best to listen. There was just this feeling she couldn't shake. It was overcoming all other emotions and it was lust. She wanted every darn thing she'd ever read about and she wanted them now. Darn what she'd told Liz. She waited for the choir to begin chortling but heard nothing.

"Toreas, I'm serious."

Okay, be careful, she warned her body. *He's getting ready to tell you he doesn't want you.* She thought that would put the incredible lust at bay. It didn't, not one iota. She still wanted him regardless of his intentions.

He was eyeing her strangely. She blinked when her eyes opened fully. The same lust she was feeling was reflected in his eyes. He wasn't going to say he didn't want her. She could listen.

"What were you going to say, Jared?"

She laughed at him. He was having the same problem she'd had only a moment ago. He was speechless. Until he pulled away from her.

Toreas watched him as he took a sip of water, then another longer one. God, he was beautiful. She no longer cared who was writing the scenes. As long as they gave her a chance to at least sample Jared, she'd be fine with that.

She smiled. "Jared."

"I'm sorry. You've got to stop looking at me like that or I'm not going to be able to talk or to stand. And there will be no way in hell I won't drag you to my room. Tell me you've changed your mind about that and we can go up now." He gave his words a moment to sink in.

"Jared."

"Yeah, I know you want the privacy," he grinned. "Maybe it's better anyway. There is something I want to say to you. I want to clear up something with you and start out fresh. You asked me before why I started attacking romance writers and now I want to tell you."

She was trying her best to listen to him. She was curious about the reason for his attacks, but even more curious about the dark hairs she saw peeping from under the collar of his shirt. She wondered if his chest hairs were soft.

"Yes, Jared, tell me." She had to at least pretend to be interested, didn't she?

"Before I moved here from L. A. there was this woman I was pretty serious about, Gina."

Okay, now you've got my attention, buster. She looked at him to see if she'd said it out loud, but since he was still talking it was safe to assume she'd only thought it.

"What does your girlfriend have to do with us?" She sat back in her chair to see if the word girlfriend would make him sweat. It didn't.

"She's not my girlfriend. Not any longer."

"What happened?"

"She dumped me."

Toreas was staring at him in disbelief. What woman in her right mind would let him go? She had to be a complete moron. Thank God for morons.

She knew he was waiting for her to ask so she did. "Why did she dump you?" She was watching him closely, wanting to see if the telling was hurting him.

"She came to a conference, one of yours." He looked around meaningfully. "And she met a male cover model and fell in love with him, or in lust, I'm not sure which." He attempted to laugh.

"Is that why you began writing derogatory stories and killing us on your television show?"

She noted he did have the grace to appear chagrined before he answered.

"Yes. I was angry. I blamed romance writers for Gina being a flake." He captured her chin in his hand. "I was going to stop, then you came along and things got out of hand."

She heard him but what he said meant nothing. There was something else she was more concerned with. "Is that the reason you didn't want me with John?" *Not again*, she thought and prepared to close her heart against him.

"Were you wishing you had done that with Gina? Maybe if you had, you'd still be with her. There might still be a chance for you with her. Perhaps you should return to L.A. and fight for her."

Toreas pushed her chair away. She was as big a moron for thinking he wanted her as Gina was for having him and tossing him aside. Now if she could only keep her hurt locked away inside, she'd be all right. She picked up her glass and drank until it was empty.

"That's not why I did it. I knew you weren't interested in that bozo. As hard as you were trying to hide it from me I saw the moment when all of that pretty brown skin turned a toasty red. You were only doing that to annoy me. I knew how embarrassed you would be later."

"So you wanted to save me from embarrassment by creating your own scene." She couldn't believe he had the nerve to smile at her.

"There was another reason. He was touching you and I didn't want him to."

Maybe he thought that was enough. It wasn't. She wanted more. She wanted to hear him say the words. "Why didn't you want him touching me?"

"Hi guys, I thought I'd find you in here."

It was Liz. As Toreas looked at her she could tell she was mouthing sorry. For a moment she wondered what she was sorry for. Then she remembered. She'd asked Liz not to leave her alone with Jared.

For heaven sakes, she thought. *Can't Liz tell the difference?* She wanted to kick her, pull her long hair, anything that would get her to leave. It was too late. Nothing she did that moment would have mattered. Their table for ten was filled and two extra chairs pulled up between her and Jared.

She had to admit that for a group of women renowned for their sense of romance they were all missing the glaring clues. Didn't any of them feel the daggers she was hurling at them? Maybe she should use spears instead.

One by one they all began pulling out their schedules trying to decide what workshop to go to. She had to admit this conference was a lot more relaxed than most. There would be no editor appointments, or agents either, for that matter.

Only a handful of the writers were upset over that. The rest thought they would benefit more from the guest speakers and workshops.

Toreas knew she would. The last time she'd attended a conference she had been so nervous the entire time that she had forgotten everything she'd wanted to say during her editor appointment.

Of course that hadn't mattered. She'd been told to send her manuscript in, as had the other two hundred writers who attended. As far as she knew, not one of the hopefuls had actually sold to the editor. All the members had done was wait anxiously wondering if the editors and agents had any idea how the writers stressed over the passing months, wondering is it okay to call and check on the status of the manuscript. The three months that most said on their various websites turned into five, seven, nine, a year. There were many of her friends who'd sent material out to editors and not heard from them for three years or more.

So this was a lot more fun. They had big name authors. She was impressed and couldn't wait to meet them. Debra Dixon she'd already met.

Now she sat listening to the women pick out their various workshops, her ears tuned to hear which ones Jared would be attending. She would be sure to take different ones.

That night it was easy to escape Jared. She had gone home and packed, and stayed in the room with Liz and Kelle. The next morning, however, Toreas had no plans to avoid Jared. Forget that nonsense. In fact, she showered quickly in order not to disturb Liz or Kelle. She'd forgotten a shower cap in her haste, and rushed from the room without blow drying her hair, knowing by the time it dried it would have reverted into an afro. It didn't matter. She was hoping to find Jared and finish their conversation.

The dining room was packed not only with writers but hotel guests. She was looking around the room trying to find a vacant table when she noticed Jared beckoning for her. She rushed toward him, wondering how he'd managed to save her a seat. It was obvious the other women were enthralled with him. Why wouldn't they be? She found herself wanting to tell them to stop drooling, that Jared was the one who'd said they wrote trash. That he thought they were all stupid.

She watched as he smiled at a woman she didn't know. It was obvious from the looks the women were giving him they wouldn't have believed her. Toreas wondered at the feelings she was having. Were they the same feelings that had made Jared pull her from John's arms? Maybe later she'd tell him John was gay, just not yet. She liked the idea of him being filled with jealousy just as she was now.

He turned his smile in her direction and she couldn't help heaving a sigh of relief.

"How much are you paying them?" he asked as he leaned in closer to her.

"Who are you talking about?"

"Liz and the others. How much are you paying them to keep us apart?"

She picked at the food on her plate with her fork. "You're crazy. I'm not paying anyone to do any such thing." She tried to act insulted but it was hard to pull it off when they spotted Liz and Kelle at the same moment, running toward them as though on a mission.

Jared said good morning to Liz and Kelle, then returned his attention to Toreas. "When this conference is over, we will be alone. We're going to stop playing around and make love." He ran the pad of his left index finger down the side of her cheek. He smiled at her wet hair in approval, surprised that she'd gone to all the trouble to hot comb it and had apparently showered without a cap knowing when her hair dried she would be sporting an afro. He smiled again, pleased by that fact. "By the way, I like your curly afro."

As if nothing had happened, as if her body were not on fire and her heart racing, he resumed talking to the other women at the table.

And she was supposed to eat as though nothing had happened? Did Jared really think he could touch her with such gentleness that it lit fires in her she'd never known she had and expect her to continue eating as though nothing had happened? She could just imagine the food lodging in her windpipe while Jared dominated the attention of the women at the table. Wouldn't that make a great headline? Writer chokes to death in a room filled with hundreds. The best she could manage was to drink her juice before rising to leave. When she did, Jared stood also.

"Remember, tomorrow when this is over, the games stop." He brushed her lips with his own. A light feathery kiss that spelt ownership. He'd staked his claim and she liked it. Right now she'd probably like it if he lifted a hundred pound club, hit her over the head and dragged her back to his cave. So she was archaic. It was what she liked, and she couldn't have wiped the grin from her face if she had tried. She touched her fingers to her wet hair, glad to know Jared loved her afro.

"You know, you're right in wanting to be watched. You're about ready to spontaneously combust right here, right now. Calm down before you scare him off."

Toreas smiled at Liz. That was sound advice. The same thing she'd say to any of her friends in the same situations, but she wasn't them.

She'd never in her entire life felt this lightness, this giddy feeling. She was determined to enjoy it.

She was surprised her internal critics were so silent. But it didn't matter. Not even they could stop the feeling of joy forcing her to smile.

For the rest of the day she saw Jared only in the company of others. The only time she sat next to him was during meals.

Liz should have been praised for the job she was doing in keeping them apart but Toreas found herself wanting to fill her backside full of buckshot.

That night a private party for two in Jared's room turned into a party for twenty, courtesy of Liz. She even persuaded a couple of the women to call and invite their husbands to come. By one A.M. Toreas was really tired and more than ready to leave for the room when Liz and Kelle both took her arms and told her it was time to leave.

She smiled weakly in Jared's direction. She was glad she couldn't read minds because he had to be thinking the whole darn chapter was nuts.

Sunday morning Toreas was nervous. With only a couple of hours left before the end of the conference it was all she could do to remain in her seat. Soon she would be with Jared. With any luck at all she would have that elusive something she craved. The thought of Jared declaring his love for her sent pinpricks of excitement skittering down her spine.

For the first time during the conference they sat together to listen to their closing speaker, Patricia Potter. Toreas barely heard what she was saying, she was so aware of Jared's nearness.

When Toreas managed to pull her attention away from Jared and focus on the speaker, she caught her in the middle of saying something about point of view.

"Listen," Jared whispered in her ear.

She was embarrassed that he knew her attention was not on the speaker. She made a concentrated effort to focus and heard Mrs. Potter saying something about a comment Nora Roberts once made about not knowing anything about point of view when she first got started. She hadn't allowed it to restrict her and it hadn't handicapped her in the least.

Toreas felt Jared smile and turned toward him. He was gloating. For some strange reason he'd chosen that particular part of writing to rebel against. He was a regular one man crusade, not accepting their reasons for the importance of clear points of view and having them not change in the middle of a scene.

Now here was a respected and best selling author telling him and them that not only did she agree with him, but so did Nora Roberts.

He turned his smile directly on her then and her heart melted. To heck if he was right. She didn't care if he continued badgering her about loosening up on the point of view. She only wanted him to continue smiling at her, as if the two of them had a special secret.

The rest of what Mrs. Potter said was lost on her. Jared was playing with her fingers, caressing them, tickling her palm, making suggestive drawings.

Toreas wondered how she'd manage to get through the good-byes with the writers she'd met from other chapters. She made her way to the dais, following Jared, to say good-bye to Mrs. Potter. Her mind was more on the firmness of Jared's behind than on what she wanted to say.

She couldn't believe it. Now he was drawing her attention from one of the writers she most admired. *He'd better be worth it*, she thought wickedly and coughed as she felt her cheeks getting warm.

When it was her turn to say goodbye to the legendary writer she could only say, "Nice to meet you." Jared had captured the woman's attention, thanking her for giving the women the freedom they'd taken from themselves to write a good and compelling story. He left Toreas with little to say.

As she turned to say goodbye to several more people, Jared's hand on her arm stopped her.

"I'll meet you at your apartment in an hour."

"I may not be home by then. I'm going to the book room."

"One hour." He smiled at her, then walked away.

She attempted to glare at him, but failed miserably. *Who does he think he is?* Toreas was doing her best to get angry at him for assuming she would rush home to meet him, but was finding it difficult.

Her entire body was tingling. Conference always stirred up her juices but this was different. Conference had never set her Southern regions on fire.

She searched for Kelle or Liz. She needed one of them to let her in their room to get her bag. She had to get home. She glanced down at her watch. She had wasted ten minutes. She only had fifty more left.

Neither Liz nor Kelle was anxious to leave the last minute farewells and they were annoyed that she was bothering them. When she refused to relent, Liz finally shoved her key in her face and told her to go to the room herself.

Toreas was aware that Liz was miffed but it couldn't be helped. She wasn't being a party pooper. Her getting home was a necessity.

Her eyes searched the meeting room for Jared on her way out. As if he had known she was looking for him, their eyes connected and he tapped his watch.

His chauvinistic attitude should have made her stop, not go to the room, stay exactly where she was, but he was smiling at her, his eyes filling with desire for her. To heck with being a feminist. She could do that later. After she'd had him, after he'd made her eyes roll back in her head.

Yeah, then she could be the independent woman. Right now it had been much too long and her toys were failing to give her the release she sought.

She could swear she had her things shoved into her bag and was back downstairs in under five minutes. She scanned the room for Jared. Not finding him, she rushed toward Liz to return the key.

The last thing she wanted was for him to get to her apartment before she did. She ignored her friend's strange looks. She was bursting to tell Liz but decided against it. This was her business and Jared's. No sharing with her friends. She was finally going to get to see what made a woman's eyes roll back in her head. *Yahoo!!*

18

Toreas barely had time to brush and gargle before Jared was knocking at her door. She wondered briefly how it was he never had to be buzzed into the building.

"Hi."

He had a bag in his hand. Toreas looked first at him then at the bag. He was moving much faster than she intended. What she wanted didn't require a bag.

"Jared...the bag... Why?" She was stuttering and feeling like an idiot because of it, but she had to clear that little issue up before they went any farther.

He closed the door, then came into the room, taking away most of the air she needed to breathe. She wanted to take a step back from him but she needed to remain close. In fact she wanted to be closer.

"I've got something for you."

She watched as reached into the bag and pulled out a thick sheaf of papers and handed it to her. Toreas's eyes fell on the questionnaire she had given him. She could feel her face start to burn.

She was too flustered to bring her eyes upwards to his. "I had no idea that you kept this."

"I had to."

"Why?"

"I've never had an offer like this before. The benefits are mind blowing."

Toreas ignored his smile. Here she was thinking he wanted to tell her that he wanted a relationship with her. She was thinking maybe he'd fallen in love with her, as she had with him.

It seemed that wasn't the case. He was here only to sleep with her. She began flipping through the pages not really reading his answers. She had to give herself a moment to keep the tears that wanted to fall from doing so.

"There was something else you were supposed to have." She made her voice cold and hard, making the whole thing appear to be a business arrangement. She noticed his smile slip a bit. Good. He was too darn sure of himself anyway.

His hand dipped back into the bag and he brought out another paper. This one she did examine. It was from a lab. He'd been checked for every possible venereal disease and for AIDS. He was clean.

"Kick his butt out." She heard the clamor of voices. "He doesn't care about you." He reached his hand out toward her. She didn't move as he lifted her chin so he could gaze into her eyes.

"Is something wrong?"

"No, there's nothing wrong." She felt a burning in her chest and it wasn't lust. It was the lie she was doing her best to suppress. There was indeed something wrong. "Kick him out," the voices chimed in again.

"No," she answered them. *"I don't want to. Even if he doesn't care, I care."*

"Toreas, why are you looking at me like that?"

"Like what?"

"Like you're disappointed in me."

She laughed then. She had to or she would have cried. "Why should I be disappointed? I asked you to sleep with me, and it appears you've decided to take me up on my offer."

She turned from him and began walking away. "You might not want to after you hear I've changed my mind about coming on your show. That was months ago, Jared. The deal is off."

"Is that what you think this is, some sort of deal for you to come on my show?"

She turned toward him, surprised at the anger in his voice, and even more surprised at the disgust on his face. "Then what is it? Why did you fill out the questionnaire? Why the doctor report if you didn't come here to sleep with me?"

"First, let's get something straight. I didn't come here to sleep with you."

Toreas felt her heart slip lower in her chest. Why did she keep setting herself up for him to hurt her?

"I came here to make love to you." He was getting angry. She was the most annoying woman he had ever loved. Hell, she was the only woman he'd ever loved. Didn't she know that?

For a long moment neither of them spoke. Then Toreas broke the awkward silence. "What is it you want exactly, Jared? A one night stand?"

She watched as his hand disappeared once again into the bag and a smile spread across his face.

"I was hoping for more." He laughed, then dumped three boxes of condoms on her coffee table. "Toreas, I filled out your questionnaire because I know you're still afraid. You were beginning to trust me. I like the feeling of your trusting me. I want you to trust me. That's why I jumped through all of those ridiculous hoops."

Toreas's eyes went first to the boxes, then to Jared. The desire in his eyes turned her to mush. She was doing her best to hang on to a little of her dignity. She couldn't give in too fast, but without a doubt she was giving in. She just had to ask him one question first.

"Why did it bother you to see me with John?"

"Because I care about you."

"You care about me," she repeated, thinking people care about plants, their dogs and cats. *I love you*, she wanted to shout at him. She leveled her gaze on him, enjoying the view. *You big goon, she thought. If you'd perhaps read one of the romance novels you're always making fun of you'd know what words win a woman's heart. Believe me it's not, 'I care about you.'*

Of course she didn't say any of that. She just stared at him, wondering how such a gorgeous man could be so darn ignorant about how to talk to a woman. She smiled at him then. Men should never be allowed to talk. They should just stand there and look pretty.

"What are you smiling about? You've got an evil look on your face, and I'm wondering if I should duck."

"No, Jared, you don't have to worry, you're a man. Why should I expect more from you?"

"I think I'll go out the door and we can start this conversation over again." This was definitely not what he had in mind.

"What's the point? You've already told me that you *care* about me. I understand that. And I *care* about you."

He wanted to laugh. So that was the problem. She was right. He was dense. He didn't even know why he'd said that instead of just telling her he loved her, other than he'd never spoken those words to anyone. And the words just wouldn't come out.

He swallowed, watching her, knowing she had to know he loved her. There was a part of him that wanted to turn her over his knee and whale the daylights out of her for deliberately misconstruing his words. A larger part of him wanted to cradle her in his arms and make passionate love to her over and over until he'd used up every foil-wrapped packet he'd brought with him. Then he'd run out and buy more. Maybe he'd buy a few thousand shares in the company.

He gazed into her dark brown eyes knowing she wanted him as much as he wanted her but seeing a struggle going on behind her eyes.

He knew without a doubt she was trying to find a reason to back out of it, anything to send him packing, to blame him for her fears.

Think, Jared, think. You're not as inept at this as she thinks you are. You always know how to charm women. Now it's for real. Charm the woman you love.

He could have just told her he loved her. He wanted to. The feeling was there, making a hard lump in his throat, but he couldn't get the words out.

"Do you really want to know why I pulled you out of that duffus's arms?"

"His name's John," Toreas attempted to interrupt but he ignored her.

"I was jealous. I didn't want him touching you." He walked closer to her, the heat from her breath warming his cheeks.

"I want you, and I don't want anyone else to have you, to touch you. I want to be the only man whose arms you're in. I want to love you completely, taste every inch of you, make you scream out my name and then start all over again."

Toreas was unsure if he lifted her up or if she vaulted up into his arms. All she knew was that she was in his arms and the smell of him was so darn intoxicating. He hadn't said he loved her, but what he had said was enough for now. She wasn't just a one night stand. She glimpsed the clock over his shoulder. It was still morning, so she wasn't just a one morning stand.

He lowered his lips to kiss her and she closed her eyes, wanting to drown in the desire radiating from him. She couldn't talk. She could barely breathe with him kissing her. So she pointed one finger toward her bedroom door, forgetting he knew exactly where it was.

"Stop." She pushed against his chest.

"What's wrong?"

"We forgot something." She bent her body over his arm to reach for the largest box of condoms. She clutched it greedily to her chest and smiled at him.

His soft chuckle delighted her, especially when he followed it up with searing kisses. She was being consumed with a fire she never knew existed. Toreas had serious doubts if they would make it to the bed.

She closed her eyes, giving in to the sweet sensations coursing through her body. She shivered slightly as she sensed her body being lowered to her bed. When her head came in contact with the pillow, she opened her eyes and stared at him. He was beautiful and she wanted him. Now she would finally know how it felt to be with a man she loved.

"Let's take off some of these clothes." Jared's breathing was ragged as his hands went beneath Toreas's sweater. He stopped abruptly, looking at her.

"I knew these clothes were big but are you sure you're in there?" He lowered his head, pushing it under her sweater, marveling at how small her frame truly was.

He began kissing her, his head still under the sweater. There was something erotic about it. He was tasting skin that he had yet to see and it was a delicious feeling. He could imagine doing it for the rest of his life.

That thought almost made him stop. Almost. Now he was glad she'd covered her body with the hideous garment she wore. He was the only one who knew what treasures lay beneath.

Well, that wasn't quite true, he corrected himself. She had admitted she wasn't a virgin. Still, that didn't mean she'd ever truly been made love to. And that was exactly what he intended.

Jared's head remained under her sweater. Toreas was getting a little anxious. She longed for the taste of his lips. He had said he was going to take the sweater off. If he didn't hurry she'd rip the blasted thing off herself. What should have been a two second procedure had turned into Jared's own personal exploration of her body. He was buried under her heavy sweater licking her skin, nibbling at her flesh, biting her lightly through her bra. His hands. Oh God, his hands were touching her, slowly, as though he knew he was driving her wild with desire.

The phone rang and for a moment Jared's hand stilled. Then he resumed his pursuit. She was surprised he wasn't trying to undo her bra. Everywhere the pads of his fingers touched she burned. If only that annoying phone would stop ringing she could focus and enjoy it.

She knew she would have to tolerate the sound until the answering machine clicked on. As soon as that was over she would take the thing off the hook. Too bad she hadn't thought to do that earlier.

"Toreas, this is Mom."

Where had that come from? Her mother was not one of her critics. Now if it was her father's voice, that she could understand, but her mother? No, no way.

"Toreas Rose, I know you should be home. This is Mom. Pick up."

She was one second from pulling Jared's hand from beneath her sweater until she felt him tweaking her nipples. She was praying her mother would soon tire of talking to dead air and hang up. Wrong.

"Tesa, Dad wants you to come home for Thanksgiving. So if you're ignoring me, let me tell you now that until the tape runs out, I'll keep calling until I'm done."

She heard Jared chuckle beneath her sweater and was grateful she wasn't looking at his face right now. She could only hope her mother would hurry with her message.

"You remember that nice Johnson boy from down the road a piece? Well, he's coming to visit his folks for the holidays so Dad made arrangements for you two to get together. I mean, you don't have anyone and neither does he, so we thought..."

"Hello Mom. I'm sorry, I was in the bathroom." She'd never meant to answer the phone but her mother was blurting out things she'd rather Jared not hear. So she'd automatically hit the speaker phone button hoping to make her mom change the subject.

"Do you have company?"

"Why are you asking me that?"

"Because you took so long to answer."

"I said I was in the bathroom." A long moment of silence followed when Toreas knew her mother was evaluating the sound of her voice to determine if she was lying. She'd always been good at that.

"Are you sure you don't have anyone there with you?"

God, Mom, can you talk any louder? "There is no one here, Mom. I'm alone."

"Good then we can talk."

Jared's head came from beneath her sweater. He was looking at her with an amused but curious expression. She wished he would stop looking at her like that. She couldn't talk to her mother and want him at the same time. The whole thing seemed somehow sordid.

He was tugging on her pants, pulling them down, his hand dipping into the waistband of her panties. She shoved his hand away.

"Mom, I can't talk now. I just got home from the conference. I need to put my things away. I'll call you later."

"If you don't have company why can't you put your things away while you're talking to me? Your phone's cordless. Besides, you've got me on the speakerphone. I can tell," her mother accused. "Tesa, are you lying to me?"

Okay, that's it, make me feel like I'm ten again and spending your leftover change from my trip to the store. "Mom, I'm not lying. I'm alone." Toreas hunched her shoulders toward Jared and held up one hand indicating it would only take five minutes.

"So what do you think of getting together with that Johnson boy? His mother says he's ready to settle down and make a commitment."

"Brian? Don't invite him, Mom. We never did get along even as kids. He grossed me out."

She was hoping this would stop her mother. It sure had stopped Jared. He was now just sitting on her bed able to hear both ends of the conversation. She wished she'd never picked up. But she knew her mother; she would have talked to the answering machine until she got tired.

"Give me one good reason why we shouldn't. Is there someone you're committed to, Tesa? Is that it, you've found someone who's special to you, someone you didn't tell us about? If you're involved with someone, bring him with you."

Toreas turned away from Jared. "Mom, I'm not involved with anyone."

"So you'll come home."

"Yes, Mom."

"Good. Your father has already deposited money in your account. Make your plane reservation, then call and tell us what time to pick you up."

"Mom, there won't be time to get a seat. I'll drive. I'll leave around seven in the morning, next Tuesday. That'll give me plenty of time to get there before it gets late."

"You'd better leave earlier than that or you'll get caught up in traffic. But be careful. It will be dark and I don't really like you driving alone."

"I'll be careful."

"What time will you leave?"

"Very early, Mom, four A.M., no later than five."

Her mother finally hung up after a bit of gossip about the town. *Now when it was too late*, Toreas thought. She'd heard the horrible squeak of the springs as Jared's weight left her bed. She turned back toward him and watched as he left her bedroom. Thanks, Mom.

She walked back into the living room and sat with her legs tucked under her in the chair opposite Jared. "I'm sorry that call took so long." She attempted a smile. "I'm sure you know how insistent mothers can be."

He wasn't answering her. The look on his face strangely resembled hurt. But she'd done nothing to hurt him. She didn't understand.

"Jared, why are you looking at me like that? I know I should have gotten her off the phone sooner but…"

"It's not that," he interrupted her. "Your mother asked you if you had anyone special in your life. You said no."

"What was I supposed to say?"

"What about me? What am I?"

"You're a man who wants to sleep with me. I'm attracted to you and you're attracted to me. It's not as though you're my boyfriend." She was trying not to become irritated but he was the one who'd defined their relationship as caring about her.

"Like I said, I came here to make love to you. Sleep was the last thing I had on my mind. Second, you're right. I'm not your boyfriend. I'm not a boy, I'm a man."

"Excuse the hell out of me, Jared. How could I possibly forget that the great Jared Stone is a man?"

He folded his hands across his torso and glared at her, the desire to strangle her pretty little neck battling his hurt feelings.

He pressed his fingers against his forehead and blew out a long exasperated sigh once, then again. He needed to calm himself. "Why am I here, Toreas?"

She returned his glare. "To make love to me. Isn't that what you said?"

He walked closer to her, so close that he could taste each breath she took. God, how he wanted her. He wanted to tell her that he loved her, but the need to know she loved him also was keeping him from reaching out to her as he wanted to do.

"Toreas, why do you want me here? Tell me." He almost whispered, praying for once she'd trust him enough to not hurt her.

"Jared, we're not a couple. You never made me any promises and I didn't ask you for any."

"Then maybe you should. Ask me for a promise, Toreas."

He watched as the flicker of doubt flashed crossed her face. She was backing away from him. He troubled his bottom lip with his teeth. Maybe he was wrong. She sure wasn't behaving as if she was in love with him.

"Jared, I don't understand why we're having this conversation. I'll take the phone off the hook and we can just pick up where we left off."

"Why don't you want me to go home with you for Thanksgiving?"

"Why would you want to go to a two bit little podunk town in Georgia? I don't even want to go."

"But you didn't ask me. You never even considered it."

Toreas was becoming more confused. All she wanted at the moment was to turn back the clock a half hour. The phone would surely be off the hook and right about now she should be experiencing everything she'd read about. Instead, here she was arguing about something as stupid as not inviting Jared home for a Thanksgiving dinner she didn't even want to attend.

"Why are you doing this?" She picked up a box of condoms from the coffee table and held them toward him. "Can't we forget about this?"

"Why don't you want me to come?"

She'd done her best not to say it, but he asked for it. What the heck? The mood was ruined anyway.

"Jared, my parents can be a little difficult?"

"How?" he asked, not letting it go.

"They're small minded and judgmental."

"Much like you?"

"I'm not judgmental," Toreas defended.

"Yeah, right."

"Jared."

"Your parents know nothing about me. But I heard your mother say that if you had someone special in your life you could bring them. I want to know the real reason you don't want me to go, Toreas."

"They wouldn't understand you or know how to take you. And you wouldn't know how to take them. I can promise you you wouldn't have any fun. My God, Jared, going there is no big deal. It's torture for me and it would be for you also. They make a big deal of my father being a deacon of Pilgrim Baptist Church and my mother being on the usher board and in the choir. Julie and William Rose are as uptight small town people as you'd ever want to meet. They belong in Georgia. It suits them."

"Those sound like a bunch of excuses. I'll say it again: Your mother said if you had someone special that you could bring them. Why aren't you asking me to come with you?"

"You're not exactly what my mother's talking about when she asked if I was seeing anyone special." That did it. She saw the smoky eyes shooting daggers at her.

"Are you saying I'm not good enough for your family?"

"I'm saying your values are different. You're not what my mother means when she talks about commitment."

"You really are a self righteous little hypocrite, aren't you? Look who's holding the box of condoms."

Toreas looked in her hand. She'd forgotten she'd picked them up.

"You know something, I'm sick and tired of you pushing your supposed morality in my face. Did you forget you're the one who first propositioned me?"

He was walking toward her. "You're right. We have different values. I would never fall in love with a woman who prostitutes her body, even, as you say, for the sake of research."

He knew he was hurting her. He saw her blink her eyes and knew she was holding back tears. He put his arm around her waist and roughly pulled her toward him. He felt her tremble against his body.

"Look at you, even now you want me. You pretend to be a prude. I should have known it was all an act. Only an expert would have asked the questions you had in that blasted survey of yours."

He stood in front of her and took the expected slap, then laughed at her. "You want a commitment. Lady, you should be committed."

With that he turned from her and walked to her bedroom. When he returned he was holding the unopened box of condoms. He glared at Toreas and bent slightly to pick up the two remaining boxes of condoms from the coffee table and toss them into the nearby wastebasket. He glared again at her before walking out the door.

Damn it to hell. If this was the way love was supposed to go then he was glad he'd never been in love before. Too much of this nonsense he'd either go insane or catch a case.

19

"Thank you. Whoever is in charge of writing my life story, thank you." Toreas was still angry, with Jared, with her mother and with fate.

She stood in shock, turning from side to side, wondering how they'd gotten to where they were. She knew she should be feeling relief at not having consummated the act with Jared, but she wasn't. She was hurt and confused, just as...

Toreas stood still, staring after the door. She thought of the look on Jared's face that he'd tried to hide but couldn't. At first she thought she'd only imagined it, but now she knew she hadn't. Jared was hurt and confused by something she'd done and for the life of her she didn't understand why. She did know he was a jackass for calling her names.

He'd told her to ask him for promises. He couldn't possibly know that the only promise she wanted from him was that he would love her forever. How could she tell him that after his half-hearted and asinine "I-care-about-you speech. That wasn't what she wanted from him. She wanted his love.

For the first time in her life since knowing Brian Johnson, she was looking forward to seeing him. She'd never have to worry about that little twerp calling her a prostitute. Her brothers would beat the crap out of him.

Maybe she should invite Jared to Georgia. Then when they were all seated she'd announce all the things Jared had said to her.

She almost smiled at the thought. Until she remembered that he said he'd never fall in love with someone like her. Now how was she supposed to stop loving him? She'd only recently admitted to herself that she did. In spite of everything that had happened, she wasn't ready to stop.

✍

Jared walked away from Toreas's apartment angrier than he'd ever been in his entire life.

Toreas was crazy. He'd known it from the first day she'd punched him. He wasn't kidding when he said she should be committed, but so should he. He would have to be given the padded cell right next to hers.

Damn her anyway. He thought they'd gotten past all of that. They hadn't. She thought he was only good enough for her to sleep with. *Correction*, he thought, *good enough to have sex with, not good enough to take home to meet her folks.*

He reached his car and threw the bag viciously in the rear seat, then slammed the door with such force he was surprised he didn't shatter the window.

He noted the time on the dash. He cringed, wondering how less than an hour ago he had been thinking of buying stock in a condom company. What a joke. He had yet to rip open the first packet and the way he was feeling at the moment he didn't want to touch Toreas Rose.

He was glad he hadn't told her he loved her. It was obvious she wanted him for only one thing. He was not into studding for hire. She could just go to hell.

Jared gritted his teeth in anger. He was as bad as Toreas. Her eyes told him she loved him, her smile, her lips, her body. Damn, he had to stop thinking like that. He wanted to continue being angry with her for being such a coward.

She was feisty when it came to punching him on live television but when it came to admitting he was now a part of her life, she'd folded. He wished she'd asked him for a promise. He would have delivered.

He was driving much too fast, trying to calm down, to slow the beating of his heart. He could feel the pounding in his chest making him want to pound something also.

He'd been right to resist getting involved with a romance writer. They were nuts, all of them.

You're one of them now, Jared. The thought came from out of nowhere. Still, he refused to take back his words. *I'm nuts to have hooked up with them.*

Jared kept trying to make some sense out of what had happened. He had no desire to go with Toreas to Georgia, to meet her parents, to play a part he was too old to play.

Alone in his car it was still hard to admit that he was hurting because she didn't seem to need him, or want him. He'd heard her mother clearly ask if there was anyone special in her life. She had not even batted an eye when she answered no.

He'd never felt like this, ever. He had thought at the time when

Gina two-timed him that nothing would ever get to him again. This was nothing like that. This was ten thousand times worse. He'd never truly loved Gina.

And I'll get over loving that snobby little prude. He banged his hand on the dash. He knew just the remedy. If one thing didn't work, try another. That had always been his motto. He'd momentarily forgotten. He wouldn't make that mistake again.

Jared was barely in his home before he had his address book out and was dialing a number. Laura answered on the second ring. She was just what he needed to take his mind off a woman he despised.

He didn't bother changing when she agreed to lunch. He turned around and made his way back to his car, heading toward Laura's home.

"You can have your Johnson boy, Little-Miss-Goody-Two-Shoes. And you can both rot in Georgia."

Laura answered the door smiling a welcome, inviting Jared in with a toss of her long hair over her shoulder and a seductive sway of her hips.

Now this was more like it. Laura was almost six feet tall with legs that went on forever. He observed her clothes, Christian Dior, no doubt. The outfit she had on easily cost eight hundred dollars.

He continued his appraisal of her as she went to the kitchen to get him a cola. Her long raven hair was silky and professionally done, her nails long and painted a bright red to match her lips. This was more like it, more how he liked his women.

Jared took the proffered drink and placed it on the edge of the coffee table. Then he took Laura in his arms, the smell of Elizabeth Taylor's Passion wafting into his nostrils.

It was nice but it wasn't the smell he'd developed a yen for. It wasn't Toreas. He stopped what he was doing for a moment and looked at Laura, scolding himself for thinking of Toreas when he was here to forget.

He brought his lips down to cover hers. They didn't taste like strawberries. He closed his eyes tightly and plunged his tongue deep into Laura's mouth. Everything was all wrong. Her mouth didn't feel right. She didn't feel right in his arms and he sure as hell knew he wasn't the only man who'd kissed her like that. Her movements were practiced and guarded. She wasn't as giving. Sure, she was squirming and moaning in his arms but it wasn't what he wanted.

Damn that annoying woman, he thought as Toreas's face flashed into his mind. He stopped kissing Laura, desperate to erase the craving for strawberry flavored lips. He plunged his hand under Laura's expensive silk blouse to touch her skin. There must be something wrong with him. Her skin felt strange.

He rubbed the tips of his fingers together trying to adjust. He pushed his head under her blouse, pushing it up higher and out of the way, ignoring her word of caution not to rip her blouse. He had to taste her. Maybe that would push Toreas out of his mind.

As his tongue licked her breast a spasm of awareness shook him. Toreas had hexed him. She'd done something to him so he'd never find pleasure in another woman's body.

He drew back, shaking, ignoring Laura's look of apprehension. She was looking at him with something resembling fear.

"I'm sorry," he mumbled, "let's just go to lunch." How could he tell her that he couldn't complete what he'd started? It sounded stupid even to him. How could he tell Laura that she didn't taste like strawberries, that he no longer liked the scent of perfume but only one woman's natural aroma?

He trailed Laura out the door. She was exactly the kind of woman he'd always been attracted to. Jared watched her behind move up and down as she walked. Nothing.

He knew she was probably wondering what had happened. It was better if she never knew. How could he tell her that his fingers didn't like touching her skin, or that she was too tall? How could he tell her that he was hopelessly in love with the most irritating woman on earth?

Despite Jared's best intentions he'd not been able to shove Toreas from his mind. His lunch with Laura had proven that. He took Laura home knowing he'd never see her again. Even if he wanted to there was no way she would ever consent to it. He'd done nothing but talk about Toreas the entire time. Toward the end she was looking at him in amusement and he didn't like it. Of course he knew the source of Laura's amusement. Him. Every few minutes he was saying how he never wanted to see Toreas again, then he'd go into a rant that told otherwise.

Now he was glaring at nothing in particular, angry that he'd not just told Toreas he loved her, that she'd not told him she loved him. And hell, he was hurt that she'd not considered him special, that she didn't want him to meet her parents. That was no way for them to start off a relationship.

Miss-Judgmental-Know-It-All-Prude had judged him one too many times and jumped to conclusions that were not true. Then it hit him. Toreas was so good at assuming and then finding the person guilty, he wondered if she'd judged her parents just as unfairly. Could it be possible she'd assumed how her parents felt? He smiled. Of course it could. Why would her parents subsidize her dream if they were so awful?

He thought of something else. She refused to accept his feelings for her and was forever throwing up roadblocks. Okay, he had to be honest. He hadn't helped matters with that 'I care about you' remark. But her parents were another thing. Maybe she'd gotten it in her pretty, stubborn head that they felt something that they didn't.

Either way Jared had to know the truth. He reached for the phone. Since the romance writer in Toreas Rose could only believe the impossible and wanted things on the heroic scale he'd have to find a way to give it to her. He'd have to let her know that his 'I care about you' meant he loved her.

"Hell no, Jared," he admonished himself, "you're damn well going to tell that woman that you love her." When the operator came on the line Jared had his plan already laid out.

✍

For the next few days Toreas did her best not to think of Jared. She'd taken the three boxes of condoms and shoved them into the small garbage can under the sink, but she neglected to empty the can on trash day.

Jared was right, she was a hypocrite. She was always judging people on the same things she did, the same things she thought. She hated that habit, had tried her best to get rid of it, but still it clung to her.

She wanted to tell him she was sorry for hurting his feelings, but was afraid he'd slam the phone down in her ear. Besides that, his remarks to her still stung. He'd been so angry when he left that he probably never wanted to see her again.

Maybe fate knew better than she. After all, she was moving back to Georgia in a couple of months anyway. It didn't really make sense to begin anything with Jared.

Still, the thought of Thanksgiving dinner with her parents and Brian Johnson made her shiver with fright. If she didn't do something they would have her engaged and married in the blink of an eye.

She could think of nothing. She'd given her word, two years to become a writer. And her father had given his money. He'd stuck to his end of the bargain. Now it was time for her to live up to hers. It was time for her to forget about romance and to forget about Jared Stone.

Toreas waited until Tuesday morning to pack her bags, dreading the long drive, dreading Georgia. Dreading Brian Johnson and her brothers' kidding, but most of all dreading the thought that she would never see Jared again.

Just as she was ready to inspect her apartment to make sure no electrical appliances were left on and that the gas burners were off before taking down her bags, the phone rang.

She walked toward it, annoyed, knowing it would be her mother on the other end. She'd already called twice, reminding her to get an early start. She'd asked both times if Toras had changed her mind, if she wanted to bring anyone with her. Where in the heck did her mother think she was going to get this person? Have him materialize out of thin air? Toreas shook her head. Her mother's question had made no sense. She reached for the phone without even bothering checking the caller ID. She was annoyed that her mother wouldn't stop calling. She wanted to ask her how she was to accomplish leaving if she kept calling every hour.

"Ask me."

Toreas gripped the phone in her hand and sank into a chair.

"Ask me."

There was no apology. No hello. Nothing. Just the silence of an unasked question hanging between them. She could have pretended not to understand what he wanted her to ask, but they both knew it would be a lie.

Her voice was thick with tears. She knew she was supposed to slam the phone down in his ear, tell him where to go, but she didn't. "Jared, would you like to go to Georgia with me for Thanksgiving?"

Her stomach was in knots and now the tears were falling. This whole thing was not happening the way it was supposed to. She was strong. She didn't need Jared, not with his cocksure attitude. But she wanted him.

"Yes."

"I'm leaving in five minutes." Toreas swiped at the tears running down her cheeks, determined not to sniffle, not to let him know she was crying.

"I'm downstairs waiting for you."

"I'll be right down." She blotted the tears with the sweater she was wearing as she raced out the door.

The elevator door opened on Jared standing there waiting for her, his look solemn. He took her bags from her hands and sat them next to his own.

He looked at her for a moment, then with one finger brushed away the remaining tears. "I'm sorry."

"So am I," she whispered as she followed him out the door and to her car.

She faced him expectantly. He pressed his body against hers, his arms at his side. She closed her eyes and gave in to the sweetness of the moment, not minding the return of her tears. His chin rested on her head before he leaned down and gave her lips a gentle rub with the pad of one finger.

Toreas waited while he hefted the bags into the trunk of her car. *There should be more*, she thought. When the last bag was placed into the trunk Jared turned toward her.

They stood for a long moment staring at each other. Then she was in his arms and he was holding her tight. Neither of them spoke and she knew it was because they were both afraid.

When they broke apart, Jared held Toreas's face between his hands and kissed away the remaining tears.

He opened the passenger door for her, ignoring the fact that it was her car. Toreas slid into the passenger seat, not objecting. She liked it. She liked him thinking he was in charge.

If her life were truly a story it would flop. Women no longer liked the same things she did. She was going backwards, loving this man who was trying to possess her, who did possess her soul and her love.

He closed the door and she handed him the map giving him a moment to see the directions she had circled. She wondered if he would go a completely different way just to prove he was the man and she couldn't possibly map out a route to drive out of state.

It didn't matter. She would follow wherever he led. She would be like Ruth from the Bible. "Where thou goeth, I will follow."

She gave him a few more minutes to adjust his seat and head for the expressway before she spoke. "Why is this so important to you?" she asked him, watching his face intently.

"Because you're important to me," he replied.

It wasn't an "I love you," but it sure as heck was better than "I care for you."

She felt the warmth surge through her veins. The knots in her stomach loosened and she relaxed in the seat. She was important to him.

"Toreas."

"Yes."

"Why do you want me to come to Georgia with you?" Jared glanced sideways at her, ready for her smart alecky answer. He arched a brow in her direction before returning his gaze to the road. "You'd better not say because I asked you to ask. Now again, why do you want me to come with you to Georgia? Why do you want me to meet your family? And why now at Thanksgiving, when it's a time for family and loved ones?"

Toreas grinned. This one she would give to Jared. She'd missed him. He was as stubborn as she was. She turned in order to look at his profile and saw his clenched jaw as he waited for her answer. "I wanted you to come to Georgia with me, Jared, because it is

Thanksgiving and it's a time for loved ones and friends and family. You're an important part of my life and we should be together on Thanksgiving giving thanks for that.

She could swear he was downright preening. She couldn't believe it. If he didn't have a swelled head before he sure would now. Toreas shook her head and laughed, not taking back one word she'd spoken.

"I have the end of my book. Want to read it?" Jared asked.

"Sure." Toreas reached for the folded paper he pulled from his shirt pocket and settled back, wondering what he'd say this time.

> *She was stubborn and pigheaded,*
> *something he'd never wanted until she*
> *whizzed into his life bringing her*
> *litany of complaints. Now he couldn't*
> *think of being without her. She thought*
> *him an immoral clod and had judged him*
> *unfairly, convicting him without a trial,*
> *not even allowing him to make a statement*
> *in his own defense. With anyone else he*
> *would not have cared. With her it was*
> *different. She'd gotten under his skin*
> *and had wormed her way into his heart*
> *and his life. She doubted him and his*
> *feelings yet she'd never bothered to*
> *admit her own. Something would have to*
> *change and shortly. He was going crazy*
> *like this. Soon, very soon, he'd make*
> *sure she never doubted him again. And*
> *if she thought she'd be the heroine and*
> *rescue him, she was wrong. He was intent*
> *on showing her that she was the one who*
> *needed rescuing. He scratched his head and*
> *sighed as he closed his eyes, knowing his*
> *thoughts were a lie. He needed rescuing as*
> *badly as she did. Maybe with his actions he*
> *could save them both. Maybe they were just*
> *what the other needed.*

She held the paper to her chest. Not exactly a love letter. She couldn't help the smile that pulled at the corners of her mouth. This time she wouldn't question him. This time she'd let it be, just enjoy the fact that Jared was here in the car with her and he was there because he'd wanted to be.

For several hours they drove in companionable silence, the only sounds in the car their breathing and the music playing softly in the background.

From time to time Toreas would look at Jared. His mouth looked pinched and she knew he was feeling the same way. If they talked they might get into a fight. So they both chose to remain silent.

Her glance fell on the gas gauge and she wondered if she should draw his attention to it. Men could be such babies about things like that and their reconciliation was teetering on the brink of fragility.

She smiled to herself. There was more than one way of getting a man to do what needed doing. Toreas had never played the game herself but she'd seen it played and she'd read about it. Now to see if it would work. "Jared, do you think we could stop somewhere for a few minutes? I'm getting tired."

He glanced at her. "I'm sorry, I should have thought about that. The next service station we'll stop." He glanced down at the gas gauge and a look of surprise came over his face.

If this had happened a week ago Toreas would have asked him why he was looking so surprised? And would have possibly added that cars didn't run on air. Now she'd rather do it this way. She wasn't used to babying a man's ego, but for the next few days she intended to try. It might prove interesting.

In a matter of moments several signs appeared and she heard the click of the turn signal as Jared prepared to pull in and get gas.

"So are you looking forward to seeing this...this... Johnson boy?"

He wasn't looking at her and she was trying hard to figure if her answer could in any way lead to an argument. "Not in the least."

"Isn't he the man your parents approve of, the man they want for you?"

"Yes, but he's not the man I want." Her eyes were glued to his face. He turned his smoky gaze on her, then brought her hand to his lips and kissed it. He held on to her hand, not letting go until they pulled alongside the gas pump.

Toreas got out to stretch her legs and stood beside Jared as he pumped the gas. She couldn't help noticing the pinched look was gone from his mouth.

"If you're tired we can get a room for a couple of hours and rest."

His eyes were teasing but she knew he meant it. "If I'm late my parents will have the highway patrol out looking for me."

"You're a big girl. You can take care of yourself."

"I know, but remember they don't know I'm not traveling alone. If they were aware you were with me they wouldn't worry. They would know you would protect me." Toreas wanted to gag. This fragile male ego thing could be a drag.

When he smiled at her she forgot that thought. She was now

turning into one of those women who were doing feminine things in the name of love. And it felt good.

Jared was enjoying the idea of being her protector. She hoped Kelle would forgive her for allowing him to believe that. But then again, Kelle had a husband, and so did Liz.

Husband. She rolled the word around on her tongue. They'd only had a few months of dating and more than a few months of fighting and here she was fantasizing about walking down the aisle with him. But God, did she want to. If someone was really writing the script for her life, she'd have to ask them if they could please do something sappy and make love between a romance writer and a romance critic become reality. *Please, whoever is listening, let Jared tell me he loves me. Let him ask me to marry him and I'll never ask for another thing as long as I live.* Toreas smiled to herself at her silliness and amended her request. *I'll not ask for another thing this weekend.*

Their hour break for gas and food was what they both needed. They returned to the easy conversation they'd shared during the two months when they'd shared dinner each night and later their secret months of dating. It wasn't until they were back on the highway that the conversation took a serious turn.

"I never should have spoken to you the way I did," Jared confessed.

"You were angry." Toreas looked out the window, not really wanting to revisit that night.

She saw him eyeing her sharply from her peripheral vision. "I was hurt." His admission surprised her.

"I'm sorry I hurt you. It was never my intention. But you made me realize that I am a self-righteous hypocrite."

"Don't," he started, but she shushed him. "I'm sorry for always judging you, Jared. I've always hated being judged. You would think I wouldn't do it to others."

"Who's judging you?"

"You'd be surprised." She laughed and he glanced again at her. Even she could hear the bitterness in the sound.

"You wouldn't really understand unless you grew up in a small town where everyone's in your business. The wrath of the Lord is constantly thrown in your face, making you fearful."

She thought for a moment before continuing. She'd never said the words out loud, not even to herself but she wanted to say them to Jared

"People of the church always thought they were teaching us to love God. I don't know about anyone else, but that wasn't what happened to me."

"What do you mean?"

"I was afraid of God. I grew so paranoid about it that he became a constant voice in my head chastising me for my wrongdoings. There was no place I could hide. He was my critic, always there."

She laughed for real then. "As I got older God got company. My father joined as one of the critics, then the entire congregation. I had to get out of there. They were everywhere critiquing my words, my walk, both physical and spiritual, my dress."

She caught his gaze on her clothes and hit him playfully on the shoulder. "I guess it would have been all right but I didn't believe everything I was told. How could I love a God that I was afraid of?"

"Is that why you chose to write romance novels? Were you rebelling?"

"No, though my father thinks so. There were many things I rebelled against. But my writing had nothing to do with that. I saw how much my mother and father loved each other and I wanted that." She blushed. "I wanted to read about it. Then later I wanted to write about love."

"So why do you have so much trouble with...," he coughed, "certain scenes?"

"That one's easy." She smiled at him. "I left Georgia, but those internal critics of mine moved to Chicago with me. I'm constantly in conflict between what I was taught and what I want to do. So you see, you were right when you called me a hypocrite."

Jared was listening to Toreas, aware that she was sharing her most intimate thoughts with him. "You picked a hard dream."

"Don't I know it."

"Why don't you write inspirational romances? Maybe that would work for you."

"How do you...?"

"I've been learning. So, why don't you?"

"Because I'm not the prude you think I am. I want to write about the sensuous side of love. You might not believe this, but sometimes I have really naughty thoughts and I want to put them on paper. I just don't want porn."

He wanted to ask her something. He could tell she was watching him and he wished they were someplace besides the car having this conversation. "How do you manage to...to make love with all the guilt?"

Toreas was blushing. He'd half expected it. Still, he was curious. How was she planning on them having a relationship?

"Let's say I've done the deed without the enjoyment."

He knew it. Had known it from the time he'd first kissed her in her apartment. "So you aren't planning on enjoying the things I'm planning to do to you?"

She didn't answer him. He reached for her hand and gave a squeeze. "Will you feel guilty when we finally make love?"

He was certain they would and making sure she knew he planned on it. By the time they left Georgia, if everything went according to his plan, they would be making love to each other for their rest of their lives. "Toreas," Jared called softly. "Will you feel guilty making love to me?"

"I hope not. For some reason, Jared, I haven't felt guilty about anything I've done with you."

Her hand was out of his and covering her mouth. He peeped at her and saw that her eyes were closed. His chest swelled with pride and his body tingled. "Any reason why?"

"You're important to me," she answered and laid her head on his shoulder. "Now can we change this conversation?"

"Not just yet," Jared said, nodding his head up and down. He'd just gotten an idea; something that he felt would help Toreas. He didn't think she'd ever be able to write love scenes as freely as most romances called for.

"What are you thinking, Jared?"

"Toreas, why don't you write a romance like we've had?" She was eyeing him with amusement then she started laughing.

"I'm serious. We've had the heat, the fire, but we haven't taken that final step yet."

"Not because we haven't tried."

"So why can't you write characters who go through much the same thing?"

"Well, Jared, I'm hoping this condition with us doesn't remain like this. What about you?"

She'd actually gone there. He didn't believe it. She was unpredictable. "Baby, you have no idea. When we leave Georgia we're coming home and the first thing I'm going to do even if I have to bind and gag you is make love to you."

"I can't put that in a book," Toreas laughed, accepting the kiss Jared gave her, but thinking that his idea was a good one, at least for a story. "Okay, Jared, I'll do it, at least I'll try."

"Good, now we have one more problem. What are you going to do about the deal you made with your father?"

"That's hard also. Can't we talk about the weather or something easier?"

Jared got a funny feeling in his gut. "Is there something you're not telling me?" He waited. She was trying to find a way to answer him. That meant trouble.

"I'm planning on moving back home."

"When did you decide that?" He was afraid he knew the answer to that.

"The night we fought. I called my mother and told her I was moving home."

"When we get there tell them you changed your mind."

"It's not that easy, Jared. I gave my word."

"What about us?" She was licking her lips and she looked so darn lonely that he had to hold her. He pulled the car off to the shoulder and gathered her in his arms. He kissed her face, her eyelids, her cheeks and still he wanted more. This was the taste he was addicted to. The taste of this strawberry flavored woman. This Toreas Rose, the woman he loved. Somehow they would work together to find an answer.

20

With Toreas's directions Jared pulled into the driveway of her parents' home and killed the engine. He looked at her. She'd been extremely quiet the closer they came to her hometown.

"Are you ready?" He brushed his hand along the side of her cheek.

"That's the question I should be asking you. Don't say I didn't warn you."

"Don't worry about me. I've been waiting for this moment my entire life," Jared said softly as he looked intently in her eyes.

Before Toreas could contemplate the meaning of Jared's words he kissed her quickly, stopping all musings. It was time to do it, face the family. *Help!*

Together they got out of the car with Jared gently pushing Toreas toward the door, telling her he would get the bags. She looked scared. He wanted to take her in his arms but was wondering if that was what she was afraid of. He watched her tug on the heavy sweater, then button her coat as if she was getting ready for inspection.

The door was opened by a woman who looked remarkably like Toreas, only several inches taller and older. The woman threw her arms around Toreas and stopped abruptly on spotting him.

He noticed the older woman's long curly hair and knew instantly that was the reason Toreas wore her own in a rapidly expanding afro. She was trying her best to disassociate herself from her mother's world.

Jared watched the silent communication pass between mother and daughter.

"Mom, this is Jared. Jared, my mom, Julie Rose."

Jared stuck out his hand and smiled. "Nice to meet you, Mrs. Rose." He stood with the bags in his hand watching Toreas shifting.

"Jared's staying with us for Thanksgiving," he heard Toreas whisper, then look defiantly at her mother. "Unless you'd rather we go into town and get a motel room."

He waited for Toreas to blush and was surprised when she didn't. A remark like that from him would have turned her soft skin into several shades of crimson.

"Jared's welcome to stay as your guest, Tesa, but what about Brian Johnson? I told you we invited him."

"Then you entertain him, Mom. I want to spend my Thanksgiving with Jared. Besides, Brian should spend the holiday with his family, not with us."

The two women stood studying each other. Jared was amused watching them and slightly confused about the reception. But he decided to give it a few minutes. Besides, he rather liked the idea of Toreas fighting for him even if there were no need. He'd already fought the battle and won.

He thought of offering to go alone to the motel, but something in Toreas's stance told him she needed to do this.

"So Mom, do we come in, or do you want Jared to hold on to those bags forever?"

He noticed a spot of color dust the older woman's cheeks. "I'm sorry, Jared. I forgot my manners. Please come in." She opened the door wide and waved them inside.

He could hear her voice as she trailed after them. "I was just a little surprised. I spoke to Tesa twice this morning and she never mentioned bringing a friend. The woman gave Jared a quick wink and put her finger to her lips to shush him. *Ahh*, Jared thought, *this will be interesting*. He was ready and willing to have a co-conspirator and a friend.

Before he could answer Toreas piped in. "That was my fault. I didn't ask him until the last minute." She smiled at Jared. "I'm glad he said yes."

For the first time since meeting her mother, Jared knew the smile was truly for him. The rest of it was a battle she evidently thought she needed to fight. Little did she know the battle had been already won. But if Toreas didn't gear up for battle he wouldn't know it was her, now would he?

"Jared, let me show you to the guest room." Before he could answer Toreas, her mother stepped in front of them both.

"I'm sorry, that room's all torn up. I think Jared will be more comfortable in the basement. He can have his own private bathroom and no one will bother him." She averted her gaze, telling him she wanted him sleeping as far away from her daughter as it was possible to put him.

Sensing Toreas's objection, Jared smiled. "That would be

wonderful. Thank you. It's really thoughtful of you to give me a bathroom all to myself."

Julie Rose turned, the look on her face saying she wasn't sure if he was being sarcastic or was truly issuing thanks. She frowned at him, then glared at Toreas before leading him down the basement stairs.

It was really better than he had expected. The room was finished and quite comfortable. The bathroom had a claw foot tub, large enough for two. He glanced over Julie's head at Toreas.

Their gazes met and he glanced once again at the tub, eliciting the blush he had known would come.

The older Rose started for the stairs, calling for her daughter to follow her.

"I'll be up in a few minutes, Mom. I want to show Jared where everything is."

"I'm sure he won't have any problem finding things. Your dad will be home soon, so you might want to take your bags to your room."

Jared grinned at Toreas when he heard the door close. "That wasn't so bad." He reached his arms out for her, sighing as she entered them. "Are you really glad I came?"

"Yes, but by the end of this trip you might wish you hadn't come. Believe me, after a few days here you'll know just why I couldn't wait to get away. This entire town is stifling. In a couple of hours everyone will not only know you're here, they'll likely have more information on you than the FBI."

They both laughed. As if on cue, Toreas's mother called her once again to come up.

Jared kissed her slowly, not wanting to stop. "Listen, Toreas, I need to tell you something. I never finished telling you about Gina." Her head went down and he took the pad of his finger and lifted it back up. "My unhappiness was never about Gina. My mother had made me promise to give her grandchildren. Even though she was half-kidding I'd still given her the promise. I'd never broken a promise to her or to anyone," he said meaningfully. "I had thought that maybe I was in love with Gina. That maybe I could keep the promise I'd made to my mother."

"Jared?"

He leaned into Toreas and kissed her forehead, holding her in his arms for a long moment before pulling slightly away to look into her eyes. "My mother was killed in an auto accident shortly after that fiasco with Gina."

"I'm so sorry, Jared."

"I know, baby. I loved my mother dearly. We'd already lost my father so it was just the two of us. The pain and unwarranted guilt made me go after romance writers. I blamed them for taking Gina from me, for my not fulfilling the promise I'd made to my mother. I couldn't get over wishing I'd given my mother the grandchildren she'd wanted." He smiled. "But there was no way I could have kept that promise then. I had not yet met the woman I wanted to spend the rest of my life with."

"Tesa, you'd better come on up here now and let Jared get settled in," Julie yelled down.

"You'd better go," Jared said, raining soft kisses on Toreas's face. "I'll give you a few minutes alone before I come up." He brushed her lips lightly with his thumb, then turned her in the direction of the stairs.

Jared nosed around the basement, picking up odds and ends, trying to get a sense of the family that lived there. He saw pictures of smiling faces that radiated love.

Toreas's face was the one that stuck out in the family photographs, her expression morose, unlike that of her parents and brothers.

He glanced at his watch. Twenty minutes should be long enough for her mother to give her the third degree. He started for the stairs but stopped near the top when he heard Julie Rose's voice.

"Why did you lie?" he heard the older woman ask her daughter.

He heard the defensiveness in Toreas's voice. "What are you talking about?"

"You said you didn't have anyone special to invite here. It's obvious you're in love with him."

Jared's hand was reaching for the knob. He stopped. This was eavesdropping, pure and simple, but he didn't care. He inched his head closer to the door to hear her answer.

Toreas's voice was raised, panic punctuating her words. "Please don't embarrass me, Mom. Jared doesn't know."

"He doesn't know you love him? How can that be possible?"

"We're too busy fighting all the time. Plus, he told me that he cares for me. Can you believe that? How was I supposed to tell him that I love him?"

"I see what you mean, honey. Men tend to be rather dense concerning matters of the heart.

Jared heard both women laugh, then Toreas's voice pleading again with her mother not to say anything to anyone.

"Tesa, honey, it's obvious he loves you too. I saw the way he was looking at you."

"He has to tell me that, Mom."

"Tesa, honey, how does he look at you and talk to you? Does he treat you like he loves you? He's here with you. You know that says something."

"But I don't want to just go on clues or hints. I could be wrong. I want him to tell me." *The way the hero does in romances,* she thought.

"Some men just have a hard time saying it."

"Not Daddy."

"Please!"

"Daddy always tells me he loves me."

"You're his daughter. But me, ha, I don't think he ever said the words to me until I laid you in his arms. A two year courtship, marriage and two sons and it wasn't until I gave him a daughter that he told me he loved me."

"Mom, you never knew?"

"Of course I knew. Are you crazy? Do you think I would have married your father wondering if he loved me? His touch, his smile, his eyes, everything in the way he treated me told me he loved me. The way he held me shouted his love to the heavens and back. That was always more important to me."

"Did you tell him that you loved him?"

"A million times."

"Didn't you get angry when he wouldn't say the words back to you?"

Toreas watched as a smile came over her mother's face.

"Tesa, honey, you have a lot to learn. The way your father has always made me feel, the way he looked at me then and looks at me now, that man could always make me melt. I knew he loved me in his arms or out of his arms. I always knew and I don't believe you when you say you don't know if Jared loves you. If you didn't know that he loves you, you wouldn't have brought him home."

"But I want him to say the words, Mom. I need to hear them."

"Did Fred ever tell you that he loved you?"

"Yes."

"Did you believe him?"

Toreas felt a shiver of dread. "No."

"Did you tell him that you loved him?"

Again the shiver. "I don't really remember. I might have."

"Honey, it's not always the words men say, it's what in their eyes and in Jared's eyes is his love for you."

This time Toreas didn't care if she was being stubborn. "Mom, I know I love him and I think he loves me. But I want to hear him tell me the words. I'm not you. I won't marry him and wait until I've had three babies before he finally tells me. He will have to tell me he loves me way before then."

"So you're planning to marry him?"

Toreas shook her head and laughed. "One thing at a time."

"But you want to?"

"Why are you being so insistent? He hasn't asked."

"But if he did, Tesa, what would you say? Do you love him enough to want to spend the rest of your life with him?"

"Mom, don't push okay. I can't answer that question until it's asked. I can't do anything until Jared tells me he loves me." Toreas cut into the homemade chocolate cake sitting in front of her wondering why on earth her mother was so bent on marrying her off to Jared. She'd only met him twenty minutes ago. Did they really want to see her married so badly that it didn't make a difference if the man didn't profess his dying love? Maybe that approach had worked for her mother but it wouldn't for Toreas. "The cake is very good, Mom," Toreas said around a mouth full of fudge, intentionally changing the conversation.

✑

Jared backed softly down the stairs. *He had to tell her that he loved her?* What the heck did she think he'd been doing for the past few months? And the nerve of them thinking men were dense. Well, he had a surprise for his lady love and when it was revealed she'd never think he was dense ever again. He shook his head in disbelief before running nosily back up, calling out for Toreas, alerting her that he was coming.

For over an hour he sat with Toreas and her mother eating chocolate cake and all the other goodies her mother put before him. Now that they were con-conspirators Julie Rose had warmed considerably. She only mentioned Brian Johnson once and that was to say maybe she should call his mother and tell her the plans had changed.

The moment she went toward the phone Toreas looked at Jared. "Now begins the small town telegraph." To which they both laughed.

He watched Toreas in her family home, testing the sound of Tesa, the name her family called her. He liked it. He also liked thinking of her as Toreas Rose, or maybe Toreas Stone, or Tesa Stone.

"Jared, you're not listening to me."

"I guess not," he admitted. "I was thinking of doing something else, but don't worry, it included you." He reached out and gave her a hug as she started to blush.

And that was his introduction to her father, William Rose. The man stood glaring at him as though he had caught him breaking into his home and stealing his most prized possession.

He tapped Toreas's shoulder. "I think your father's home." He stood then, his hand outstretched. "Hello Mr. Rose, I'm Jared Stone."

He watched as the man's glare became even fiercer. Jared looked toward Toreas, then back toward her father.

"Jared Stone. Why are you here? Aren't you the critic who was hounding my daughter on national television?"

The man's angry gaze swung to his daughter. "Tesa, what is the meaning of this? Why did you bring this man to our home? He's the critic."

"I know, Dad. Since I've always had critics in my life, I thought it was time I invited another." Both men looked at her, watching her grin in amusement.

"Jared's my friend." She refused to look away from the fury in his eyes. "Actually he's a lot more than that. He's important to me, Daddy, and it's important that he spend Thanksgiving with us. He's going to be in my life for a long time. I want you to be nice to him."

She smiled at her father, then went to hug him, hugging him so tightly that he tried to pull away. "I love you, Daddy, please be nice to him," she whispered in her father's ear. She wanted to whisper that she also loved Jared.

She felt her father's arms tightening around her and knew he would do his best. She'd forgotten to tell him that she'd made peace with Jared, that he was no longer the enemy.

Before anyone could say another word, both of her brothers bounded into the room and rushed toward her, lifting her high into the air and passing her back and forth between them as though she were nothing more than a football.

Toreas wished that Kelle had taught her something to do in this situation. They were literally throwing her and from the sound of their laughter, enjoying it.

"Would you two baboons put me down? We have company."

For a split second she was suspended in midair as both brothers momentarily forgot her while turning toward Jared. Then in the same instant they both put out their arms, catching her between them.

They deposited her on the floor, hugged her to them, kissed her cheeks and turned to Jared all in a matter of seconds.

"This is Jared Stone." She introduced her brothers.

"You kicked this big guy's butt?" Billy asked.

Billy and Michael laughed and shook hands with Jared. Toreas had expected they would be as angry with him as her father but their attitude was entirely different. They seemed to like him. For that she was thankful. But something strange was going on. It was as if her entire family already knew Jared. They were being much too calm, not drilling him. The more she thought about it, even their initial glaring had been too mild. What the heck was wrong with these people?

"What the heck do you have on?" Her brother Michael looked at her, frowning. "Your clothes are ugly."

"And too big," her oldest brother Billy chimed in. "What are you doing, buying your clothes from a flea market?"

She turned toward Jared, seeing the smirk she had known would be there on his face. She wished she knew a karate punch that would take the three of them down in one fell swoop.

Then her father got in on the act, surveying her. Apparently he hadn't noticed her clothes before in his anger at finding Jared sitting in the middle of the kitchen with her in his arms.

"Tesa, the boys are right. Why are you wearing those clothes and where on earth did you get them?"

"I've been trying to save money, so I sometimes buy my clothes at secondhand stores." She was praying that for once she wouldn't blush.

"Why? You could have asked me for money." Then she watched as her father frowned. "What happened to the clothes you had before? You never dressed like this when you were dating Fred. Where are those clothes?" He growled at her and frowned more fiercely, then glared at Jared. "And you cut off your beautiful hair."

"Don't blame Jared. I cut my hair because it's easier to manage. And I changed my wardrobe before I ever met him. This is more my style." She pulled on the huge sweater, then twirled around, pretending not to be mortified. It was one thing for Jared to call her clothes ugly. She didn't even mind her brothers' comments, but for them to do it together, they were ganging up on her.

"You're going shopping with your mother tomorrow."

"No, Dad, I owe you enough already."

"This isn't a loan. It's a gift."

"I like my clothes."

"I don't and you're not going to church with us looking as if you've no family to take care of you."

"Why don't you just have Mom tell Mrs. Johnson that I dress like this on my own? The town should know in a minute that my dress is not your fault." She knew immediately she had gone too far.

The four men she loved were staring at her. Her father's face wore a wounded expression and her brothers wore identical looks of contrition. Jared's look was embarrassed amusement.

"I'm sorry." She hugged her father, then kissed his cheek. "I'll go shopping in the morning with Mom for a proper dress to wear to church on Thursday." She felt like what she'd always tried to be, Daddy's good little girl. "But Daddy, I have enough money to pay for the dress myself." She held up a hand. "No argument, I'll buy the dress."

During dinner Jared talked with her brothers. He appeared to be enjoying their good natured teasing and she wondered at that. Their teasing was always a bone of contention with her. It annoyed her.

Hours later when she went to bed, Jared was still being entertained by her family. They barely seemed to notice when she said goodnight, except to yell a cheery goodnight back to her.

She lay in her old bed fuming, feeling a weird jealousy. Her family had stolen Jared's attention, and he had stolen theirs. She was the only one not having a good time with any of them.

Her family had never been this much fun. Why was Jared enjoying them? Why wasn't he bored out of his skull? She heard hearty laughter coming from the living room, causing her to shove a pillow over her head. They were disproving everything she'd told Jared about them, everything she'd thought of them. Where the heck had this family come from? And what had they done with her true family?

Wednesday she barely had time to see Jared. Immediately after breakfast her brothers and father took off with him. When her mother appeared in the door of the kitchen as she was finishing up with the breakfast dishes, she informed Toreas they were going shopping.

By the time they returned home she had been hugged by so many people she was sure she had people burn from their rubbing their cheeks against hers.

When had this town become so loving, so fond of her? They behaved as if they genuinely loved her and had missed her. How could that be possible? She'd always been as obnoxious a brat as she could get away with.

Of course obnoxious for her was refusing to accept a piece of cake from one of the neighbors her mother had forced her to do errands for. They probably hadn't noticed, or else they had forgotten.

Toreas was glad she had a moment alone with her mother. She had some worries about her relationship with Jared. As much as she didn't want to tell her mother she seemed unable to keep it from her.

"I'm worried about the way Jared and I are always fighting," she began.

"Why?" her mother answered. "All couples fight."

She took a moment to digest that word, *couple*. Was that what she and Jared were? *A couple*? "I want to be like you and Daddy," she confessed. "You guys never fight."

Her mother laughed till tears ran down her face. Toreas frowned, looking at her mother as though she were a stranger.

"Mom, stop laughing. I'm serious."

"I know, honey, that's why I'm laughing." Toreas watched her serious mother in awe as she clamped both hands over her mouth. Still the tears rolled down her cheeks and her eyes held a devilish twinkle. Her mother bit her lip, shaking her head in amusement.

"Honey, your father and I fought from the moment we met. When you kids were little we'd hire a baby-sitter so we could go out and fight."

Toreas was staring at her mother. Now she was sure something had happened in this town. Maybe aliens had invaded and replaced all of the people she knew with pod people. Her brothers were fun, the townspeople loving, and now her mother was telling her the one ideal couple Toreas knew fought.

"Tesa, fighting is healthy for a relationship. Especially when the two people love each other as much as your father and I do. If you want a relationship like ours, then you're on a good road toward getting it." Toreas saw the change come over her mother as she smiled before continuing. "When you love each other, there is a level of respect even to your fighting. The making up is always a lot of fun." Her eyes twinkled and Toreas's mouth fell open in shock.

"Mom." Toreas had to know, and it would tell her if this was truly her mother.

"What is it?"

"Can I ask you a personal question?"

"Sure, go ahead. You're my daughter."

"Were you a virgin when you married Daddy?" She watched as her mother, who never blushed, turned a bright shade of red.

"Billy was a nine pound preemie."

Okay, this was proof that her family had been replaced by aliens. Her mother had drilled in her head the evils of fornicating the moment she'd learned to crawl. "Mom, I don't believe it. You? You and Daddy were always teaching us not to fornicate, that it was a sin. I'll bet I was the only ten-year-old who even knew the meaning of the word fornicate."

"Tesa, grow up. Do you think you and your generation invented sex or temptation? That doesn't mean that we wanted our children to give in to it."

"Mom." Toreas voice was still shocked. "Did you enjoy it?"

"Of course I did. And I still do for your information."

"You didn't feel guilty?"

"A little the first time. We weren't married, but I loved your father. I got over it." Her mother's look became intense. "Do you feel guilty with Jared?"

It was Toreas's turn to blush. "We've never…"

"Never?"

"Never." Toreas was glad her mother didn't ask if she'd ever. Both women were silent for a moment. Then Toreas broke the now awkward silence. "Do you think God forgave you?"

"I know he did. God loves us. He doesn't expect us to be perfect. He just expects us to try our best."

The door opened then, ending any further conversation. Jared came in with her brothers and her father, his eyes finding hers.

"Did you have fun?" He came up to her and kissed her lightly on the lips in front of her entire family. Toreas waited for the explosion, the protests, but none came. They were behaving as if he had the right to kiss her. Who the heck were these people?

She watched all of them warily, including Jared. She felt as if she was the only person whose body had not been snatched. All the others were different and happy.

When they sat down hours later to a dinner of pizza, she had to do something to shock them back to reality. Her father eating pizza for dinner? More proof. Something must have happened to her world while she was in Chicago.

"Tesa, your brothers want to know when you're coming home. They'll come up and move you."

She caught Jared eyeing her. This was her chance. "I've changed my mind, Dad. I'm not moving back and I'm not going to stop writing romance."

"We had a deal, Tesa. Are you telling me you're going back on your word?"

"Yes, I guess that's what I'm saying. I'll pay you back every penny."

"It's not the money." Her father looked at her, his expression unreadable. "You gave your word. Tell me why you choose to break it now." He glanced at Jared.

"God gave me a talent. He gifted me with an imagination and I think I would honor Him if I use it to the best of my abilities."

"Writing smut? You think that's honoring God?"

"Romance isn't smut, Daddy. Besides, I can write it in a way that won't compromise my beliefs." She, too, looked toward Jared. He'd given her the idea.

"I thought you told me you had to write those sex scenes or no one would read the books."

"I could be wrong, Daddy." She was still looking at Jared, his golden brown eyes telling her he was proud of her. "I think I can do this in a way that you'll still be able to hold your head up and I'll still be following my dream."

"So your word means nothing." Her father looked around the table then. "How do you plan to support yourself or to pay me back? You said you needed to be home to write. Surely you don't expect me to continue subsidizing you when you've broken our agreement? By your own admission you can't write and support yourself at the same time."

"How much longer do you think you'll need?"

Toreas glanced at her brother Billy, surprised he was asking her this instead of telling her to stick to her end of the bargain.

"Probably another two years."

"I'll take care of your expenses for a year," Billy offered.

"I'll take care of the other year," Michael chimed in. "You keep writing, Tesa. We're behind you."

A lump filled her throat and tears poured down her face. She was right. Someone had taken her family.

Her father was standing beside her pulling her up. "Is this really so important to you that you're willing to defy me?"

"My writing is important," she answered her father, not wanting to say it was important enough to defy him. She felt as well as saw his hand coming up to her cheek. For a moment she thought he was going to smack her but he didn't. He rubbed the tears away with the pad of his thumb, his touch rough and loving.

"I'm proud of you, Tesa, for standing up for what you truly believe. You've always been so rebellious that I thought this writing thing was just to annoy me. I never knew you considered it a gift from God. A talent. I'm sure if that's the case the good Lord will send you the words to express what you both want to say." He hugged her close. "And I'm proud of you boys for standing up for your sister."

"So am I." Toreas disentangled herself from her father's arms and went to her brothers, kissing and hugging them both. "Thank you. I'm so surprised I don't know what to say."

"Surprised? Why should you be surprised?" It was her father's booming voice. "Your brothers have always looked out for you and taken care of you, even volunteering to take your spankings. You should have known they would come through for you."

Toreas's thoughts were muddled. She glanced first at her brothers, then at Jared. Nothing was as she remembered. Suddenly it was as if a veil were lifted and she saw clear images of her brothers battling bullies in her defense, of them giving her their last piece of candy, of them sneaking the spinach off her plate and eating it because she was crying and their mother refused to let her down from the table until she was done. They all hated spinach, but they'd both eaten hers countless time to stop her tears.

Toreas wondered where she had buried those memories. Until now she only thought of her brothers as the two baboons who tortured her, teasing her endlessly. She'd completely shoved aside all the loving acts. Maybe she was the one who'd been replaced by a pod person. They seemed to have always been here for her. She wondered what had happened, how she had managed to twist everything up so horribly.

Again she sat on the sidelines listening to the men talk, wondering at the overwhelming feelings of love she had for her family.

Every once in awhile one of her brothers would ruffle her hair or throw an insult her way. She noticed them constantly smiling in her direction. They loved her, they always had.

21

Toreas stayed up with her family, following Jared down the basement stairs when everyone decided to turn in because of the seven A.M. Thanksgiving worship service.

"I'll be up in ten minutes, Dad. I need to speak to Jared." She wanted to assure her father that she wasn't trying to rebel at this moment. She wouldn't dare attempt to stay in the room where Jared was sleeping. Her brothers would kick her butt and Jared's if she tried. Her memory hadn't failed her on that score.

She didn't know how to begin. She didn't want to offend Jared but she had to warn him about the church service, so she dove right in.

"Jared, I was thinking you might not want to come with us to early morning worship."

"Why?"

He wasn't making this easy for her. "In this town…in this family…" She stopped again. "Going to church together, us, the two of us," she pointed toward Jared, then herself, "we will be considered a couple."

"Aren't we?" He smiled at her as though there was no problem.

"We've never defined our relationship but yes, I think we are a couple but we're just beginning to be a couple. We haven't had an opportunity to prepare for the expectations. My family, the church, they're all going to make more out of this. They're going to assume we've made a commitment."

He was staring at her, an amused smile on his face. His brown eyes filled with passion and she doubted his mind was on church. Still, she had to get it through to him that church was very serious to her family and to her.

"What will you think if I want to come to church with you, Toreas? Will you think that I'm making a commitment?"

"No, I'll probably think you're being stubborn and that it's another opportunity for you to show that famous testosterone."

"As long as you're clear on what it would mean, then I don't think we have a problem."

He smiled at her and she wanted to hit him and kiss him in that order. "Jared," she had to try again. She wound her arms around his neck, twisting her fingers in his hair, wishing they were back in Chicago, in her bed. The phone would definitely be off the hook. "I'll make coffee for you. When you get up just turn it on. We should be home around nine." She kissed him then and walked up the stairs, satisfied that she'd put an end to that discussion.

At six A.M. she found Jared up with her family, drinking coffee and dressed for church. She frowned at him and he smiled at her, coming to kiss her good morning.

If it didn't feel so right she would have pushed him away. Didn't he know that a proper Baptist girl didn't go around kissing guys in front of her family? Especially a guy she wasn't married to? Even if that girl was almost thirty. It just wasn't done.

✍🏻

It felt strange and right to have Jared sitting alongside her in the family pew. She barely heard the minister. Jared was holding her hand, squeezing her fingers, lightly scratching the palm with one fingernail, making her hotter than anyone should ever be in church. She deliberately searched her head for her critics. Nothing.

The service ended and she heard the minister ask if anyone wanted to say thanks for some special gift. She felt Jared tug his hand free from hers and stand. Her eyes followed his movement, the flow of his body up and up. Liz was nuts to think she preferred small men.

Jared was what her mother referred to as a long drink of water. She watched as his full height extended higher and higher up toward the rafters. He was so tall and she loved it. Toreas waited, expecting to hear Jared say he was thankful to be with her family. That wasn't what he said at all.

"I'm thankful that I've fallen in love with the woman I want to marry and I was wondering if you would marry us right now, sir."

At first Toreas was stunned. She had to be dreaming, but the smiles and clapping of the congregation told her she wasn't.

He's kidding, she thought. That is, she thought that until he pulled gently on her hand, forcing her to stand.

"Toreas Rose, I'm madly in love with you. Will you marry me?"

"Are you crazy?" she attempted to whisper. "It's not a requirement to make a commitment. Let's sit down."

"Women can be so dense," he whispered into her ear. "Didn't you hear me? I love you."

Apparently he wasn't concerned with her answer on marrying him.

He'd turned his attention back to the minister and was asking him again to marry them.

"You need a license," she heard the minister say.

Then another voice piped up and said he would go to the courthouse and come back with one. Toreas couldn't believe it was Brian Johnson's father. "I have the keys. Give me a half hour," he offered.

Jared looked at her again. "Well, what do you say?" His eyes clouded and he frowned. "I'm sorry, you probably want a gown and a big wedding. What was I thinking?"

"No, that's not it. None of that's important."

He dropped to his knee and reached for her hand. "Will you marry me?" He was smiling, a little nervously, she noted, and that pleased her. He wasn't being his usual arrogant self.

"Jared, we haven't had a chance to talk about this. Look, I don't know what's gotten into you but," Toreas looked toward the pulpit, "let's go somewhere so we can talk in private."

"Do you love me, Tesa?"

Tesa. He was calling her by the name her family used for her, he wasn't playing fair.

"Te...sa..."

Now he was caressing her name.

"I love you, Tesa."

"But, Jared, we don't really know each other. This is crazy." Her heart was pounding. How she wanted to say yes, but she didn't want Jared to be caught up in the moment.

"How so?"

"Get up, Jared."

"Not without an answer. You tell me no and I'll get up and I'll go back to Chicago alone because I know what I want. There is no need for any more games."

"All we do is fight. If we marry we'll probably be divorced in less than a week."

"You have no faith in me, do you?"

"Jared, let's go someplace and talk."

"Not until you tell me if you've ever thought about this, my asking you to marry me." He gave her a stern look. "And tell me the truth, Tesa. Have you had thoughts about spending the rest of your life with me?"

Toreas's eyes shuttered closed. She licked her lips.

"Don't lie to me, it's too important," Jared whispered roughly.

Toreas opened her eyes and glanced around the sanctuary. She couldn't believe Jared was doing this.

"Answer me, Tesa, or I will walk out of your life forever and I'm not kidding. Do you want to marry me?"

Threatening her was not exactly the most romantic way to go about it but Toreas was not stupid enough to let him leave either. "Yes, I've thought about marrying you."

"Then I'll ask you again. Will you marry me?"

Toreas fell to her knees beside him and whispered in his ear, "We've never made love, Jared. What if you don't want me after…what if I don't satisfy you…what if…"

He kissed her thoroughly then, while they were both on their knees in the church.

"Is that a yes?" the pastor asked above the noise.

"It's a yes," Toreas answered. "Yes, Jared, I'll marry you, right here, right now, without a wedding gown."

"You could wear my gown."

Toreas looked up into her mother's eyes which were brimming over with tears.

"I know it's much too long but we can pin it. I'll go home and get it." Her mother was turned around to make the trek back to the house before Toreas could even say thank you.

"How long will that take?" she heard Jared asking. She was still in shock.

"The whole thing shouldn't take longer than a few minutes."

Toreas watched as her very own mother took orders from Jared. She stood there in amazement as he confirmed the time with the minister.

There were so many people talking at once that Toreas was lost. She saw her parents leave for home and the gown and Mr. Johnson leave for the license. She heard someone say they were going for flowers and another woman began to organize the women into groups to prepare food.

She heard enough of the conversation to know they would have a wedding breakfast.

People were kissing her and pumping Jared's hand, congratulating him. She watched as one by one they disappeared to complete whatever chore had been assigned to them.

Finally she was left with Jared. The two of them stood alone in the sanctuary. Everyone else was milling about outside the door, ecstatic about attempting to pull off a wedding and a wedding breakfast in less than an hour from the ending of service.

"You never said if you love me. Do you love me, To…re…as?"

He was caressing her name, making her want him more than she'd ever wanted him. Her heart was pounding so loudly she could hear it in her ears. "I love you, Jared," she whispered, then quickly looked around the room.

"Tell me again, Tesa. This time look at me. I love you and I want to know, do you love me enough to spend the rest of your life with me, fighting, making up and making babies?"

She was blushing. "We're in church, Jared. Stop looking at me like that."

"Why?"

"Because I love you and I want to spend the rest of my life with you, fighting, making up and having babies. And right now I want you so much that if you don't stop looking at me like that, I'll be forced to give you the most passionate kiss the Lord has ever witnessed."

"Perfect," he answered her. "Who better to witness our commitments."

She was suddenly in his arms and he was kissing her. Her feet were dangling in the air. It felt right, this acknowledgment she'd spent her entire life trying to run away from.

It was only right that she stop running from love and accept it here in this church. It felt right that this was done in front of God.

"I love you, Jared," she murmured as he slid her downward. Her mother was there waiting with capable hands to help her into her own wedding gown. She'd not known she'd returned. Toreas had not checked her watch when she left but she knew her mother had not been gone nearly long enough to have gone home, found the gown, and made it back to the church.

Toreas looked at the cleaner bag the dress was in. The thing looked like as if it had just come from the cleaners. This was all too suspicions. "Mom, where was your dress?" Toreas asked.

"Tesa, honey we don't have time for questions. Let's get you into this thing. We need to see how much we have to take it in."

Before Toreas could protest her mother had shoved her into the minister's study and a group of women had jostled her into the dress and were making on the spot alterations, all which seemed to be minimal. The dress fit her much better than she would have thought, much better than it should have.

"Mom, your dress, it's beautiful and it almost fits. How can that be possible?"

"Tesa, honey, thank God for that. Now come on, let's get started."

In what seemed to her only a matter of minutes she was standing before the minister telling Jared once again that she loved him, hearing him tell her, her parents, God, the congregation and the hallelujah choir that he loved her as well.

In a whir of activity they accepted the kisses from the congregation and followed the ministers and the others out of the sanctuary, down the stairs and to the huge community room where the breakfast had been laid out. Toreas gasped in amazement at the lavish decorations and tables laden with food and flowers. How the heck had they done all of this in such a short time? she wondered.

"Anything wrong, Toreas?" Jared asked.

"I can't believe everyone did all of this for us."

"They did it for you. They all apparently love you," Jared whispered and kissed her lightly on the lips. "Just as I do."

As they ate their wedding breakfast, Toreas continued to marvel at the array of food the women had whipped up in so short a time. These nosy people who butted into everybody's business. God bless them.

It appeared she'd also forgotten the generosity of her town, the love and caring they had for each other and the skills. Three of the women, along with her mother, had altered the gown to fit her body in record time. They'd prepared a feast and all because they loved her. She was one of them. She wondered how all of this had escaped her notice. Why had she not seen it all?

"You were too busy running away. Now enjoy their love."

It was her internal critic. She intended to do just that.

When a wedding cake was wheeled out and stacks of wedding presents uncovered on a nearby table, Toreas knew she'd been had. She got up and walked toward the cake, smiling. Okay, so she'd been wrong about her family and her town but come on, did they all think she was stupid? This was not some last minute planning that had been put together in an hour. This was planned ahead of time. She tilted her head and glanced across the room at Jared standing with her family. They all lifted their champagne glasses up at her and laughed.

"How did you do this, how did you know?" she asked, walking toward them.

"How do you think," Jared teased, sliding his arm around her waist.

"You?"

"Of course."

"But how, Jared? I didn't even ask you until the last second and when would you have had time? You almost didn't come."

"Now there you're wrong. Did you think I was going to leave you to that Brian Johnson? No way. I got your parents' number from information and I called and asked your father for permission to marry you. I did it the old fashioned Southern way, the way you kept pretending you hated. I didn't believe you."

"But this weekend, why so soon?"

She could feel his hand pressing gently on her back, caressing her. She didn't dare look up.

"Because it was perfect. Thanksgiving is a time to give thanks. It's a time for family and friends and those we love. I thought it was a good time for us to begin a new life as husband and wife.

"But what if I had said no?"

"You didn't."

"But what if I had?"

"In that case I would have had to convince you that we belonged together." He stared at her for a moment before kissing her until her knees turned weak.

When she could breathe again, Toreas looked at each member of her family in turn. "I can't believe you all went along with this scheme."

"He loved you and we could tell something was up with you in the past months. We just didn't know it was love. That's why I drilled you and that's why I cancelled Brian." Her mother looked up at Jared. "Your husband told me in no uncertain terms that he didn't want you anywhere near Brian Johnson or any other man. Once he asked your father for your hand, things just kind of snowballed. You were the only fly in the ointment.

"But, Mom, you did all of this not knowing what I would do."

"Believe me, there were a dozen urgent calls between us and Jared. Why do you think I was suddenly calling you every fifteen minutes. That morning when you were all packed and ready to leave I almost had a heart attack. Jared never called to say that you'd agreed, just that he was coming."

Toreas couldn't help laughing. "So that's why you asked me if I was sure my gas was off or if I was sure I didn't want to bring a friend." Toreas laughed harder. "I was wondering if you were beginning to lose your memory. You'd already asked me that a dozen times." She looked at Jared. "I should have known."

"You should have known I loved you and I had no plans on your moving anywhere without me by your side."

Someone had put on music and was yelling for the bride and groom to dance. When they were cheek to cheek, Toreas looked around the gaily decorated church community room and whispered to Jared. "You know you've outsmarted yourself, don't you? There is no way we're doing what's on your mind in my parents' basement."

"How about upstairs in your bedroom?"

"Ha ha, don't think so, buddy."

"But we're married now."

"I don't care," Toreas answered. "If you're planning on making my eyes roll back in my head, I think we need to be alone."

"Then I guess when we get back to your parents' home you'd better help your mom make dinner so the preparations can go quicker."

"I can't believe you're not rushing me out of here."

"Why not? I have you and we have a lifetime together." He pulled her hard against him.

"I don't believe you."

"You shouldn't." Jared laughed. "We have a honeymoon suite here in town, I made reservations. As soon as we have Thanksgiving dinner with your family we're off." He leered at her.

He could see the wheels turning and shook his head. "No, Tesa, I didn't sleep with anyone when I was so angry with you. How could I when all I could think about was you and the fact that if I had you'd probably tack on another year and make me retake the test and fill out another questionnaire."

"Jared?"

"Okay, baby, I didn't want anyone else but you. I love you."

"Say it again," Toreas purred, looking up at him with adoring eyes.

"I love you, Toreas Rose Stone. There is something I've been meaning to ask you about that first time when you were glaring at me as though you hated me. It was so personal. Why?

"You don't know?" Toreas teased.

"No."

"I'd had a little crush on you for months and then you opened your mouth and spoiled it."

"Now?"

"Well, now is now."

"How about telling me how much you love me and that you wouldn't think of living without me."

At that moment the music ended and Toreas smiled at Jared and walked toward her father.

"Toreas," Jared called, and she ignored him, taking her father's hand and leading him to the dance floor. Of course she loved him but she couldn't let him get a big head, now could she? "I love you, Jared, and I can't think of living my life without you," she yelled at him from the dance floor. She looked at her father and grinned, surprised not to feel the heat from embarrassment that she normally would have felt.

"I like him, Tesa."

"So do I, Daddy," Toreas said as she leaned against her father's chest. "So do I."

After the dancing they sat and ate and talked with old friends until everyone began cleaning. It was time for them to go home to prepare their own Thanksgiving dinner.

Several people walked up and kissed her goodbye, pressing envelopes that she knew contained money into her hands. Some of them gave her rolls of film and three different people gave her video cassettes of the wedding.

She returned to her parents' home a married woman. Through it all she was in a daze, helping her mother with the meal while listening to her husband. *Her husband.* She loved the way it sounded in her head.

Her husband was now a part of her family and it also felt right. She couldn't wait until she told Liz and Kelle. They would never believe it. No matter how talented, she didn't believe any writer could have come up with such a wonderful beginning for her new life.

Hours later when they were climbing into the car she held each of her brothers tightly to her. She would never forget again how much she loved them or how much they loved her. She would remember always.

"Tesa, thank God you went shopping with Mom. Your outfit looks beautiful."

Toreas hit at Billy but he grabbed her and gave her a hug. She twirled around for them in her new outfit the same as she'd done in her thrift store clothes. She had to admit the purple silk dress melded to her curves like a glove. Her mother had even insisted on buying her a stylish new black coat. It all made sense now why her mother had taken her from store to store on a manic shopping frenzy, telling her to hush up every time she'd attempted to pay.

Her father reached out a hand and touched her hair. "I thought I would have a stroke when your mom called to warn me that you'd cut off your beautiful, long hair. But you look just as beautiful in an afro."

Throwing her arms around her father Toreas hugged him as hard as she could. "Thank you, Daddy, for everything," she said and kissed his cheek.

"Tesa, I'll still pay for that year for you to find your dream." Michael hugged his sister close.

"So will I," Billy chimed in.

Jared grinned at them both. "Sorry, guys, she's my wife and I'll take care of her."

Toreas shook her head at the men in her life. "You're all the greatest but I've decided to go back to work." She took in their looks. "Don't worry, I have no plans on giving up but I also have no plans on not doing some of the real struggling to get there. I truly thank all of you but I need to go about this in a different way. I have the inspiration I need and I have the passion." Toreas grinned. "I don't think it will be nearly as hard to write now."

Her father was the last one to kiss her goodbye. "You no longer have a debt to me," he whispered into her ear. "It's paid in full."

"No, Daddy, I'll keep my word on that."

"Consider it a wedding gift. After all, I didn't have the expense of giving you a wedding. This is a fair trade." He hugged her, hard. And she felt his body shake.

"Be happy," he said to her, then pushed her toward Jared. A few more waves and they were off.

"Now, Toreas Tesa Rose Stone, let's see what I can do about making your eyes roll to the back of your head," Jared whispered as they got in the car.

"In the car, Jared."

"Baby, before we're done we're going to make love in places you've never before imagined." He glanced at her and saw her grin. "What?" he asked.

"I'm a writer, Jared, I have a very vivid imagination." She fished in the dash box for a piece of paper and a pencil, then started writing, listing some places worth considering.

"What are you doing?" Jared asked.

"Oh, just starting a list. You'll be lucky if you manage to do even half of the things on my list."

When he laughed out loud she laughed with him and continued writing.

22

Sitting next to Jared as he drove, Toreas wondered a few minutes later if she was dreaming it all. She was married to Jared and her family had been in on it. It was too unbelievable. She chuckled softly and pinched herself.

"What now?" Jared asked, grinning.

"Just pinching myself to see if this is real."

"It's real, baby. You can't run from me any longer."

"I have no plans to run, Jared."

"How do you feel, Mrs. Stone?"

"Wonderful. How about you?"

"I feel lucky."

"Does any of this strike you as hokey?"

"Yeah, but who the hell cares? I have you in my life and nothing else matters. I knew from the moment I began falling for you that I would have to work my ass off to get you."

"You haven't worked it off yet, Jared," Toreas joked.

She couldn't believe she'd laughed with her mother only a couple of days before about the denseness of men. This was without a doubt the most romantic thing Jared could have done.

"What are you thinking?" he asked.

"How much I love you and how much like a dream this all seems. I found my family, the church, God and a husband all in one neat bundle."

"You didn't find us. We were never lost. We were just waiting for you to want us." He smiled. "I'm speaking for myself. As soon as we get home I'm going to prove that to you."

She leaned into his body, as close to him as she could possibly get. *When we get home,* she thought. *Okay, Toreas, she coached herself. It's up to you to change your husband's mind about waiting till you reach Chicago. Just once more. Just a little wifely manipulation.*

"I can hardly wait until we get home." She tried to sound innocent as her hand began roaming up his thigh. "I wish we didn't have to wait so long. I thought you had the honeymoon suite here in town."

She felt Jared looking at her and she looked up into his eyes. They were finally on the same page.

"I wasn't talking about waiting to make love to you. I was talking about proving we belong together. But you're right, and I think I can prove that to you in just a few minutes."

His voice was husky with desire. Toreas smiled. She was aware of what he was thinking. She could feel it. Her hand was directly covering a huge bulge. "Now that's more like it, Mr. Stone."

Jared was grinning. "By the way, there is something I want to tell you."

"What's that?" Toreas asked coyly, waiting to hear him tell her he loved her.

"I want you to keep a few of those bulky sweaters. I want to bury my head under them and taste my own private buried treasure."

His hand touched her face and she burned. When he tried to use his right hand to burrow through her coat he gave up after a few seconds and grinned at her. "I can't caress you and drive, at least not while you have on that darn coat. Please tell me what you're dressed for. It's not that cold."

"Cold enough for a coat," Toreas replied, smiling at Jared.

"But I don't have on a coat."

"That's your body, I get cold easily."

"Do you heat easily?"

"I think you know the answer to that."

"I'm not sure, not really. You could have been lying to me. After all, you always managed to say no. Are you planning on saying no to me today?"

"Would it do any good if I were?" Toreas laid her head on his shoulder, her hand feeling once again for the evidence of his arousal, finding it and feeling emboldened. She stroked him, laughing as his body shuddered and his foot pressed harder on the gas pedal.

"You like teasing me, don't you?" Jared placed his hand over Toreas's. "We're going to see how well you like it in about thirty seconds."

He pulled off the highway and turned into the parking lot of a hotel that looked liked heaven to Toreas.

"Now I'm going on a treasure hunt," Jared informed her, "and I get to keep the prize."

Before Toreas could count to ten, they were out of the car, in the lobby and being led to the honeymoon suite. When the door closed behind them, Toreas turned and saw the way her husband was looking at her.

"Jared," she whispered. Before another word could leave her mouth he was beside her. The moan died in her throat. Jared was kissing her, and her body surrendered to his touch. This time when the feeling of floating overcame her she opened her eyes and grinned. "I love you, Jared," Toreas said softly as she gazed into her husband's eyes.

"No more interruptions," Jared rasped hoarsely.

Both their eyes fell on the phone. Toreas laughed and took it off the hook. "Is that better?"

"Much."

"Jared, this is all so crazy. Liz is going to think I'm nuts."

"Do you care?"

"Not really."

Then why are we discussing your friends on our honeymoon?"

"Maybe I'm just a little nervous." She looked toward the bed, then at Jared.

Jared raised a brow. "Do you doubt that you love me, that you want to be married to me, or do you doubt that I can fulfill your request?" He too glanced toward the bed.

Toreas smiled and turned toward the window. Her breath was coming in short pants and she was feeling flushed. She'd waited her entire life for this moment, for Jared. It was hard to believe this wasn't a dream.

She heard him move, felt the rustle of air. Then his hands were on her, pulling her close. He pulled her into him and she went willingly.

Jared's lips traversed her neck, his tongue licking a path of fire, of want and need. Toreas shivered as he continued raining kisses along her jawline, his fingers caressing the side of her face.

A slight breeze caressed her skin as he moved the zipper of her dress an inch. More kisses rained down on her back and the pull came from her womb while her knees buckled.

"This is one of the few times I've seen you in a dress," Jared teased. The wedding gown and now this one. Your body is suited to silk. It feels almost as soft as you but not quite," he purred and slipped the zipper down a little lower. "Did I happen to mention that purple is your color?"

"Jared…" That was the only word she could utter. He nuzzled into her so close that not even air could get between them. She felt his erection pressing into her, and his groan shook her body as he attempted to hold her even closer. He was moving so slowly, only taking her zipper down an inch at a time, laving her skin with liquid fire, his tongue doing magical things to her libido.

Toreas didn't know how much longer she could remain standing. He'd once again turned her into melting butter. "Jared," she moaned softly, "what are you doing?"

"I'm tasting every inch of you, just like I promised myself I would. I had to make sure I wasn't crazy."

"For marrying me?" Toreas sucked in a breath and felt him nip her lightly with his teeth.

"No, silly, for thinking you tasted like strawberries. I thought I must have been losing my mind, that no one's body could taste like fruit. But guess what, Toreas, yours does. It's so yummy. Have you ever tasted it?"

With that Jared licked a path from her neck to the three inches of skin he'd exposed. If he continued to go that slowly she'd surely die.

Jared's hands were trembling. He'd waited so long to be able to touch his wife in just the way he was doing. He'd thought for sure he would enter her the moment the door closed behind them.

This wasn't in his plan, this slow seduction of his wife. But when she'd turned her back to him it hit him squarely in the gut how much he truly loved her and wanted to make her his in every way. Every inch of her he wanted to touch, taste and savor and he was doing just that.

If she thought the slowness wasn't having an effect on him, she was nuts. Still, he was determined to know her body. Jared's hand found the clasp of her bra and he undid it. He sucked in huge gulps of air as his hands found her breasts and he cupped them.

Toreas was moaning his name, wanting more and truly he wanted to turn her to face him, bury his lips in her breasts, pull her plump nipples into his mouth, but he'd forgo it for now. He was finding too much pleasure in the tremors he was producing in his wife's body.

For once Jared was glad of the difference in their height. He didn't have to remove his hands from Toreas's breasts as he used his teeth to slide the zipper farther down her back.

He groaned, kissing her skin, licking it, making his own flesh harder. For a moment he stopped and held her, nuzzling her close, afraid of coming right then and there. What kind of honeymoon would that be?

"Jared."

He heard her whispering his name so softly that it gave him goose bumps. She was close to the edge. He could feel the vibration of her body clear to her legs.

Jared chuckled and picked up the pace just a bit, pulling the zipper farther down. When the dress pooled about her waist, he dropped to his knees and laid his head in the small of her back, his hands trading her breasts for other areas.

He moaned as his fingers came into contact with silk. He smiled. *So they weren't cotton.* Jared rubbed one hand up and down over his wife's nether regions, not wanting to go there yet, just enjoying the feel of her through the material.

He moved lower, bringing his hand around to trace the roundness of her firm buttocks. Jared kissed each cheek. His hand trembled as his fingers traced a path up and down her before going into the dip of her behind. He felt her heat, her shiver, and her effort to pull away but he groaned and held her close, and shook away the need. Then he turned Toreas to face him. Her face was contorted by lust and she was shivering so hard that Jared remembered her leg hitting the table when she'd propositioned him.

"Toreas, baby, are you scared? You did tell me you weren't a virgin, right?"

"No, I'm not a virgin, I've done it eleven and a half times."

"Eleven and a half," Jared chuckled. "How the half?"

"Don't ask."

"How long has it been?" He thought at first she wasn't going to answer, but then her voice came, trembling and breathy.

"It's been three and a half years."

"You're kidding!"

"No, I'm not.

"So you're probably ready by now," Jared teased.

"What do you think?"

"I think I haven't finished with the taste test. He pressed his face into her abdomen and flicked his tongue into her navel and swirled it around, again feeling her heat. Her scent was rising up to meet him as he moved farther south, his mouth kissing her through the silk, his nose nudging the material aside. He had to have a taste. Toreas had gone still and was pulling back.

"Have you ever done this before?"

"No."

"Do you want me to?"

"Jared, how am I supposed to answer that?"

"Honestly."

"I can't."

"Why can't you?"

"Jared."

He grinned. "I'll make the decision then, how's that?" he said and this time used a hand to move the material aside. Before he could taste her, she'd scooted out of his grip and made for the bed.

"Just for that, Mrs. Stone, you're going to have to tell me what you want."

Toreas stepped out of her dress and crawled across the bed, kicking out as Jared's hand pulled on her ankle, trying to bring her back to him.

"You're trying to get away from me?"

"If you think that you really are dense. I'm just trying to get in a more comfortable position." Toreas flopped on the pillow, expecting Jared to come alongside her. When he didn't she raised up and glanced downward. He was eyeing her foot.

"Jared, what the heck are you thinking of doing?"

"Like I said, I want to know if you taste like strawberries all over." His hand snaked out and grabbed her leg as she tried to get away.

"Jared, if your mouth goes anywhere near my foot, I'm not kissing you."

"I don't believe you. Besides, I don't think if I do it right you'll object. And I'm planning to do it right. I'm going to taste every inch of you, Mrs. Stone."

Before Toreas could object further Jared was kissing her foot as his hand caressed her leg. Then he moved upwards. He felt her shiver as his tongue connected with her bare skin.

"Jared?"

"Tesa, you said you wanted your eyes to roll back in your head. I'm trying to make that happen but you're interrupting me."

"But, Jared, you're having all the fun."

"I waited long enough. I deserve to have fun, don't you agree?"

"But you're only going for the appetizers. What about the entrées?"

Jared shook his head and grinned in disbelief. His little Baptist bride was a fast learner. "I have patience. I had to in order to wait all these months and you're not going to deter me. I intend to finish."

"Do I?"

"Do you what?" Jared smiled, lowering his head to lick her brown skin, heading higher toward her thigh.

"Do I taste like strawberries?"

"That you do, baby." He moved higher still and the faint wetness tickled his nostril. He moved the silk aside with one finger and touched her wetness. A sigh filled the room and he smiled, thinking how hard he'd worked before to get her out of her pants and now here she was.

Jared's flesh throbbed with wanting. *Too fast*, he thought. If he kept his finger there it would be over in a matter of minutes. He rubbed his hand over her mound, felt her shudder, and he groaned. Damn. He gritted his teeth. He was determined to remain strong, he was on a mission. He would make his wife's eyes roll back in her head or die trying.

Mercy. He moved upward, dropping a kiss a mere millimeter from where his lips wanted to land. He would save that for later, he thought as he kissed her smooth abdomen, his tongue dipping into the valley of her navel. He should have known she'd have an innie. Such discoveries. Jared was unprepared for the moan that slipped out as one of his hands disobeyed him and sank down between his wife's thighs. He found her wet, hot and wanting and touched her with the pad of his finger. A ripple of pleasure burst through Toreas and caught him in his very soul. Her essence combined with his and he held her tight.

"Jared," Toreas was moaning, her breath ragged. "You could continue the taste test later. We have forever."

"Mrs. Stone, don't you know that the best part of any journey is the getting there? The little stops you make along the way are what make it totally worthwhile. Trust me, baby, I will make it worth your wait."

"Jared, I don't want to wait any longer. Didn't you tell me to tell you what I wanted? Well, I'm telling you." Toreas groaned, knowing her husband was not going to give in to her demands. He was enjoying this sweet torture he was inflicting on her.

He was moving his hand away, not what she wanted. She felt his hardness pressing into her. She wanted him to make love to her. She was ready for the main course.

The feelings that were flooding through Toreas had never touched her before. She'd never wanted to be touched between her thighs. Now she wanted to beg Jared to touch her, to finish the game they'd only played at. She couldn't believe it, all the times she'd slapped his hands away and now when she was giving him an open invitation he was taking it so slow. She wanted to touch him but he was too low for her to reach.

"Jared, I want to kiss you." She heard his chuckle. "Jared, I want to touch you."

"Which?" he teased.

"Both," Toreas answered.

Again Jared's flesh quickened. He couldn't deny that he wanted his wife's hands around him. She was right, playtime was over. He sat up to remove his shorts, shivering as Toreas's fingers trailed down his back and came around to his front. "Ummm, no fair, baby." His hand fell away and he kept the shorts on.

"It's fair," she purred. "I want to do to you what you did to me."

"What's that?"

"You were driving me crazy." Toreas pushed Jared back on the mattress. "You said I had to tell you what I wanted and I'm telling you.

Now you just lie there quietly and let me work."

Toreas teased his small pebbled nipples, nipping him lightly as he'd done her. She used her tongue in much the same manner as he'd done, tasting him. His sweat, the scent of soap, of cologne. It was nice. She ran her hands over his bare chest and smiled. No wonder Jared had taken it so slowly with her.

Toreas liked touching him. Nothing about Jared's body was soft, he was hard. Her eyes gazed downward, hard and firm. She kissed him slowly, touching him, getting to know his body with the tips of her fingers. Without warning Jared moved downward and captured her lips. "You're moving much too slowly," he said in a whisper against her lips.

"Fair's fair, you did it to me." Toreas smiled beneath her husband's lips.

"Well, I can't take it." He was over her, leaning down. "I want you," Jared moaned. "I've never seen you naked."

"And I've never seen you naked," Toreas answered.

"It wasn't for my lack of trying," Jared said and with one swift motion he yanked Toreas's panties down from her hips, down her thighs and kicked them from her legs with one foot. Then he rapidly rid himself of his shorts. For a second his eyes lingered on her body. He smiled at her. "Perfect, I always knew you were hiding a treasure."

Jared's head bent to suckle her while his hand made a home in her warmth. She was so hot and wet. The wetness pooled within her and spilt out. Her muscle constricted, bringing his finger in deeper.

Sexual heat raced through his veins. Not a cell in his body was left untouched. Jared stared at Toreas, his question answered at last. He knew he was without a doubt the reason for his wife's ability to blush. He knew now that despite whatever hormonal change produced the phenomenon in a Black woman that it was her sexual heat that flooded her skin and warmed it from the inside out, changing her cinnamon color to a tomato red.

She stroked him and he stayed for a moment rooted to the spot, enjoying the touch of her soft, hesitant hand. God, he must have been crazy to have worried about her inexperience. Now he was thankful.

Need pulled at Jared, stabbing him with heat in the center of his groin. A grunt of pleasure fell from his lips. Toreas's touch was electric. He glanced at her, filled with wonder at her shy smile.

"Am I doing okay?" Toreas asked.

Damn, was she doing okay? Have you ever touched a man? His words slammed into his brain. Toreas had not really answered that question, Jared realized. But he knew the answer. She'd never touched a man. Virgin or not, Jared was without a doubt Toreas's first real lover. The knowledge filled him with pleasure.

"More," Toreas moaned to Jared's amazement. He hadn't believed that she would ask for what she wanted. He inserted a second finger and felt the shudder it produced. He glanced upward. Her eyes were closed. "Hey, how am I going to know if I'm doing it right with your eyes closed?"

"You're doing it right," she whispered.

"I want to see," he pleaded, moving into position. "Are you ready?"

"I've been ready, Jared."

That was all he needed to hear as he drove into her wetness. The tightness rocked him and had him wondering if she'd lied about not being a virgin. It sure as hell felt like she was.

"To…re…sa?" He caressed her name. "Baby, I love you." He drove deeper, harder, faster and faster. Her legs clasped tightly behind his back, her writhing pushing him even deeper into her heat. He shuddered from the pleasure, felt hers, and took it into his body. Her breath was hot and hitching in her throat. That he took as well and kissed her, giving her his own.

Never had it been like this, never. The thought struck Jared that he was also a virgin in a way. This was the first time he'd truly made love. Sex, yes, making love, there was a difference. It meant commitment, something that a woman like Toreas Rose Stone deserved.

God, he was definitely committed to love her and bring her pleasure for the rest of their lives, and he was praying that God granted them a long life. Each thrust was becoming unbearable, the pleasure bringing him to the brink.

Jared didn't know how much longer he could hold out, but he refused to climax until he fulfilled his wife's request. He plunged deeper into his wife's body and her wet heat sealed him, burning him with their combined passion.

"Oh God, Toreas," he groaned. "Baby, I can't stop it." And then it happened. Jared smiled in satisfaction as his wife's body rocked beneath his. Her eyes rolled back in her head and she screamed his name, digging her nails into his flesh. Still Jared continued, taking each shiver of her climax and riding it to his own release.

A low guttural groan came up from his soul tearing through his flesh, ripping through his lungs, filling his vocal cords and exploding from his mouth. He couldn't believe the primal scream that issued from his mouth.

Jared grabbed Toreas to him and held her tightly, riding out the last of their release together. Shudder after shudder tore through them like the aftershock of an earthquake. "I love you, baby," Jared moaned. He heard her soft sobs and smiled. "What's the matter, baby?"

"You did it, Jared, we did it."

"To your satisfaction?"

"I'm not quite sure, Jared. I might need to get my notepad and write this down. Do you want to show me again how it's done?"

Jared grinned to himself as his semi-soft erection swelled back to full attention. He was surprised when Toreas changed position.

"This is my story, Jared," Toreas said as she looked down on her husband, moving her hips, watching him close his eyes in ecstasy. "Now it's time to make your eyes roll to the back of your head."

"You already did, baby, and you're wrong, this isn't just your story, it's our story."

"Agreed, but still I want to make your eyes roll to the back of your head."

"You already did baby."

"But I'm going to do it again." Toreas grinned as she moved up and down clenching her muscles, determined to give to him what he gave to her.

"I love you, Jared," she whispered as his hands came around her waist to help guide her toward his release. This she'd accept for it was their combined pleasure that she was after.

And as Jared had said, the journey was to be enjoyed and she was definitely enjoying the trip. Her body was burning with passion for her husband. She grinned down at his face distorted by desire, her belief in fairytales renewed. With Jared thrusting upward to meet the downward sway of her hips, she knew all things were possible if you only believed.

With that thought Toreas gave herself over completely to Jared's love and to the burning desire flowing through her body.

"What a lovely way to burn," she whispered to Jared as another orgasm crested and she floated away to fulfill the promise.

***

Hours later Toreas woke from a sated sleep. She was lying with her full weight on Jared. She grinned as the memory flitted through her mind that Liz thought Toreas preferred small men. Good thing Jared wasn't a small man. As she began to disentangle her limbs and climb from the bed, she felt her husband's flesh stirring to life.

"Where are you going, baby? We're not done." Jared's arm snaked out, holding her in place.

"I want to put something on for you."

Jared leaned up an inch or so and observed her from one eye. "You're kidding, right? You're perfect naked.

"I think you're going to like this."

"I don't need anything but bare skin."

"This I think you'll like."

"Ten seconds," Jared said, pulling her to him and placing a kiss in the small of her back. "I forgot I have something for you also," he said, watching her rummage through her bag. She glanced at him, then carried the bag into the bathroom.

Jared laughed. It was pretty hard to hide a nightgown when one was naked. Jared grinned and went to his own bag and got out his surprise and lined up the boxes across the desk in the room. Then he stood back and waited for his new bride to come out of the bathroom.

When Toreas returned from the bathroom in panties and a bulky sweater, he burst out laughing. When the laughter died the lust returned. Jared's heart was pounding in his chest as he gazed at Toreas. He'd never known he would feel like this.

Dreams Jared had never known he had had been fulfilled with his falling in love with Toreas Rose Stone, this tiny, perfect, beautiful woman who tasted so much like strawberries. He ought to know, he'd tasted almost every inch of her, and was saving the best for last. Now he'd finally get to see just what the rest of her tasted like.

"Why are you looking at me like that?"

"Why do you think?" Jared grinned. "Besides, just how am I looking at you?"

"Like you want to eat me."

"You're extremely perceptive, Mrs. Stone. Now get over here."

"No." Toreas shook her head slightly. "You get over here." Her head snapped up and she glanced at the desk. "Condoms! I don't believe it. My God, how many boxes do you have here?" She walked over and began counting. "You've got twenty boxes here."

"And more at home. I'm a stock owner. Now get over here, Mrs. Stone."

Toreas couldn't stop grinning. This marriage of theirs was going to be fun. "If you want me, Mr. Stone, you're going to have to come and get me." She grabbed three boxes of condoms and shook them in Jared's direction.

For a moment they stared, wondering which one would give first. They both wanted to move. Toreas took one step. Jared grinned and did the same. "Romance writers," he groaned and took another and another, giving in.

This was one battle not worth fighting. He'd waited his entire life to make a commitment. He reached out and pulled his wife into his arms. Hogtied, that was him. His lips came down to cover hers and the groan came from the bottom of his soul and made him tremble. He felt her shiver.

"You still scared, baby?"

She shook her head no. "Is this real, did we really get married, Jared, or am I dreaming? I can't believe you planned all of this that you..."

"That I what?"

"Jared, what made you do it now?"

"Because I love you and there was no way I was going to lose you to that Johnson boy."

"Is that really why you did it? You were just jealous?"

Jared looked into her eyes. "Are you kidding? Do you still doubt my love?"

"No, I don't doubt you anymore. I trust you implicitly enough that I'll tell you now you're not going to need those condoms. Besides, we didn't use any before."

"Ah, but we were so hot we were using luck. I don't think that will work for long," he grinned. This time he shook the condoms at her. "Besides, you're still not on the pill. And I don't want to share you with anyone, not even a baby, for at least a couple of years." He picked her up and grinned at her. "Ready for another round?" Her sparkling mischievous eyes gave him her answer.

Dropping Toreas on the mattress, Jared quickly went for what he was after. He felt the material hitting him lightly on the head, Toreas's wonderful, beautiful, bulky sweater. A smile tugged at the corners of Jared's lips as he thought about how it had felt to have his head buried beneath Toreas's sweaters. Even though the other one was a bit larger, this one would do.

"I love your clothes. They're beautiful."

Toreas laughed and snuggled in to enjoy her husband's touch. "Sometimes the things that are worthwhile are hidden from view," she teased. She ran her hands over Jared's back. "Like us falling in love. Who would have thought it?"

"Yeah, who woulda thunk it?" Jared said, his voice muffled underneath her sweater.

Toreas grinned and opened a box of condoms and dumped the contents on the bed. She was in agreement with Jared, she wanted to enjoy him also. A moan escaped her lips. "Ummm," she whispered, "you're right, we need lots of time."

Epilogue

Two years later, Mr. and Mrs. Jared Stone were sitting in the packed auditorium at the ARW national convention in Colorado. They had only a few minutes before the announcement of the best first book category. Toreas Stone turned to her husband and kissed him lightly, not caring who saw her.

For their first wedding anniversary she'd given Jared her form filled out for The Purple Plum. The entry was the story of their love. Not only had she won but the story had been bought and it was now entered in The Bard, the contest for published writers. That anniversary had been the turning point in Toreas's writing. She'd thought often about how it differed from the previous one when she'd agonized over spending fifty dollars for The Purple Plum.

Now, because of her marriage to Jared, Toreas had fulfilled her dreams. She'd kept her promise to her father and combined her talent with her beliefs. Her father had written her a note after her book came out acknowledging that he had known all along that she could do it.

When she'd received notification that she was a finalist for the coveted statue, Jared had bought her a diamond studded charm. He promised to buy her a bracelet to wear it on after she won.

The two years since they'd been married had been the best time of her life. Winning The Bard would be wonderful, but if she didn't win she was aware she already had the biggest dream of her life fulfilled. She had Jared.

She noticed John Cain coming toward her, waving. She saw the muscles in Jared's jaw tense with dislike. She'd forgotten to take care of that little matter, so unimportant it was to her. "Jared, stop glaring at him. John's gay." She watched as Jared turned toward her, surprise forming his mouth into a circle. She sat farther back in her seat and began to rhythmically stroke her husband's arm, to assure him he was the only one she wanted.

Together they listened to the program, to the entertainment, and Toreas began to feel the apprehension she had thought she didn't have.

"Don't worry, honey, you're going to win."

Toreas looked at Jared's smiling face and was still looking at him when a few moments later she heard her category called. She refused to take her eyes from Jared.

Her name was called. Her novel, *The Critic*, had won the annual Bard for best first novel. She sank against Jared's massive chest, needing to feel him before walking up to the stage. His lips covered her possessively, releasing her finally to walk to the stage and pick up her trophy.

Jared was waiting for her when she descended the stairs. He lifted her in his arms and spun her around. "You did it," he shouted before kissing her again.

She could barely get Jared to contain his excitement and sit until the end of the program. She prayed for it to be over soon. She had another gift for her husband.

When it was over finally, Toreas stood rubbing her hand across the golden statuette, moving her fingers lovingly over the base, working her way to the quill in the figure's hand.

Liz and Kelle were running toward them, excitement and joy for her etched on their faces.

"Wow, you did it," Liz exclaimed breathlessly before looking over at Jared.

"You wrote your own reality and look what happened. You won The Bard."

"So what are you writing next, how you won the lottery?" Kelle grinned at her, then reached for Toreas's statue, rubbing it in awe.

Toreas looked from her friends to her husband. "From now on I'm only writing what I know." She paused for a moment, her gaze focused only on Jared. "Books about babies are always popular."

She watched his eyes as her message sank in. Then like magic she was floating in her husband's arms, his lips pressed against hers.

"I love you," he whispered into her mouth.

"And I love you. And, Jared, you're going to be able to keep that promise you made to your mother after all. She'll know, Jared, trust me, she'll know." Toreas Stone accepted her husband's kisses wondering what would happen if she did write them a story about becoming millionaires.

Author Bio

Award winning author, Dyanne Dvais lives in a Chicago suburb with her husband Bill, and their son Bill Jr. An avid reader, Dyanne began reading at the age of four. Her love of the written word turned into a desire to write. She retired from nursing several years ago to pursue her lifelong dream. Her first novel, *The Color of Trouble*, was released July of 2003. the novel was received with high praise and several awards. Dyanne won an Emma for Favorite New Author of the year.

Her second novel, *The Wedding Gown* was release in February 2004 and has also received much praise. The book was chosen by Blackexpressions, a subsidiary of Doubleday Book club as a monthly club pick. The book was an Emma finalist in March 2005 for Steamiest Romance, and for Book of the Year. *The Wedding Gown* was also a finalist for Affaire de Coeur Reader's poll.

Dyanne's *Misty Blue* is a sequel to *The Wedding Gown*. It received a four star rating from Romantic Times. In December of 2006 *Let's Get It On* also received a four star rating from Romantic Times. In February 2007, *Misty Blue* was a finalist for best cover and best romance sequel. Dyanne was a finalist for author of the year. *Misty Blue* garnered an Emma win for best book cover.

Dyanne has been a presenter of numerous workshops including several workshops for teens at Chicago and Suburban high schools. She has a local cable show in her hometown to give writing tips to aspiring writers. She has guests from all genres to provide information and entertainment to the audience. She has hosted such notables as USA Today Best Selling erotica author, Robin Schone and vampire huntress L.A. Banks. Dyanne is also writing for the first time under a pseudonym, F.D. Davis, for her new vampire series.

When not writing you can find Dyanne with a book in her hands, her greatest passion next to spending time with her husband Bill and son Bill Jr. Whenever possible she loves getting together with friends and family.

A member of Romance Writers of America, Dyanne is now serving her second term as Chapter President for Windy city. Dyanne loves to hear feedback from her readers. You can reach her at her website: www.dyannedavis.com. You can email her at davisdyanne@aol.com.